P9-CQQ-538

JOAN
JOHNSTON

NO LONGER
A STRANGER

POCKET BOOKS

New York London Toronto Sydney

An Original Publication of POCKET BOOKS

 POCKET BOOKS, a division of Simon & Schuster, Inc.
1230 Avenue of the Americas, New York, NY 10020

ISBN: 0-7434-6979-8

First Pocket Books printing February 2005

10 9 8 7 6 5 4 3 2 1

POCKET and colophon are registered trademarks of
Simon & Schuster, Inc.

Front cover illustration by John Harris

Manufactured in the United States of America

For information regarding special discounts for bulk purchases,
please contact Simon & Schuster Special Sales at 1-800-456-6798 or
business@simonandschuster.com

"You asked for this," Kincaid said, picking her up and throwing her over his shoulder.

"I couldn't tell you the truth," Reb protested.

Kincaid tossed her on the bed. "Why the hell not?"

"I was in love with you!"

Kincaid's hands went to his hips in triumph, and a huge grin stole across his face.

"You don't have to be so smug," Reb said haughtily. "I didn't *want* to be in love with you."

"Rebel, Rebel," Kincaid said lovingly as he wagged his finger at her.

"I'm not a kid," she said, throwing the pillow at his head. "I'm a woman!"

"Act like a brat, get treated like a brat!" Kincaid responded good-naturedly as he flattened Reb under him on the bed. "Act like a woman, get treated like a woman," he added in a voice that had thickened in passion.

"Johnston writes brisk romance chock full of compelling conflicts and strong local color."

—Publishers Weekly

"Delightful!"

—The Atlanta Journal-Constitution

For Hugh

1

Laramie Mountains
April 1865

Reb Hunter kneed her bay mare, Brandy, and when the animal grunted, she tightened the cinch on the saddle one more notch. She led her horse out of the barn and hitched her to the rail in front of the log ranch house. One of the few things Reb enjoyed about being a rancher's daughter was owning her own cowhorse. She gave the horse's silky jowls a comforting pat and darted inside. Brandy snorted twice at being left standing in the cold, the foggy air billowing from her nostrils like smoke from some mythical dragon.

"Where do you think you're going?"

Reb closed the door behind her and stood, feet apart, facing her father. Matt Hunter leaned against the heavy pine trestle table that dominated the room. Steam rose from the mug of coffee cupped in his hands. Behind him Reb could see her younger sister, Dillon, working on some flapjacks at the iron stove and trying not to appear to be eavesdropping.

"Where I go every spring at this time—to take supplies to Blue in the mountains," Reb replied.

"I can't spare your brother to go with you this year. Spotted Tail's Brulé Sioux tribe is under guard at Fort Laramie on their way to a reservation they don't want any part of, and Standing Buffalo's band of Brulé renegades are raising hell. I have to get the roundup finished before that powder keg blows up," her father said.

Reb raised her chin an inch and crossed her arms under her breasts. "Fine, then. Adam can stay here and help you. I'll go by myself."

"No, Reb. It's too dangerous. You saw what happened to the Morgan family."

Reb's face paled. One of the many groups of settlers that passed by on their way to the promised land, the Morgan family had stayed overnight at the ranch before continuing their trip north to the Oregon Trail. After dinner Reb had held the little blond girl in her lap, and the towheaded boy had played with her younger brother, Jesse. Even now, the picture of what had been left of the mutilated couple and their two children when she and Adam had discovered them an hour north of the house made her sick. Reb swallowed back her nausea at the memory of those bloody, hairless heads.

"That was March. This is April, almost May. I'll be careful," she managed to say.

Her father rose to his feet. Tall and lean, the golden-haired man hardly seemed old enough to have five children, the eldest of whom was twenty-two. But there was no question he was the final authority in the house and expected obedience.

"Rebecca, don't argue with me. I said no."

Calling her by her full name was a sure sign of his distemper, a reminder that she was a seventeen-year-old girl, and there were limits to what she could do. The setdown was not surprising, just frustrating.

Reb had been prepared for her father's attempt to keep her from making the journey. In the past he'd found other excuses. One year it had been a threatening blizzard. Another, she'd just gotten over a bad cold. Each year she'd overcome his objections and made the trip.

This year there was a difference. She no longer had a strong ally to support her. Perhaps invoking her ally's name would be enough.

"If Mama were alive, she'd let me go."

It was Matt's turn to pale. His eyes fixed on the empty chair where his wife should be sitting. In six months the loss hadn't gotten any easier to bear. Reb was right, of course. If Rachel were alive, she would insist Reb be allowed to make her yearly pilgrimage to see the mountain man who'd been like a second father to her. And to please Rachel, he would have agreed.

For most of his adult life, Matt had trapped beaver with his friend Blue in the Laramie Mountains. Six years ago they'd parted ways. Matt's eyes narrowed and his jaw tightened in anger until a muscle in his cheek jerked. He'd trusted Blue and had been enraged at the discovery that his best friend had deceived him.

In his first fury at that betrayal, he'd almost killed Blue, who wouldn't fight back when Matt attacked him with a knife, stabbing Blue in the ribs. Rachel had grabbed his arm, begging him to spare Blue's life. That had only infuriated him more. It was not until she reminded him what Blue meant to Reb that Matt dropped his knife, and turned his back forever on his friend.

Matt had left the mountains and moved his family down to this road ranch along the Overland Trail, one of the many way stations where the Overland Stage changed horses while its passengers enjoyed a meal. Over the years he'd established a good-sized herd of cattle so that he operated more as a ranch now, with the station a service he continued to provide. Through it all, Matt had hidden his bitterness and anger from his children.

He regretted that decision now. He couldn't explain to his daughter why he didn't want her to go near the mountain man, especially now that Rachel was dead and couldn't answer the questions that were sure to arise. The Indians provided a valid reason to forbid the sojourn without any further explanation, so he turned away from Reb without answering her charge.

"It's time for breakfast. Call your brothers," he said, dismissing her.

Reb had planned to eat before she left anyway. Hiding her exasperation, she moved to the front door and called Adam from the barn, then called Garth and Jesse from their wing of the house.

Dillon flashed her a conspiratorial grin that crinkled her green eyes at the corners, and then flipped her auburn curls back from a breathtakingly creamy complexion.

"You could help by setting the table," Dillon said. When Reb passed her at the stove, Dillon murmured so their father couldn't hear, "I'm surprised you gave in so easily. Or did you?"

Reb just grunted and pulled some dishes from the cupboard. If she'd been more desirous of male attention, she might have been jealous of her sister's beauty. Her own short black locks and mahogany brown eyes did not seem to have the same effect on men.

Actually, Reb had the same flawless complexion as her sister—except for the freckles. Her straight, boyishly cut hair fell onto her brow haphazardly and hid beautiful arched brows that framed her large, expressive eyes. She had a delicate, aquiline nose, but a stubborn mouth and chin.

When Reb finished setting the table with the good china, she poured herself a cup of coffee and seated herself at her place to the left of her father. He didn't seem to notice when they were joined by two of her brothers.

When it appeared that Jesse's fidgeting might break her father's reverie, Reb shot a warning glance at Garth, who, at twenty and the second son, was least like his sire. He silently nodded his head in understanding and immediately proceeded to distract the youngster.

Garth's quiet demeanor, dark hair, and penetrating black eyes evidenced their grandmother's Indian heritage. Garth made up in wiry strength what he lacked in size. He also lacked the flamboyant sense of humor their father seemed to have handed down intact to Adam, his firstborn.

The quiet was broken when Adam burst into the house, rubbing his hands together and blowing on them to warm them. As he passed by his youngest brother's chair, he placed his frigid fingers on Jesse's ears.

"Hey, stop that!"

Adam tousled Jesse's hair, then plopped into his chair next to the youth.

Jesse was a miniature physical copy of Adam, and it appeared from his gangly limbs that he would grow to equal his brother's six-foot size. Both had their father's sandy blond hair and their mother's green eyes.

"Jacks coming up," Dillon announced. She handed the plate of flapjacks to her father and joined the rest of the family at the table, where they joined hands in the traditional short grace their father still said in deference to their mother.

"I've got the mules packed," Adam said, pouring honey on his pancakes.

"Well, you can unpack them," her father snapped. He threw Reb an aggrieved stare.

"What's going on?" Adam asked, looking from Reb to Matt and back again. "I thought you told me Dad was letting us go."

"He didn't say anything about not going until just now," Reb said. "How was I supposed to know he would go back on the promise he made when Mama was alive?"

"This has nothing to do with my promise to your mother," Matt said, knowing as he spoke that it had everything to do with just that—the promise Rachel had forced him to make and the sanctity of which she'd protected all these years—that Reb be allowed to visit Blue each spring. He rationalized that it was a promise to Rachel, but didn't say that aloud. Instead he growled, "I'm trying to keep you from ending up with your scalp hanging from some Sioux lodgepole. Standing Buffalo and his braves are on the prowl, and there's no reason for you to expose yourself to that danger just to deliver some supplies to Blue."

"I'm not afraid of any Buffalo Man—"

"Standing Buffalo," her father and Adam said together.

"Standing Buffalo," Reb repeated irritably. "For that matter, I can just as easily be attacked when I'm searching for cattle in some gully during the roundup. That's no good reason to keep me here. You promised Mama when we moved down from the mountains that I could visit Blue every spring. Well, it's spring, and even though Mama's not here, I'm going to hold you to your promise."

Reb pushed her chair back and stood at her place, fists balled at her sides. "Unless you plan to keep me tied up or locked in my room, you can't stop me," she said through clenched teeth. "If you do lock me up, I'll never forgive you," she added in a harsh whisper. "Don't you understand? I *need* to go."

Her brothers and sister shifted uncomfortably, but no one joined in the private battle of wills.

Reb was as close to pleading for permission as her pride would allow her. She let her stricken eyes rest for a moment on her father's stony visage. She didn't know how to explain in words the sense of freedom she found in the Rocky Mountains, isolated from civilization of any kind. Not that their road ranch was a hub of society, but they were visited frequently by travelers on the Overland Stage and by those pioneers headed for the Oregon Trail to the north. Her father's previous trapping partnership with Blue also had made his ranch a haven for those mountain men who craved the sound of a human voice.

Reb loved to sit by their campfires at night and listen to their stories of survival in the wilderness. She vicariously lived each of their adventures and yearned for the one week of each year that she and Adam took off for Blue's cabin on their own. She refused to be cheated of the time in the mountains she'd enjoyed every year since she had turned eleven.

"At least eat your breakfast before you leave," came a calm voice from the shadows in the corner.

Reb turned to where her grandmother, the Old One, sat in her willow rocker. The perfectly straight white hair framing her face in two braids that hung forward nearly to her waist proclaimed that the Old One possessed Indian blood, but not even she herself could say how much, or what kinds. Her flesh seemed to have shrunk over the years so it was stretched taut over her facial bones like a pelt staked out on a willow hoop to dry. Reb had found the Old One's dark black eyes to be wells of wisdom, always providing the cup of promised knowledge. So, as in the past, she let them sway her now.

"You're right," she agreed. "I would only get hungry on the trail." She sat down and picked up her fork, although her trembling hand revealed the tension in her lithe young body.

The sound of the Old One's rocker creaking on the wooden floor filled the silence that had settled on the table. Occasionally a pewter fork would scrape against a china plate, but they ate without speaking.

The Old One felt the charge of lightning in the room waiting to strike. It was bound to come to this, she thought. Maybe if she and Rachel had not been so much at loggerheads . . . but they'd been as different and as evenly matched as two adversaries could be, and Reb had been caught between them.

The Old One had warned Matt against marrying the green-eyed woman with milk-white skin and auburn hair; she had never expected Rachel to fit in to the wilderness life her son led. Who would have believed that the daughter of a Philadelphia historian traveling with the first party of missionaries and settlers along the Oregon Trail would have adapted so well to the hardships endured by a trapper's wife?

But the Old One had to admit she had. Rachel had clung tenaciously to values of the civilization she'd left behind, but she'd been intelligent and realistic enough to adopt the wisdom of mountain customs as well. The bony point of their contention rested on the fact that Rachel never compromised in her belief that the mountains would not remain isolated for long.

She could remember the lecture Rachel had given to the children more than once. "When civilized society finally arrives in the West, as it will in your lifetimes," Rachel had preached, "you'll need certain talents not only to survive, but to excel."

The Old One had scoffed at Rachel's ideas, equally sure, as her Indian forebears had been, that the white man was only passing through. She couldn't swallow the possibility that her daughter-in-law might be right without a lump in her throat, and had looked for ways to thwart Rachel's efforts to prepare her children for "civilized society." Reb had been by far the best tool for that job.

While Rachel instructed Reb on how to read and write, using everything from Shakespeare to obscure philosophies provided by her father, held regular dancing lessons, and observed strict etiquette at the table, the Old One made sure Matt instructed Reb on how to shoot straight, trail game, and trap beaver. When Rachel insisted a dress was proper attire for Reb in and around the cabin, the Old One was equally adamant that buckskin shirt and leggings be donned for Reb's forays into the mountains.

She gladly would have made the same arguments on Dillon's behalf, but Dillon, two years younger than Reb, had different priorities. Attracting a man was more important to her than dressing like one. Reb chuckled to herself at Dillon's one-track mind. No, Reb had definitely been the better tool with which to antagonize her foe.

The Old One had more than once encouraged Matt to let the child try her wings merely as a goad to Rachel, who didn't approve of Reb's increasing deviation from the accepted feminine role. Reb was adept at the things her mother taught her, but she enjoyed doing the things her father taught her more. As the Old One watched Reb meet and conquer every challenge, she developed a curiosity to see for herself how far the girl could go.

Unfortunately, time had proven that Rachel was right, and she was wrong. The Overland Stage ran a regular route through the territory now, and a telegraph line sang along the plains. There was even serious talk of a railroad coming across the country.

The Old One understood Reb's fear that the wilderness she loved was escaping her grasp; she felt the same fear herself. That understanding made her decide to support her granddaughter's wishes in spite of the pain she knew it would cause her son for Reb to seek out Blue. How strange that in this first confrontation between father and daughter without Rachel there to act as mediator, she should find herself taking the side her daughter-in-law would have argued. She consoled herself with the thought that what Rachel had really cared about was that Blue see Reb. The Old One wanted Reb to see the mountains.

Her thoughts were interrupted when Dillon had the temerity to speak to her rebellious sister.

"I don't see why you want to go up there. Except for Blue there's not another man around for fifty miles."

The reactions to that statement were as varied as the personalities at the table, but Adam's hoot of laughter irked Reb onto her feet.

"I'm going to see Blue, and I'm staying the week," she said. "Adam is welcome to join me, if you can spare him." Reb left the table and stalked outside to await her brother.

Adam turned to his father with a quizzical look, awaiting his decision.

Under his breath Matt swore. "Damn!" Reb had more than a little of her mother in her.

A firm, soft voice broke in to soothe his consternation.

"The danger is not greater than in the past, only of a different nature. She's a woman, not a child. You trained her yourself. She's a better shot than any man you know, and coolheaded. She's Adam's match at reading signs. Let her go."

Matt considered his mother's words carefully. He was not so ignorant of Reb's nature as to think he would be successful in keeping her confined against her will. Nor could he blame her for missing the mountains when he missed them himself. If she were a man, he'd know how to handle her. If she acted more like a woman, he would not have felt so at sea.

But Reb was something in between—a woman who knew everything Matt could teach her about being a successful mountain man. He refused to let the bitter gall that rose when he thought about Reb with Blue make him alienate his daughter any further. This year he would let her go, but he knew he had to find some way to end these hellish confrontations each spring.

Maybe he could send Reb away to one of the finishing schools her mother had suggested for the two girls shortly before the accident. Settling on this possible solution to an apparently insoluble problem, he turned to Adam.

"Your brothers and I are going to start the roundup. I'm not so sure General Dodge's attempt to put the Brulés on a reservation won't backfire, and I want Garth to get the cattle back on the range before the repercussions start. Go, but keep your eyes open and get back here as quick as you can. We can use the help.

"Come on, boys," he called to Garth and Jesse. "We'll see you at dinner, Dillon."

Reb eyed her father warily as he stepped onto the porch. When he reached his arms out to her, however, she stepped into them and laid her head against his buckskin shirt, drinking in the familiar earthy smell of him.

"Be careful," her father whispered in her ear as he held her close.

"I will." She hugged him tightly.

At last, he stepped away and headed for the corral.

"Are you going to bring me a baby bear this time?" the irrepressible Jesse asked Reb on his way by.

"Let's hope not," Garth said. He pushed the eight-year-old toward the corral, then paused to search deep into Reb's eyes. She automatically lowered her gaze to protect her private self.

"Have a good trip. Keep your eyes open, and don't do anything you'll regret later." Garth kissed her lightly on the cheek and headed after Jesse.

Reb was still musing over Garth's admonition when Adam came to the porch with his arm on Dillon's shoulder. Dillon hugged herself to stay warm in her frilly, bright yellow cotton dress, which was flattering, but too light for the cold snap they were having.

Adam pressed a kiss to her forehead. "So long, little sister. Don't let any beaus get too friendly while I'm not here to protect you."

Dillon giggled and gave Adam a hug. "No one you wouldn't approve of, anyway," she reassured. "So long, Adam. So long, Reb. Take care."

Adam and Reb mounted, and he pulled the pack mules loaded with supplies behind him as they rode toward the sun-rimmed Laramie Mountains.

Reb longingly eyed the broken ridges silhouetted in an orange daybreak. "If I were a man, I'd live in the mountains and never leave."

"But you're not," Adam reminded. "You're only a girl. So dream, dear sister, of something more practical, if you please."

"Well, it doesn't please!" Reb shot Adam an impish grin and urged her mare into a canter. "This girl is dreaming of at least a week in the mountains, and that's as practical as she gets on a cold, beautiful April morning. I'll see you at Blue's cabin."

"Hey, Reb, wait for me," Adam shouted. He kicked his horse and pulled the pack mules forward, but their broken trot was no match for Brandy's distance-eating lope. Reb left him behind as she answered the beckoning call of the Rockies.

2

Kincaid had reached the limit of his patience with the garrulous woman who balanced her overdressed bulk on the narrow seat facing him and babbled incessantly about her daughter and the successful San Francisco merchant the fortunate young woman had met and married in New York.

For the past fifty miles of the ride west, while the stagecoach had swayed on its heavy leather traces like a ship in a turbulent sea, he'd heard how they begged her to join them and how much she would uplift the cultural and moral fiber of San Francisco when she arrived.

When he recognized a lull in the conversation, he tipped his dark blue felt hat and agreed politely, "Yes, ma'am, I'm sure you're right," although he had no earthly idea what she'd just said.

He let his gaze wander out the window to the receding view of the Laramie Mountains. Spring had barely touched the plains they now crossed, and the dull brown flattened grasses grudgingly gave way only here and there to the green of new growth.

Eula Thomas held a much higher opinion of the Yankee officer seated across from her, whose physical presence filled the cramped interior of the Overland Stage. She would have given a lot to be twenty-five years younger and a hundred—no, she admitted honestly with a cackle—a hundred and fifty pounds lighter.

Eula perused the mobile mouth and square jaw. She guessed he was used to having his own way. A scar below his right eye lent his face a rakish look, but his eyes were what caught her imagination. Steely gray, rimmed in sooty black lashes and capped by finely arched brows as black as the errant curls that he brushed back occasionally from his forehead, they seemed to look right through her. Her knees went to jelly at the thought of those eyes turned on her in anger or in passion.

He was massaging his right thigh again. She'd questioned him earlier, and he'd reluctantly admitted it was a war wound. He probably was a hero of some Civil War battle. He looked the type. He hadn't volunteered a tittle of information to satisfy her curiosity, however.

All she'd been able to find out was that he was from New York, and his name was Kincaid. Not "Major Kincaid," mind you, although she could see his rank perfectly well from his uniform. Just "Kincaid."

He seemed preoccupied, and she had to tap his knee with her fan to get his attention when she spoke to him. "I noticed you're headed away from Fort Laramie, Major—I mean Kincaid," Eula said with a girlish blush.

"Yes, ma'am," he replied.

"Are you headed someplace in particular?"

"Yes, ma'am."

"Can you tell me where you're going?"

"No, ma'am."

One of the soldiers in the cavalry escort from the fort drew alongside the coach and addressed Kincaid.

"Sir, we've sighted a couple of renegades."

"I'm just a passenger, Corporal Jennings. I don't have authority to give you any orders."

"Yes, sir, I understand, sir. I just thought I'd let you know we're planning to go after them."

"Do you think that's a good idea?" Kincaid could hear the painted braves baiting the recruits—"Come fight us, you sons of she-dogs!"

"We don't have to take that from those red devils, sir!"

The youth crimsoned when it became apparent Mrs. Thomas had heard the taunt as well.

"No need to be alarmed, ma'am. We're going to rid ourselves of those two vermin in the shake of a beaver's tail. Begging your pardon, ma'am," the lad added, tipping his hat to the rotund woman. He raced with the rest of the escort after the two Sioux rapidly disappearing over a rise to the west.

Kincaid shook his head at the soldier's misguided exuberance. At the same time, he pulled his Colt from its holster to check the rounds. How many kids had he heard make the same brash promise about some Johnny Reb? He hoped the results were not the same for these inexperienced recruits.

He scanned the countryside keenly for signs of danger, then laid the gun down on the worn leather seat next to him with his finger wrapped around the trigger. God, he was glad the war was over. It had been over for him for a while now, he thought ruefully, as he rubbed the ache in his leg. He wished he had more space to stretch out and ease the stiffness.

His father had pressured him to take this assignment from General Dodge, outlining the details he and Dodge had worked out, but Kincaid hadn't resisted much. The task had the intrigue of being a secret mission, and although he'd resigned his commission from the army, he'd been authorized to perform his investigation in uniform.

He'd harbored no desire to become one of the northern carpetbaggers that ravaged the South, nor could he seek solace by assisting those he'd helped to defeat, since that meant acknowledging his complicity in the events leading to the death of his wife during the war.

To his mother's dismay, two days after the talk with his father, he'd headed west. A wry smile widened on his face. His mother would consider it poetic justice to know his hurried timing had gotten him to the Overland Stage depot at the same time as Eula Thomas. They were nearly at his destination, and she hadn't talked him to death yet—although it was a very near thing.

All in all, Eula Thomas was certain to make him appreciate the opportunity this mission offered for solitude.

Standing Buffalo bared his teeth in a cruel smile as he watched the progress of the Overland Stage toward the gully where he waited in ambush with half his braves. The other half hid beyond a rise to rain arrows on the raw recruits being led to them by the two decoys. They had used the plan successfully many times over the winter. So far it was working perfectly, despite High Forehead's whining complaints that they should quit raiding and join Spotted Tail at Fort Laramie.

It had taken some convincing to overcome High

Forehead's objections. Standing Buffalo had reminded the hawk-nosed brave—who should have been named for that prominent feature, rather than his moderately low forehead—about the thieving agent of the White Father, who stole their goods and left them to starve and freeze in the winter. He'd argued that they could not trust the white devils and must kill those who came to drive the buffalo away. Before they returned, he'd shouted, his knife must taste the white man's blood and leave his bones as bare of flesh as the hungry women and children of the tribe.

The graphic picture of starvation, too vivid in their memories, had convinced the other braves to join him, and at their urging, High Forehead had capitulated and this attack had been launched.

The inexperienced soldiers, fresh from duty in the East, did not get far before a hail of arrows decimated their ranks. Then a cluster of Indians charged from behind a slight rise in the flat terrain. The Sioux suffered casualties when some of the soldiers had the presence of mind to fight back. But of the eight troopers, only three remained alive to rue their underestimation of the enemy. They turned back to the stagecoach in panic.

The two decoys, Spotted Elk and Strangling Wolf, gave chase, exhibiting superb horsemanship as they closed the gap. Guiding their ponies with their knees, they used bows and arrows to summarily end the lives of two of the fleeing men.

Corporal Jennings raced his lathered horse onward. When he located the stagecoach, the full folly of their escapade became apparent. The four stage horses were down in their traces, peppered with arrows, and the driver had already been scalped. The Indians were mutilating the body in a way they believed made it difficult, if not impossible, for the white man's spirit to find its way to the land of Wakan-Tanka. Not waiting to see more, and convinced he was the lone survivor of the raid, the soldier thundered away toward the nearest Overland Stage station.

Had he paused a moment longer, he would have seen a very tall man emerge from the interior of the coach to take a stand before the open door, his hand-gun blazing. Several warriors screamed and fell before the rest sought refuge out of range.

Kincaid was unaware that Standing Buffalo crouched above him, hidden amidst the baggage on the coach. He threw the emptied Colt aside in the sagebrush and stood boldly facing the Indians, empty-handed, in obvious contempt of their prowess.

The Sioux yelped in glee. Here was an adversary worthy of their attention.

"I will be first to count coup," Black Horse shouted exultantly.

"First after me!" Rolling Thunder bellowed back in the voice that gave him his name.

The two painted braves raced away on their ponies, competing for the honor of counting coup first on the large man. It soon became apparent that this was a rash action on their part.

Soundlessly, Kincaid reached out with his bare hands to unseat Black Horse, who was then brained with his own tomahawk. Seconds later he swiftly and accurately threw the bloody tomahawk at Rolling Thunder, who tumbled backward off his horse, dead.

It was a sign of their admiration for his courage that the Indians did not then attack the white man with bow and arrows. The deaths were unfortunate, but within the rules of this deadly game that allowed the opponent on whom the Indians attempted to count coup to do his level best to kill them.

More wary, however, they raced back and forth in front of their tall adversary, waving their lances and screaming insults. Unarmed, the man faced them calmly, seemingly undaunted. He brushed a black curl back from his chiseled face and waited.

Standing Buffalo's younger brother, Smaller Bear, took up the silent challenge, seeking to count coup with the tip of his lance, a little safer distance than the coup stick allowed.

Standing Buffalo watched in satisfaction. *It is good for my brother to fight as a man*, he thought.

Sadly, it was the end of Smaller Bear's life as a man. As he raced past, Kincaid rolled over in front of the Indian pony with a grace and speed that defied his size and his lameness, causing the animal to rear in fright. In the moment before the pony could speed its rider to safety, he disarmed the boy, broke his neck with a sharp upward jab of the lance, and then backed up slowly in his halting gait to the stagecoach, lance in hand, to await the next foe.

Stunned by this turn of events, each Indian searched his heart to determine whether he stood in as good stead with the Great Spirit as this white man obviously did.

Wakan-Tanka smiles upon him, Standing Buffalo thought, noting that the white man was not even breathing hard from his exertion.

The tension mounted as several warriors in turn danced their ponies toward the white man, only to wheel them back into the crowd.

Standing Buffalo realized that if he did not take matters into his own hands soon, it was possible all his warriors would be sent to the Happy Hunting Ground one at a time.

Moving stealthily, he reached the edge of the coach above the powerful white warrior. Swinging with all his might, he brought his stone and rawhide war club crashing into the man's right temple. The giant dropped to his knees, still clutching the lance, then fell forward like a mighty tree cleaved from its trunk.

The Sioux thanked the Great Spirit for this good fortune with whoops of delight. Such a great warrior was strong war medicine, and they rushed up to obtain talismans from his person.

Rides-Two-Ways, one of the younger braves, had already stripped the shirt from Kincaid's body before the groan sounded that evidenced life. Startled, and more than a little fearful, the young brave raised his tomahawk.

Standing Buffalo descended from the stagecoach in time to grab the youth's arm on its downward arc.

"He is mine. Do not take the scalp that protects his soul. I want his strong spirit to find its way to the Happy Hunting Ground to serve my brother and the other braves who died today. I will test the limits of this man's strength. Then we will truly know the worth of this enemy that took my brother's life.

"But you may keep the shirt," he said.

"Another enemy, but already dead," High Forehead yelled. He referred to the heavyset older woman discovered inside the coach, who'd been killed by a stray arrow in the first attack.

"Let me help," Rides-Two-Ways offered, joining the braves in dragging the woman's body out onto the ground and stripping it. Others tore through the baggage.

"Look at me!" one commanded, as he paraded cockily in a bright lavender opera cloak.

Standing Buffalo ignored the cacophony, concentrating instead on his prisoner. He checked the man's pockets, looking for booty. A grin spread across his face when a heavy gold pocket watch, bearing the inscription, "To Kincaid with Love from Laurie," appeared in his hand.

He searched the other pocket eagerly, but was disgusted to find only a folded piece of paper. He opened it up and perused it but, as with the inscription, the writing meant nothing to him.

April 15, 1865

Christopher Lyle Kincaid
Fifth Avenue and 28th Street
New York, New York

Dear Major Kincaid:

After our successful association in Atlanta during the war I am ready to set another task of equal, or perhaps even greater, importance for you now that General Lee has surrendered.

I realize you have barely had time to recover from your wound, but your father and I have discussed the necessity of your participation in this effort on behalf of the Union Pacific railroad and are agreed you are the best man for the job. Your father can fill you in on the significance of making the right choice between the two alternate routes.

I need you here as soon as possible. Meet me at the second Overland Stage station west of the Laramie Mountains no later than May 15. I'm counting on you.

Maj. Gen. Grenville M. Dodge, Commander
Dept. of the Missouri

Standing Buffalo started to let the wind carry the paper away, but on second thought folded it again and stuck it in the sacred medicine bag that hung around his neck. Perhaps some of the white warrior's powerful aura might wear off on him.

Having completed their destruction, the braves who had attacked the soldiers rode up to join the rest of the band. They were greeted by the excited shout of Rides-Two-Ways, who said proudly, "I have the shirt of a great white warrior. It will ensure my conquest of the white man."

Each group of Indians boasted of their bravery, but the exploits of the unconscious man, when recounted by the Sioux who had seen them, acquired a little of the supernatural in the telling.

Standing Buffalo ordered several braves to take their dead comrades back to their families, along with

the soldiers' horses, with instructions they would follow soon. "Strangling Wolf, you and Spotted Elk put
our captive on my brother's pony," he commanded.

It was a struggle for the two short, stocky Indians to
move the large man. "Rides-Two-Ways," Spotted Elk
shouted to his friend, "stop bragging and help us get
this big man up here."

He panted with the effort of getting the captive up
onto Smaller Bear's pony, which had been chosen to
bear this last burden before its life ended. As the
dead Indian's favorite mount, the little mare's head
and tail would be cut off and tied to the scaffolding
supporting Smaller Bear's body, enabling the pony to
serve her former master in his travels in the afterworld.

With extra-human effort, the three Indians completed the task. When they stood back to survey their
work, Rides-Two-Ways could not suppress a snigger.
He was joined by Strangling Wolf's raspy chuckle and
Spotted Elk's outright guffaw.

Seeking the source of this mirth, the other Indians
took one look at the prisoner and convulsed with
laughter. The white man's fingertips touched the
ground on one side of the pony, and the toes of his
boots dragged the ground on the other. Even
Standing Buffalo, weighed down by the sorrow of his
brother's death, could not keep his lips from quirking.

"The Council will long sing the praise of our cap-

ture of this white man who is too big for horses,"
Standing Buffalo said solemnly.

"Yes, Too-Big-For-Horses was a brave warrior in
battle," High Forehead agreed, sealing the label on
the man.

"Let us go now to tell Spotted Tail we will return to
the Powder River and hunt the buffalo. We will test
the strength of Too-Big-For-Horses along the way, and
tell his tale to our children around the campfire."
Standing Buffalo grasped the rawhide lead on
Smaller Bear's pony and headed north.

The Indians rode far into the night, then camped
high in the mountains, where they believed themselves safe from pursuit. Always cautious, however,
Rides-Two-Ways was selected to stand guard while
the others slept. With sunrise only moments away, the
boastful brave was tired, but still exuberant over his
prize. It was a good thing that the sun was rising,
since it meant his vigil as lookout was nearing an end.

He noticed the white man they had named Too-
Big-For-Horses was awakening. The prisoner stood
where they had tied him spread-eagled between two
ancient spruces. He had not died from the blow to the
head from Standing Buffalo's war club that would
have killed an ordinary man. Soon the other braves
would be stirring, and the testing of the white man
promised by their leader could begin.

We will find much pleasure today helping Too-Big-

For-Horses seek the Great Spirit, Rides-Two-Ways thought, fingering with pride the white man's dark blue shirt that dwarfed his figure. He hoped Too-Big-For-Horses manfully withstood the exquisite torture planned for him, since that would make his token all the more valuable.

"Today your trip to the afterworld begins. Be strong, Too-Big-For-Horses," he chanted. "This conquering brave wills it so."

3

Kincaid woke to the throbbing pain in his massive shoulders and arms, which were stretched out taut away from either side of his body. The effort to flex his benumbed hands resulted in agony as tightening thongs bit into raw wrists. His head hung forward, so that when he blinked open his eyes to the early-morning light he saw only the muddy ground, strewn with pine needles, below him.

A slight turn of his pounding head in either direction revealed his black-booted feet, spread far apart and secured by rawhide at the ankles. His eyes followed the rawhide on one side to where it wrapped around a thick spruce.

Kincaid closed his eyes and struggled mentally to orient himself.

A pulsing ache in the muscles of his right thigh took him back to a scene from the past. The scream of the shrapnel that had left him with a slight but permanent limp resounded in his ears. He jerked unconsciously at the memory of that first awful impact of metal on muscle. It was a nightmare he relived time and again, but always with the same painful ending. He remembered anxiously watching the slender woman, her long blond hair windblown around a terrified, heart-shaped face, racing toward where he had been pitched from the saddle by the blast. He'd warned her to get down, but was unheard amidst the chaos of defeated soldiers fleeing on horseback and on foot.

Suddenly, a blossom of red unfolded on the front of her high-necked gray wool dress. A tentative hand reached up to admire the deadly corsage, and she sought Kincaid's steel gray eyes with her own silvery blue ones, a poignant sadness replacing the fear for him on her face. Stumbling unsteadily, she took one more step. Then he watched helplessly as his wife crumpled, like a flower trodden to the ground.

He dragged himself to her side, forced to pause occasionally by the bursting shells around him. Finally, he cradled her head in his arms as he lay full-length beside her on the red clay. He searched her face for signs of life, but when he saw none, gathered her close to him, their long bodies molding perfectly, and pressed gentle kisses on each closed eyelid, and finally on the still-warm mouth. The taste of his loss was bitter on his lips. Tenderly, he laid her head down and rested his own cheek beside hers on the cool clay.

His throat constricted so that he couldn't breathe without turning his gaze away from the precious young face to the sky above, dotted with ugly clouds of black smoke. If only she hadn't insisted on being where she didn't belong in the first place. If only he'd demanded she obey him and leave. But, oh, how he'd secretly admired her for staying.

"Damn you, Laurie!" he raged. He hugged the lifeless body to his own in frustration, while tears of anguish squeezed from eyelids drifting closed in unconsciousness.

But the war of brother against brother was over now and had been for more than a month. Kincaid realized he'd remembered too far back in the past, and wished he hadn't. He'd awakened an ache in his heart as persistent as the one in his wounded thigh. He forced his mind to focus on solving the puzzle of how he had come to be tied, spread-eagled, between two trees in the middle of a forbidding pine forest.

Two other minds worried over the same problem from another perspective.

"I count nine Sioux, including the lookout," Adam whispered to his lanky, buckskin-clad younger sister. "Too many for us to kill before one of them kills him."

"Why do you suppose they kept him alive?" Reb asked, as they observed the unknown man from their hiding place behind a mammoth boulder.

"Don't expect we'll ever know. Could be his size. That is one *big* man. Maybe they just want to see if the extra inches give him extra courage."

Millions of pine needles and spruce branchlets rustling in the wind muffled their voices, and the strong breeze carried the softened sound away from the Indian camp.

Reb appraised the body that was stripped to the waist and suspended between two trees. She found no fault in the impressive shoulders and chest, the defined muscles across the abdomen, or the strong, sinewy thighs molded into a pair of Union Army pants. She was curious to see the face that went with such a body, but the head hung forward, hidden in the shade of the forest.

They were several hours' ride south of Blue's cabin, on their way home with the beaver skins they'd picked up from the loner in exchange for the coffee, flour, and beans they'd delivered to him. Located where the Laramie River crossed the plateaulike summit of the mountains, the cabin was more than fifty miles, as the crow flies, from Fort Laramie on the plains directly to the east, and equally distant from their home at the base of the mountains to the southwest.

Reb wondered whether the presence of this captive meant another massacre of soldiers on patrol like the many throughout the winter. "Aside from the blood on his forehead, he doesn't appear to be hurt," she said.

"Not yet," Adam replied. "Those eagle feathers identify that lookout as one of Standing Buffalo's renegades, the ones Dad warned us about. I've seen samples of their handiwork. The kindest thing we can do for that stranger is shoot him."

Reb's senses rebelled against the mutilation planned for the magnificent specimen of mankind she saw before her. Surely the fates that had caused them to stumble onto this warrior camp could not have intended they pass without changing the now dismal outlook of this stranger's life.

"There must be a way we can save him. Think, Adam."

"Whatever we do should be done soon, before those sleeping Indians wake up," he said, "Or we could take a chance that they're planning to postpone their entertainment until they get to wherever they're headed. We might be able to steal their prisoner away during the journey."

Adam figured the band was headed for the Powder River far to the north near the Black Hills, where Red Cloud's Oglala and other Sioux less inclined to peace than Spotted Tail were congregating. If so, he didn't like the idea of trekking across mountains and plains after the Indians. They were too likely to be discovered and share the stranger's fate. He said as much to Reb.

"You're right," she agreed. "What about a trade?"

"We don't have a snowball's chance in the sun of bargaining with Standing Buffalo for that man's life, even if I were willing to give up Blue's beaver skins, which I'm not. Those Brulés won't trust us as far as they can throw us. They'll kill him sure if we charge in there. No, I'm afraid he's a goner, Reb. There's nothing we can do."

As he finished speaking, a far-fetched idea came to Adam of how to save the doomed man. He rose, a smile tugging at the corners of his mouth. "Yep. The kindest thing we can do is shoot him."

Adam clamped a hand over Reb's open mouth as she jumped up to protest.

"Listen," he whispered excitedly. "I've got a crazy idea, but it just might work. What's the first thing those Sioux will do if we start shooting?"

Reb mumbled against Adam's hand, but he ignored her in his exuberance.

"Kill that stranger, that's what! So we're going to 'kill' him first. That is, we're going to make them *think* we've killed him, so they're more concerned about escaping our ambush than hanging around here to carve up a dead body."

The large, liquid brown eyes rimmed with long black lashes, together with the light dusting of freckles visible across Reb's nose above his callused hand, reminded Adam of a startled fawn. When she mumbled again in frustration, he took his hand away from her full, still-parted lips.

"How?" she hissed.

"You're going to shoot him. I think if you hit him just above the heart, that ought to convince them he's dead."

Reb sucked in a breath of air between clenched teeth, but said nothing.

"I'll sneak around to the far side of the clearing. When I'm set, I'll shoot the lookout. That'll leave eight Indians. We've got two seven-shot Spencer rifles, four Colt repeaters, our knives, and the element of surprise on our side. We can't lose," he said with a lopsided grin.

"When the lookout falls, you shoot the stranger," he continued. "I'll unhobble the Indian ponies so that they stampede when the noise starts. Don't stop firing till they're all dead or gone. I'll be doing my part from the other side. Any questions?"

"What if I miss?"

"You miss those Indians, and we'll be dead ducks."

"You know that's not what I mean," Reb said. "What if I accidentally kill that stranger?" She gnawed her lower lip with her straight white teeth, her forehead wrinkled in concern. She was a crack shot, but had never aimed her gun at a man before, only at animals and standing targets.

"Like I said, the kindest thing we can do is shoot

him. Besides, you're too good a shot to miss. If it both-
ers you so much, we can just leave the way we came.
He's no worse off if we leave him dead than if we
leave him alive."

Adam might be a pragmatist, but Reb was an eternal optimist. Besides, she very much wanted to see
the stranger's face, and she was more likely to get her
wish if they tried to save him.

She had no qualms about killing the nine Sioux
when she remembered the Morgans. Those horrible
deaths, among others over the winter, were evidence
that a state of undeclared war existed with the
Indians—at least, undeclared on the white man's
side.

The previous November, Colonel John Chivington
had ordered the murder of Cheyenne men, women,
and children waiting at Sand Creek to begin peace
talks. The unprovoked attack of the army on the peaceful Cheyenne was the last straw. In retaliation, the
Sioux, Arapaho, and Cheyenne had indulged in what
many mountain men considered a quite justifiable
rampage.

The Indians began paying the white man back for
the degradation of drunkenness caused by his
whiskey, for diseases brought back to Indian husbands
by wives who prostituted themselves with the soldiers
for scraps of food, for the theft of government annu-
ities by dishonest Indian agents, and above all, for the

lies of the White Father who broke treaty after treaty.

The Sioux were incensed by the story of how the Cheyenne chief White Antelope, who stood alone and refused to fight the white man at Sand Creek, was shot down, then scalped and castrated by the soldiers. When his story was told, the Sioux smoked the war pipe gladly. They became the scourge of the Overland Trail, killing soldiers and settlers indiscriminately and pillaging or burning everything in their path.

The atrocities committed over the winter had included the riddling of one body with no fewer than ninety-seven arrows. Both sides had given sufficient warning that when one met the other, the rule was "Kill or be killed."

"All right, I'll shoot him," Reb said at last.

Adam disappeared silently into the forest. She lifted her Spencer to her shoulder and sighted down the barrel to a spot several inches above the stranger's heart.

Reb's hands shook at the enormous responsibility she'd undertaken. Knowing that she held the stranger's life at the tip of her trigger finger, she wanted to know very badly who he was and where he'd come from. She wanted to know the color of his eyes, to hear the sound of his voice. She wanted to know if he had a sweetheart, or worse, a wife and children.

"Look at me."

She willed the stranger to respond. As though reading her thoughts, his head rose slowly on his shoulders until he stared proudly forward, directly at Reb.

His whole face wasn't visible, only his eyes, lit by a narrow shaft of sunlight that blazed through the towering spruce and two-hundred-foot lodgepole pines, so named for the use to which the Indians put them. She was unable to discern the color of the unwavering orbs that bored into her own, compelling a response, demanding her soul.

Lost in his piercing gaze, Reb momentarily surrendered to the stranger's power, willingly giving to him a part of herself never before offered to anyone. In that fleeting instant Reb experienced a feeling of belonging so intense that it took her by surprise. This feeling was not the same sense of well-being that had always been provided by the support and love of her family. It was much more.

Unused to domination of any kind, Reb's spirit shook off the pleasant, but still unwanted, yoke of attachment. As the daughter of a onetime trapper and mountain man, Reb had learned not to give without taking a fair trade.

"I will never belong to any man, including you," she whispered in response to the stranger's unspoken demand for her soul, "who does not also belong to me."

She took careful aim once more and waited for Adam's signal. Her eyes drifted to the lookout, who had begun strutting boldly before the stranger.

At that moment, Adam fired.

Pandemonium hit the camp. Rides-Two-Ways clutched the gaping hole in his chest, his dying thought one of furious anger for the ruin of his wonderful shirt. The Sioux threw off their blankets and buffalo robes, grabbed weapons, and looked through sleep-crusted eyes for an enemy to fight.

"We are attacked!" Standing Buffalo cried.

"But I see no enemy," High Forehead said, uselessly holding his tomahawk.

Reb took a deep breath, her smooth white cheek pressed to the equally smooth brown rifle stock, and squeezed the trigger. Surprise registered on the stranger's face before it sagged forward.

"Too-Big-For-Horses has been shot!" Strangling Wolf exclaimed.

The Indians howled in outrage, certain now where at least one enemy lay. Reb chose another target immediately, knowing she must make each shot count. Her repeating rifle roared in her ear, and an Indian died.

The gunfire stampeded the unhobbled ponies through the camp, increasing the confusion.

Adam aimed and fired again. He caught High Forehead, who had paused in hopes of taking the "dead" stranger's scalp, with a bullet in the middle of his namesake. Adam struggled to avoid a charging brave who ripped open his right arm when he raised it to deflect a slashing knife blow. He hit the Indian in the throat with his left fist, crushing the windpipe.

Reb killed two more Sioux who were barely awake enough to realize they were meeting their eternal rest. Then Strangling Wolf and Spotted Elk attacked Reb. She dropped her rifle, grabbing for her two revolvers. She barely had time to free one gun and fire before Strangling Wolf fell dead on top of her with a final garbled cry.

Adam's revolver spoke from a spot near the stranger, and Spotted Elk screamed his death song before reaching Reb. Adam rushed to his sister, who was shoving her way out from under Strangling Wolf's corpse.

"Are you all right?" he asked anxiously.

Reb felt oddly disconnected from the death all around her. She answered calmly, "I'm fine, Adam. Did we get them all?"

Adam counted quickly, confounded to discover they were one Indian short. Colt in hand, he searched the forest surrounding the camp, but found no sign of his prey. He checked each dead Indian, but none was Standing Buffalo.

"Damn! That renegade will probably hightail it back to Spotted Tail for reinforcements. He isn't going to find any help there, thanks to Dodge. All the same, I'm not sure enough of what any Indian will do to stake my life on it. We better pack up and get moving."

Noticing several Indian ponies still lingering nearby, he added, "We can probably make sure he stays on foot for a while if we scatter the rest of these ponies. I presume your stranger is still alive?"

"He's alive, but he's unconscious."

"It makes the most sense for us to go back to Blue's cabin. It's closer than going all the way home. You can tend your stranger there."

Reb looked around at the slain men, then said so softly he barely heard her, "Let's get out of here, Adam."

Standing Buffalo watched the white man, who was nearly as tall as his former captive, cut down Too-Big-For-Horses, wrapping him securely in the blanket offered by his partner. When they lifted Too-Big-For-Horses across High Forehead's pinto and tied him down, Standing Buffalo smiled grimly and thought again how well the name fit the man, whose arms and legs nearly touched the ground on either side of the larger pony.

He waited patiently as the rest of the Indian ponies were scattered in the forest by several shots. He noted the direction of his favorite mount and set out at a brisk trot after him. He was not a superstitious man, but his former captive seemed to be having more than his share of good luck. He would leave it in the hands of the Great Spirit to bring the white man back to him, for he did not doubt that Too-Big-For-Horses still lived.

Now he must meet Spotted Tail at Fort Laramie and tell of the daring theft of Too-Big-For-Horses, and of the white man's evident favor with the Great Spirit.

It was not until they had traveled some distance that Reb came out of shock sufficiently to notice the blood covering the front of Adam's shirt.

"You're bleeding!"

"You call that bleeding? Why, I've seen a stuck pig do better than this," Adam replied.

"Adam, be serious." She was more annoyed with herself for failing to notice his injury than with him for joking about something so serious. She was startled to realize it was well past noon. She had no recollection of the trip from the Indian camp and was surprised to see she was leading the pony that carried the stranger.

Although he'd pressed his injured arm against his body in an attempt to stop the bleeding, Adam so far had been unsuccessful. The result of this tactic, however, had been to soak the front of his shirt with blood, so it looked like he had a belly wound. He might have been more concerned if the danger of pursuit was greater, but they soon would be able to stop, and he was confident Reb would be able to take care of him.

"It's just my arm, really, see?" He held out his arm to Reb, who raised an eyebrow appraisingly. "We should be back at Blue's cabin soon. You can play doctor for both me and your stranger there."

"Yes, and you can play nurse," Reb retorted irritably. She realized she would need to take care of both men, and dreaded it. Her doctoring experience had been gained as an assistant to the Old One. What Reb hated most was inflicting the necessary pain that so often accompanied the cure.

The fact that Adam could never be serious about anything was an irritation she'd learned to live with. In fact, the more dangerous the situation, the more he tended to treat it humorously. But, those who knew Adam well never underestimated him because of the smile on his face or the laughter in his voice.

She tried to look objectively at her brother. His green eyes glittered in a tanned face topped by sun-streaked, sandy gold hair. Clean-shaven, unlike most frontier men, his face revealed a firm jaw. He'd joked that he wanted the ladies to be able to find his lips. He did have a good mouth, she admitted, with pleasant, full lips prone to smile, and to quirk when he was teasing, which was often. His nose had once been aquiline, but it had been broadened at the bridge by a break when he was ten, adding character to an otherwise too-perfect visage.

Adam yanked on the pack mule line with his good hand. "Blue's skins will just have to get delivered a little later. Come on, cheer up," he cajoled. "Not only did we rescue your stranger, but we're still alive and well enough to greet him when he comes to."

"He's not *my* stranger," Reb protested, out of patience with his constant ribbing. He was a little too close to feelings she was not yet willing to admit existed.

Adam's knowing grin was too wide to be measured.

She turned away to hide the embarrassing blush that rose in her cheeks. His reference to the motionless man made her consider for the first time what she would say to the stranger when the opportunity finally arose to have a civil conversation. What should she ask? What would his first question be? It's rather like stumbling onto a sleeping mountain lion, she thought. The action doesn't begin until the lion wakes up.

4

"Home again, home again, jiggety-jog," Adam recited as he straightened up after helping Reb place the stranger on the long, extra-wide bed that was centered along one pine wall so that it took up most of the space in Blue's one-room cabin.

"Take your shirt off, Adam, so I can check the damage," Reb commanded from her place beside the unidentified man.

"And all the king's horses and all the king's men couldn't put—"

Reb's flat-brimmed hat interrupted him as it sailed into his face.

"Yes sir, yes sir, three bags full," he said, bowing comically.

Reb surveyed the room where she'd lived as a child as a potential infirmary. The furniture consisted of a wooden chest Blue and her father had fashioned from cottonwood planks, a rough-hewn table and two chairs of the same material shoved against the wall opposite the bed, and an iron stove in the corner that they'd salvaged from that great dumping ground to the north, the Oregon Trail, and carted here for her mother at great effort.

A high window sealed with a thin layer of animal skin let in the light, if not the heat, of the late-afternoon sun. It blazed a bright spot on the dirt floor she'd so recently swept in anticipation of their departure for home.

A cupboard was built in along the mud-daubed wall near the table, with numerous cracked dishes, also salvaged property, arrayed on the open shelves. Several barrels for flour and beans were stacked next to it.

"I expected Blue to be here," Reb said.

"I know what you mean," Adam said. "I guess he must have gone out somewhere. He'll be back soon, I'm sure." His fingers fumbled at the strings that tied his shirt.

It never occurred to Reb that anything could have happened to the mountain man. That was unthinkable. Blue could take care of himself. Still, his absence was puzzling. When they'd said good-bye to him that morning he hadn't talked about any plans for the day. He'd said he planned to sit back and relax, maybe even whittle some.

Once Reb started thinking about Blue, the question she'd asked herself more than once rose automatically to her lips. "Have you ever wondered why Blue didn't join Dad to start the ranch?"

"Why don't you ask Dad?" Adam said.

"I did. He told me that if Blue wanted me to know, he'd tell me."

"Sounds like Dad. So?"

"Blue's never said, and I've never asked."

Reb focused for a moment on the dark bruise and scrape marring the rugged beauty of the stranger's face. "How old do you think he is?"

"Oh, about forty-five or so."

"No, he can't be! He doesn't seem much older than you."

One look at Reb, whose eyes were riveted on the stranger, told Adam why the conversation had gotten so confusing. He was still talking about Blue. She was talking about the stranger. "I'd guess *he's* twenty-five or twenty-six," he said, an amused grin on his face.

Realizing she'd been caught staring, Reb turned her back on Adam to check the injured man. She tentatively lifted the wool blanket from around him enough to determine that it was stuck to the wound with dried blood. At least the bleeding had stopped. She checked the pulse at his throat and found it steady, the breathing regular, if a little shallow.

"He's not likely to get any worse in the time it'll take me to fix you up," she said.

"I just have a scratch," Adam said.

She knew that the seemingly innocent slash could be dangerous. She decided, as rationally as a sister could, that Adam needed attention now. The stranger could wait. "You first," she insisted, "or I don't take care of either of you."

Adam shrugged in submission. She watched him finish unlacing his buckskin shirt nearly to the waist and make a one-handed attempt to pull the blood-soaked leather up over his head. He grunted as he painfully raised his cut arm to ease the torn shirt off. As the grunt became a groan, Reb came around the bed to push him into a chair.

"Sit down and let me help." Reb carefully skinned the shirt over Adam's head and down his arms until he was free, revealing the jagged slash that ran along the length of his forearm from wrist to elbow.

"That needs stitching," Reb said when she could see the cut clearly. "I'll get some water from the creek. You'll find Blue's whiskey stashed behind the stove. There should be a needle and some thread in that chest beside the bed. See if you can find something in there to use for bandages."

Noting the steady drip of blood running off his fingers, she added, "Try not to dribble blood all over everything!"

She grabbed a chipped blue Dresden china pitcher from the cupboard and hurried out. Avoiding patches of melting snow, her moccasined feet literally raced to the narrow creek that burbled downhill at the left end of the cabin. She sat on her haunches, chasing away a feeding trout as she dipped the pitcher into the icy water, then paused, finally locating the beautiful violet-green sparrow perched singing on a budding willow above her, its feathers varying from bronzy green at the head to purplish bronze at the tail. Her eyes were drawn to the pine-covered ridges laced with snow, visible through the naked cottonwood trees along the creek.

She wondered what had brought the stranger to these mountains. She might never know if he didn't recover. But surely he wouldn't die! It wouldn't take long to stitch Adam. Then she would tend the stranger's wound. He'd survived the flight from the Indian camp, and the blood had clotted around the bullet hole. He was strong. The bullet had hit him in the exact spot where she'd aimed. The wound was serious, but not deadly, she tried to convince herself.

But who was he? Probably another Yankee seeking his fortune in the West now that the war was over, she thought. Most of the skinny, white-skinned easterners she'd seen passing through with the wagon trains had trouble staying on their horses at more than a trot. Their aim was so poor she didn't mind their shooting at the buffalo, because they seemed to enjoy it, and it didn't hurt the buffalo.

Reb believed most easterners didn't have the strength of body and spirit demanded out here. That was why they didn't stop in the Rocky Mountains, but kept on going to Oregon and California, the lands of milk and honey.

At least this stranger had a powerful body, as evidenced by the knotted shoulder muscles and bulging biceps that had supported his Herculean form between the trees.

"Reb! What are you doing down there? Taking a bath?"

Reb started at Adam's shout from the doorway, flushed at the reason for her delay, and retorted, "I'm coming. Hold your horses, if you can do it one-armed!"

Besides the needle and thread, Adam's rummaging had turned up an old sheet, which he deemed a fitting sacrifice for bandages. He observed that the stranger was still unconscious and more than a little pale.

As Reb reentered the cabin, Adam said, "Don't you think you ought to take care of him first? With this arm, I don't know how much help I'll be, but he looks awful." He gestured limply toward the unmoving man, leaving red bubbles across the floor that were gradually absorbed by the hard-packed dirt.

"He'll be fine," said. "Let me get your bleeding stopped. Then I'll see about him."

Adam sat down while Reb rinsed his arm as free of blood and dirt as possible, trembling from the combination of icy water and pain.

"It's a deep cut," Reb murmured, carefully prying the flesh apart. "Give me the whiskey, Adam." She accepted the bottle from Adam, uncorked it with her teeth, and poured whiskey liberally over the slash.

"Damn, Reb, that stings like the devil," Adam yelled.

"Sit still and stop acting like a baby," she scolded. She set the bottle aside, then wrinkled her nose as Adam handed her a whiskey-dipped threaded needle. Before recorking the bottle, he helped himself to a healthy slug of the golden liquid to counter the pain.

"You certainly have chosen the hard way to find out whether I can sew a neat stitch," Reb said.

Adam's laugh was stifled by his gasp as Reb inserted the needle through a flap of skin on his wrist and pulled it through to meet the skin on the other side. By the time she finished her work, the needle had been rethreaded several times, and two sets of lips had tightened into grim lines.

Reb used a strip of the sheet to make a sling in which to rest and protect the wounded limb. As Adam stood to escape her attentions, she reached her arms up around his neck to tie the sling in a knot. She was tall enough to manage easily without the need to rise on tiptoe.

"It's getting dark. Light a lantern, please, Adam," she said quietly in his ear. Then, turning back to look at the stranger, she shivered noticeably.

Adam rubbed his good hand up and down quickly along the golden fringe of her buckskin shirt to create some warmth. "You're cold. I'll light a fire, too," he said.

Reb nodded, although the shiver was more a reaction to the silent stranger than to the frigid early evening air.

Blue still had not returned, and knowing she could avoid him no longer, Reb moved to the wounded man. She watched his face as she unwrapped the blanket that had been so hastily slung around him at Standing Buffalo's camp. There was no reaction as the material was dampened and cautiously pried away from the dried blood that crusted the gunshot wound. Reb reached carefully behind the stranger's shoulder, probing with her fingertips, expecting to find that the bullet had passed all the way through. She groaned inwardly when the search revealed only hard, taut muscle.

"The bullet's still inside. I'll have to dig it out."

Adam gave Reb a sympathetic look, but didn't offer to relieve her of the job.

She pulled her knife from the brightly beaded sheath at her belt. The feel of the beadwork gave her courage as she remembered the occasion on which the beautifully ornamented object had been bestowed.

On the eve of her first trip to Blue's cabin with

Adam, her father had advised her to use her head, to think carefully before she acted, and to heed Adam, since he had five more years of living under his belt. It was then he'd pulled out an intricately worked beaded sheath made to fit her knife. She would never forget his words as he'd bestowed the gift.

"As your knife will always be with you, protected by this sheath, my love will always be with you, safe in your heart wherever you go."

Almost to himself, but loud enough for her to hear, he'd added, "Someday you'll understand that the love in a Hunter's heart is a great and powerful thing. It can withstand disappointment and pain, and be stronger for the testing. Remember that."

He'd offered her the beaded sheath as a symbol of infinite love. She'd promised to keep the precious token with her always. And she always had. Reb ran her fingertips comfortingly over the familiar pattern of knobby beads, then once more uncorked the whiskey bottle and poured some of its contents over the knife. She walked over to the lantern on the table, removed the globe, and ran the blade back and forth through the flame, in preparation for the overwhelming task before her.

I can do it, Daddy, she thought, as she watched the whiskey burn in muted orange and blue glory. *You taught me well.*

Adam glanced up from the fire beginning to smolder in the stove and said, "If I can hold my horses one-armed, I can hold him still for you."

Reb rewarded his effort to lighten the situation with a weak smile and, rather than say out loud how much she appreciated his support, merely nodded. She set the sharp knife down on the chest, taking care that the blade didn't touch the surface. Tossing the bowl of bloody water out the door, she refilled it from the now tepid water in the pitcher, tore several more strips of cloth from the sheet, and laid them on the chest.

Then she sat down on the edge of the bed at the stranger's side to wash the area around the wound. Once she had disinfected it with whiskey, she alerted Adam and waited for him to take his place near the head of the bed.

Both men were naked from the waist up, and Reb couldn't help making a physical comparison. She'd seen Adam shirtless innumerable times. Indeed, her father had encouraged his five children away from modesty, and much to her mother's chagrin, when they were younger, she and her sister had gone swimming in the nude several times with their brothers.

The sight of a male body was not a new, or even unusual, sight, so she had no explanation for her sudden avid curiosity. It didn't occur to her that this stranger was neither a relation nor a youth, or that she herself had matured since her last playful splash with her brothers in the swimming hole.

Both men were deeply tanned and broad of shoulder, although she reckoned the stranger must be broader by at least the width of her outspread fingers. Reb's glance paused at the stranger's collarbone and followed it to the small hollow of his throat.

She avoided looking at the destruction wrought by her bullet in the area of the left shoulder, concentrating instead on the distance between the dark nipples, turgid from the cold, that indicated the breadth of the stranger's chest. Missing was the small triangle of sandy-colored curls that accented the center of Adam's chest. She found the bared muscle oddly enticing, and nearly reached to caress the stranger's smooth skin.

Instead, she counted the several ribs that could be seen before the stranger's form narrowed to a waist as slim as Adam's. The black line of curls leading from his navel boldly downward into a pair of dark blue britches was an exciting contrast to the light down found in the same place on Adam. Reb again fought the desire to touch.

The uncharacteristic direction of her thoughts was unsettling. Her gaze leaped guiltily to the stranger's face, offering penance for so intimate an examination. But the closed, wide-set eyes, framed by thick, sooty black lashes, denied her absolution.

Adam patiently watched Reb's visual assessment of the stranger, attributing a more clinical purpose to her darting glances than was the truth. When she finally lifted her solemn face to him, he questioned with his eyes whether she was ready.

Reb directed with the knife for Adam to grip the man's right shoulder. When she began probing for the bullet, the stranger cried out hoarsely and writhed upward under her hand. "Hold him!" she said.

Adam's strong left hand pressed the stranger down as. Reb turned to the task before her, inserting the knife into the torn flesh as though it were not a totally new experience. The stranger wrenched once more under Adam's firm, one-handed grip, but made no sound as he slipped further into unconsciousness.

The work was not clean, or as neat as Reb would have liked, although she tried to minimize what she knew would be a sizable scar.

"The bullet got caught by the shoulder blade. That's why it didn't go all the way through. There are bone splinters that have to come out. This may take a while."

Before long, perspiration glistened on her high cheekbones and dotted her forehead and chin. Unable to use her bloodied hands for relief when a drop of sweat rolled down to tickle the end of her nose, Reb stuck out her lower lip and sent puffs of air upward in an attempt to dislodge the offender.

Adam grinned at her unsuccessful efforts.

"Don't just stand there, help me!" She sent him a ferocious look, meanwhile twitching helplessly.

"All you had to do was ask, Miss Independence." He gently brushed back the short, straight black hair covering her forehead. In the same motion he swiped his thumb across her damp brow, then down her small, straight nose, scratching the rounded tip lightly until Reb's relaxing features indicated relief from the itch.

"Ahhh," she purred. The uncontrollable locks settled back down on her arched eyebrows even as Adam finished his favor.

Reb had cut her waist-length black hair as short as a man's for the first time when she was fourteen. The deed had angered her mother, amused her grandmother, and left her father in the middle, reluctant to side with either of them. The incident was typical of the constant dichotomy in her upbringing, caused by the differing outlooks on life held by her mother and grandmother.

It had always been a challenge for her to please equally the two demanding and headstrong women. That she could shoot the stranger in exactly the spot she chose, ride half the day escaping from the Sioux, and then calmly treat both Adam and the stranger, who at this very moment was under her knife, with capable medical skills gleaned from her apprenticeship with the Old One and her recent study of *Gray's Anatomy* was a tribute to the success of both women's campaigns.

Sometimes Reb wished that they hadn't both been so thorough—times like now, when she found herself digging splinters of bone out of a man's shoulder.

She finally located the bullet and retrieved it from the bone where it had lodged. She gratefully rinsed her hands and the knife in the bowl of water, then cleansed and disinfected the wound one last time before binding the shoulder with strips of sheet. The sun was all but gone by the time she finished.

"All we can do now is wait for him to regain consciousness and hope he doesn't develop an infection," Reb said. "I can take care of the bruise and scratches on his temple. Get a blanket from your bedroll to wrap around you before I have to treat you for pneumonia," she told Adam.

"Yes, mother," Adam said dutifully as he headed into the dusk, throwing back at her, "If you're sure you'll be safe all alone with your stranger, I'll make sure the horses and mules are bedded down and fetch some more water and firewood, too."

Reb gave Adam a disgusted look as he disappeared. She moved the lantern so that she could better examine the unknown face she found so inexplicably tantalizing. The bruise and knot at the temple had darkened somewhat, but the break in the skin was superficial.

Already annoyed and confused by the depth of emotion the stranger aroused in her, Reb tried to detach herself from the hand that lifted aside the soft, midnight black hair from the scratch at the temple. Yes, her fingertips told her, as they threaded through the wavy mass, his hair was very soft.

She dabbed a damp cloth on the scratch and then set it aside. She hesitated only slightly before her fingers obeyed the impulse to trace an old scar highlighted on the man's cheekbone. She brushed away a small amount of dust and dirt accumulated there, and the tips of two fingers drifted down his cheek of their own volition to touch the stranger's full lips. She waited for the sleeping man to wake or react in some way to her touch, but he didn't. As she watched her fingertips glide from edge to edge of the full mouth, unbearably pleasant sensations registered in a region far removed from their source.

Reb fought, but couldn't control, the desire to smooth first one thick dark brow, and then the other, the gesture ending each time in the creases of tiny smile lines at the corners of his eyes. Her forefinger tested the bridge of a Grecian nose, then gravitated once more to the smooth scar across the prominent cheekbone.

Reb closed her eyes in the hope that by shutting the face away from view, she could end its temptation. But inexorably her hands reached up until she cupped the stranger's face, gently feeling with her fingertips the heavy black stubble along square jaws. Her thumbs drew the strong chin for her mind, then retreated to the soft lips.

Reb had never been kissed by any man except her father and brothers. Nor had it ever entered her mind to encourage such a thing. Now, she imagined the taste of the stranger's lips on her own, imagined his breath smelling of the good brandy from the East her father treasured. Unconsciously, Reb's parted lips moved downward toward a destiny of their own.

The emotional turmoil of such unaccustomed behavior finally forced Reb's eyes open in alarm. Her hands still framed his face, and her mouth was poised an inch above the stranger's lips. She jerked herself upward, hands flying outward in knotted fists, as though escaping the strike of a rattlesnake. She expected his eyes to flash open accusingly at any moment. His peaceful visage, totally unaware of the conflict stirring within her breast, forced a savage, inarticulate cry from deep within her throat.

At the sound of her own voice, Reb lurched away from the bed, appalled at what had transpired. *What's happening to me? What are you doing to me?* Dillon might welcome such emotional entanglements, seek such sensual attraction, but not Reb. "Besides, you're probably married and have three kids," she threw at the figure on the bed.

It occurred to her that she'd never checked for a wedding band. She rushed back to the bed and grabbed the lantern in one hand and the stranger's left hand in the other. No ring! Unaccountably, however, there were numerous abrasions, cuts, and scratches from the tips of his fingers to his knuckles that she hadn't noticed before.

She dropped the hand and leaned across the stranger to check his other hand, her firm breasts brushing lightly across his naked chest. She tried to ignore the exciting sensation that resulted. Both hands were in the same condition. Raw places on his wrists also should be treated. Reb set down the lantern and once again prepared a bowl of clean water and tore more rags from the decimated sheet.

Forced once more into contact that she considered too personal, Reb held the stranger's long slender fingers tenderly in her own. She couldn't have guessed in her wildest dreams how she would feel. The man's abraded fingertips burned into her own, and the tingling that began in her palm traveled up her arm until she was shivering, whether from delight or fear she couldn't have said.

She concentrated on removing all traces of dirt and pebbles from hands that were covered in the same black curls found on his belly. When the job was complete, she brushed the unmarred portion of one ravaged hand across her cheek. It was happening again. She was not in control. She was no longer sure who was possessor and who was possessed.

"No!" she whispered through gritted teeth, firmly setting the stranger's hand down upon the bed next to his body.

With the dearth of women in the West, she'd faced such male temptation before, and she'd conquered it. True, the magnetism hadn't been this strong, but if she hadn't given way to flowery words or tentative and not-so-tentative touches, she'd be damned if an unconscious man would melt her resolve!

Reb knew she enjoyed the company of men, but she chose to focus on the opportunities for competition they provided. Deep down was the fear that if she submitted to their caresses, she would lose the freedom to be one of them—to dress in buckskins, to hunt and ride, and to enjoy their laughter around the campfire after a long day.

She told herself frequently that she would never make a choice between the two different lifestyles offered by her mother and grandmother—one as a member of civilized society, the other as a roaming free spirit.

So she tried to find a compromise between the two worlds. She observed her manners at home, learned to dance and read and write, but continued to cut her hair, downplay her femininity, and meet the mountain men on equal terms. She avoided physical or emotional relationships with them and worked at being reasonable and practical and not allowing her emotions to govern her life.

Consequently, the independent souls who often sat by the Hunters' campfire accepted her on the terms she demanded. Because she earned it, they bestowed on her the respect and admiration usually reserved for their male peers.

Reb had no plans to give up her hard-won status at the tender age of seventeen. It was absolutely infuriating to find that she'd become the aggressor. Her traitorous body simply couldn't resist touching this stranger for the pure pleasure of the feeling.

"It must be the mystery of discovering an unknown man in the middle of nowhere," she muttered to herself. Well, if mystery was the problem, she could solve that.

"Just wake up, stranger, and tell me who you are," she growled softly, "and then we'll see who controls whom!"

5

"I've been thinking," Adam began, a spoonful of beans poised in midair before his mouth, "about what we should do now."

"And?" Reb helped herself to another cup of coffee from the black pot on the stove.

"Ummmmm," Adam modulated, indicating with the now empty spoon that, in obedience to his mother's training, politeness forbade talking with his mouth full.

"I've been thinking, too," Reb said. "If we hadn't run into this stranger, we'd be home by now. Dad expects us to show up to help with the spring roundup. One of us ought to ride down to the ranch and let him know what's going on. The other could stay here with the stranger until Blue shows up to take over."

"I agree," Adam surprised Reb by saying, then left her aghast when he added, "You stay here with your stranger, and I'll go down and round up cattle with Dad and the boys."

As Reb started to object, Adam hurried to explain his logic. "Blue should be back any time now, but until he shows up, you're the one with the medical skills. Besides, even one-armed I'm a better roper than you." As Reb grimaced he said, "You're not afraid to come down the mountain alone, are you?"

"Of course not," she replied indignantly. "It's just that I thought you should be the one to stay since . . . I mean, since the stranger is a man and . . ." She was unaccountably embarrassed to admit to Adam, the same Adam to whom in the past she'd always confided the antics of the forward swains she rebuffed, the effect the stranger had on her.

"Yes?" Adam waited while Reb stammered helplessly, then said matter-of-factly, "He doesn't have anything you haven't seen before." Ignoring her rolling eyes, he continued, "He'll be incapacitated, so you shouldn't be in any danger of physical harm from him. What's the problem?"

Reb didn't know whether Adam was being purposely blind to her dilemma. She struggled to think of a valid reason, besides her inexplicable attraction to the man, why she shouldn't stay alone with the stranger.

"The Indians?" she ventured.

"No." Adam watched Reb's shoulders visibly sag in defeat. "You ought to keep an eye out, but I'm not expecting any trouble. We've put Standing Buffalo out of commission for a while, and all the other Indians have gone to the Powder River except Spotted Tail's Brulés. They're now considered 'prisoners of war' and on their way to a reservation, thanks to that idiot Dodge."

"Just because he was a good general during the War between the States doesn't mean he knows how to deal with the Indians. How Washington could have assigned him to command the army out here is beyond me. If he thinks Spotted Tail's tribe will sit still for being moved to Pawnee country . . . Doesn't he realize the Pawnee and the Sioux are mortal enemies?"

The question was rhetorical, of course. Adam mounted a soapbox when he wanted to change the subject painlessly. Reb listened, knowing that, if past experience held true, the oration would be short-lived, and the subject would be changed by the time he finished speaking.

"And do you know why he's made this unbelievably stupid move of holding Sioux who've come to make peace as 'prisoners of war'?"

"Why?" Reb obediently asked.

"Because it's an embarrassment to have Indians making friendly overtures while he's planning a grand revenge campaign against the Sioux. No matter that these are 'friendly Brulés' and he's after the 'unfriendly Oglalas.' If that bastard Grenville Dodge keeps it up, he'll eliminate any difference between the 'friendlies' and the 'unfriendlies.' They'll all be out for scalps. Dodge has got to be stopped," he said, slamming his fist on the table.

"Shhh," Reb soothed. She placed her hand on Adam's fist to calm him. "You're making enough noise to wake the dead. We'll figure out a way to control Dodge so that we can get the result we want," she said, all concern at the problem of staying alone with the stranger forgotten for the moment, as Adam had intended.

The "dead" had indeed been awakened by Adam's outburst, which intruded on Kincaid's senses, nudging him to consciousness in time to hear Reb's last remark about "controlling Dodge."

"If only we knew who this stranger is," Reb said, "we could contact his people and have them come to get him. That would solve a big part of our problem."

Where am I? Kincaid wondered. The last thing he remembered was waking up in the Indian camp, and just when he'd begun to worry about how he was going to get out of the fix he was in, being shot.

And who were these two? Had they learned of his mission and captured him to thwart Dodge's plans? No, that couldn't be the case, since they didn't know who he was. If they wanted to be rid of him, why not just let the Sioux kill him? What was the problem they needed to solve?

Kincaid was confused and knew he was missing some pieces. They planned to control Dodge, he thought foggily. He must find out their plan, if possible, yet keep his own identity and mission a secret. He surreptitiously glanced at the pair seated at the table in the shifting lantern light.

The larger and apparently older of the two had leaned his chair back against the wall, one hand stiffly holding a buckskin shirt while his other hand sewed the sleeve. His left boot was up on his right knee, the right toe holding the chair in place.

The smaller had shoved the chair back far enough to stretch long legs out fully, heels resting on the table top, hands cupping a mug.

Both had short, shaggy hair, one sandy colored, the other pitch black. The older one had a day's stubble on his chin, while the younger had a face as smooth as . . . he struggled for something to compare it with.

The more he examined the complexion turned peach by the flickering reddish light, the more he thought "baby's bottom" appropriate. The lad probably hadn't reached puberty yet, and his husky voice spoke from a mouth and jaw that seemed too soft for a man. He gave the youth the benefit of the doubt, guessing that the face would strengthen as the boy matured.

One of these two probably had shot him. Time enough later to figure out the reason for that, if they didn't know who he was. He tested his shoulder by lifting slightly. Pain raced briefly across his upper body, and it was with great effort that he suppressed a groan. Clearly he would be in the custody of these two for some time. Certainly until he healed enough to think moving was preferable to dying, he told himself wryly. His tongue felt thick and fuzzy, and his head ached.

"Why is it so important for you to know who he is?" Adam asked.

"I'm just curious," Reb fibbed, admitting to herself that that was only half the truth. She believed the stranger's identity was the key to unlocking the tenacious hold he seemed to have on her heart. "Don't you want to know what happened to his companions? Surely he wasn't out here all by himself."

Kincaid absorbed this additional information. Although they didn't know who he was, their discussion suggested they would ask questions he couldn't answer. If only his head would stop hurting so he could think. Of course! He'd been hit on the head. The ache in his head eased as he put into action a plan he thought might solve some problems, even if it created others. At least it would give him some time.

"Water," he rasped.

Reb froze in her chair. Adam poured a cup of water and offered it to the man, who took it weakly in his right hand. While Adam supported his head, the thirsty man greedily drank the entire cup.

Reb rose slowly and moved as in a trance to a spot beside Adam. *He has gray eyes*, she thought. *Such sad gray eyes.*

The stranger held out the cup when he was finished. Reb was forced to reach for it, since Adam had no free hand. Trying to avoid contact with him, she inadvertently dropped the cup, which landed with a thud on the floor. She quickly retrieved it, mumbling an apology for her unusual clumsiness. She set it on the table, then returned to stand slightly behind Adam's shoulder.

Adam eased the stranger's head back down onto the pillow and stood with one hand on his hip, waiting for the silent man to speak.

Reb was dying of the curiosity she'd so recently professed to her brother. The revelation of the stranger's identity would free her from his spell. She was sure of it. When the unknown man had a name, he would lose his indefinable lure. She leaned in slightly to catch his faint words.

"Who am I?"

"What?" she blurted incredulously.

"Of course!" Adam said. "The blow to his head! We should have suspected something like this might happen."

"What are you saying?" Reb said.

"He seems to have lost his memory." Adam asked the stranger, "Can you remember anything at all about yourself, or how you got here?"

Reb held her breath.

The stranger stared intently first at Adam, noting his genuine concern, then at Reb, noting her nervous anxiety, and answered positively, "I'm sorry. I can't seem to remember anything."

"Well, I'll be damned," Adam said.

Reb groaned out loud. She turned to Adam, pleading in desperation, "You can't leave me here now. Not with this . . . this . . ." She turned to look at the virile young man, who'd cocked one eyebrow speculatively in anticipation of her description. "Mindless Yankee tenderfoot!" she finished.

A fleeting smile crossed the stranger's face.

"Watch me," Adam replied. "Come morning I'm heading down the mountain. I'll check at Fort Laramie to see if anyone knows who you are," he told the stranger.

Kincaid unclenched the hands he'd fisted under the covers. They believed him. It was going to work. And he couldn't believe his good fortune. The older one was actually going to leave the younger one here alone with him. "Thank you. By the way, where am I?" he asked so quietly Adam had to bend down to hear him. "How did I get here?" The last question came out as a kind of sigh.

Adam realized the stranger was struggling to keep his eyes open. "Tomorrow's soon enough for all that. You just rest now. Reb'll tell you anything you want to know tomorrow."

Reb gave Adam an angry glare and crossed her arms defiantly across her breasts.

"Reb?" the stranger whispered, eyes closing. A chasm opened, and Kincaid plunged into an exhausted sleep.

"Yeah, my baby sister Reb—" Adam stopped when he realized the stranger hadn't heard him. "He's asleep."

"I can see that," Reb snapped, letting the full measure of her anger at the stranger fall on Adam. "Adam," she began in a loud voice.

"Shhh." He placed a finger before his lips. "You don't want to wake your stranger."

"You're not seriously going to leave me here with him in this condition, are you?" she hissed back at him.

He folded his sister in his good arm to comfort her. "Reb, Reb, think what an opportunity this will be. He's like a clean slate—a man with no bad habits to contend with. With total ignorance like his, you can turn him into a right fair human being by the time Blue shows up," he teased.

Reb didn't see the twinkle in Adam's eyes as he smoothed her shorn locks. His suggestion, although humorously intended, put a bee in Reb's bonnet. She jerked out of Adam's grasp in her excitement.

"You're right," she said. A grin broke across her face for the first time since they'd encountered the stranger. "I wouldn't miss an opportunity like this for all the prairie oysters in the world. By the time I get through, he may still be a Yankee, but he won't be a mindless tenderfoot," Reb said smugly. "I'll teach him a thing or two. Why, he'll be *so* polite. I can't wait to get started!"

Adam looked askance at Reb. "Don't overdo it."

"Don't worry." Reb smiled with the knowledge that she was once more absolutely in control of the situation. "You just go brand and castrate calves with Dad and the boys and don't worry one little bit about me and *my* stranger. I'll be fine. Now, are we going to let this man sleep in his boots?"

"Uh, no." Adam was too concerned that Reb had a little castrating of her own in mind to focus on her question. "I'll take his boots off. You want his pants off, too?" he asked suggestively.

"Yes," Reb said, ignoring his leer. "Take everything off and give it all to me."

Adam did as he was bid, both of them registering in silence the extensive scar on the stranger's right thigh. Finally, Adam covered the naked man with the sheet and wool blanket on the bed.

"Now we'd better think about getting some sleep

ourselves," Reb told Adam. "Dawn comes early, and the sooner you get started, the better."

Adam followed her lead, but wondered whether he'd made a mistake in his evaluation of Reb's feelings toward the nameless man. He'd thought she was attracted to the stranger, but her plans to "remake" the poor man made him stop to reconsider. He didn't want to leave Reb in an uncomfortable situation if he'd misjudged her feelings. He decided to give her one last chance to trade places with him. "Maybe I ought to stay here, after all," he suggested.

"Oh, no, you don't," Reb replied. "I'm planning this party, and you aren't invited. Pillow?" She offered Adam a folded-up blanket, a serene smile adorning her flushed face.

Adam thought at that moment she was beautiful. He wondered what the stranger would think. He lay down, wrapped up in his buffalo robe, and, not aware how much the efforts of the day had drained him, immediately fell asleep.

"Adam?" Reb called from her place beside him on the floor several minutes later. A small snore indicated that Adam was no longer of this world. "I only wanted to ask," she whispered anyway, "whether you think my stranger isn't a handsome man?"

6

Adam uttered a last good-bye, visible in the frosty air, and moved down the mountain, pack mules in tow. Reb watched and waved until he disappeared into the dim forest, prolonging until the last possible moment her reentry into the quiet cabin. At last the chilly wind and cloudy skies forced her back into the somewhat warmer refuge.

Like a homing pigeon, she headed for the stranger, approaching hesitantly, then more surely as she noticed he seemed feverish. Immediately concerned for him as a doctor for her patient, Reb placed her palm on his forehead. It was hot to the touch. She pressed the back of her hand to his whiskered cheek, also hot.

Suddenly a powerful hand grabbed her wrist in a paralyzing, but not painful grip, and she found herself gazing into the flinty gray eyes of the fully wakened man.

"You have a fever," she said, attempting to free herself. "I need to check your wound."

"Who are you?" He tightened his grasp.

"My name is Reb."

"As in Johnny Reb?" he asked menacingly.

"No, no," she reassured him. "It's . . ." She hesitated, unwilling to let him know it was a masculine shortening of Rebecca. "It's just a nickname."

Kincaid suspected the young man was hiding something, but continued his interrogation. "That other fellow . . ."

"Adam," she supplied.

"Are you his brother?"

"He's my brother," Reb answered evasively. Apparently the stranger didn't recognize her as a woman. So much the better.

"Where is he?"

"He's gone. Don't you remember? He went to Fort Laramie to see if he can find out who you are. Do you remember anything about yourself this morning?" she questioned hopefully.

"No." He sighed, already regretting the necessity to pretend amnesia.

"I need to check your wound," she reminded him.

He released her hand, then waited stoically for the changing of bandages with which he had such recent familiarity.

"Go ahead." His face closed to all emotion.

Reb watched the hardening features age the young man before her eyes. She proceeded to quickly unwrap the bandages with a deft yet gentle touch.

Reb gasped when she saw the wound.

Kincaid braced himself for bad news. "Infection?" He refused to look at himself, having seen enough of his own torn flesh.

Reb's gasp had been the result of surprise at what she did *not* find. There was no bright red skin, no oozing pus to indicate the anticipated infection that would explain the stranger's fever. The wound looked—ordinary. A scab was forming, and the skin surrounding it had the expected colorful black and blue bruising.

Reb met the stranger's gaze and answered in amazement, "No infection at all."

Kincaid frowned at her contrary diagnosis.

Reb rebound the wound snugly with clean strips of sheet. Forced to look for another cause for his fever, Reb started asking questions, fearing the answers she would get.

"How do you feel?" she asked, flustered by the turn of events.

"How should I feel?" he retorted.

"How do you feel!" she shot back impatiently. "Are you hungry?"

"No!" That answer surprised him even as he admitted it. He should be hungry, since he hadn't eaten in over twenty-four hours.

"Are you thirsty?"

"Yes." His tongue felt furred, in fact.

"How about your head?"

"I have a headache. Is that any surprise?"

Reb reached out to lay her fingertips on the pulse at his throat, and the stranger once again stayed her hand.

Kincaid wondered at the slenderness of the wrist he held, which reminded him once more of the youth of his physician. The commanding tone of the boy's next words belied his apparent youth.

"I need to feel your pulse."

"Are you a doctor?" he demanded, curious about the competent self-confidence of the lad.

"Do you have someone else in mind for the job?" she asked, gesturing around the deserted cabin.

Kincaid allowed the boy to place his fingertips on his throat.

The increased rate alarmed Reb. "I want to listen to your breathing," she said as she lowered her ear to his chest. The labored breathing, rapid and shallow, revealed the answer she sought.

"Are you always so irascible?" she asked, to postpone thinking about what her examination had revealed.

"I don't know. Are you always so kind to your patients?"

Reb laughed out loud, surprising Kincaid with the warmth of the sound.

No infection for this huge, irritable, and irritating

man, she thought, amused at the ludicrous conclusion she'd been forced to draw by her examination. This stranger, unfazed by a bullet wound that had narrowly missed his heart, had caught a cold from exposure. The head and shoulder wounds probably hadn't helped. God only knew if he would develop pneumonia.

"You have a fever, and I think it's the result of your exposure to the cold. You should drink lots of water, and it would help get the fever down if I applied wet cloths. Are you willing to cooperate?" Reb wasn't sure what she would do if he refused.

Kincaid studied the serious young man. It disturbed him to hand over his well-being to the youth, but he had seen younger men handle even greater responsibility during the war, so he was hesitant to deny himself the boy's services. He avoided answering by asking another question.

"How did I get hurt?"

"The head wound you had when my brother and I found you strung up by the Sioux. I . . . I shot you. It was the only way we could think of to rescue you," she rushed to explain.

"You see, there were too many Indians for us to kill before one of them would have finished you off, so we decided to 'kill' you first. The bullet broke your shoulder blade. I guess I miscalculated a little," Reb finished lamely, unwilling to continue in the face of the stranger's obvious skepticism, and angry that she should feel the need to apologize.

Kincaid heard in the story the excuses of a child caught doing something he shouldn't, and seeking parental expunging of guilt for the wayward action.

"Are you that good a shot, that you had no qualms about shooting someone to 'save' him?" He was not yet ready to oblige in the matter of forgiveness.

"Yes," Reb answered, then added defiantly in response to the eyebrows rising in disbelief, "You're alive, aren't you?"

"Just barely," he muttered under his breath.

Reb heard him, and an unwanted blush began to rise at her throat.

Returning her earlier sarcasm, he asked, "And I'm to believe you and your brother risked your necks to save a total stranger?"

"You can bet I'll think twice before I do it again," she spat as she headed for the door.

"Hold it, kid," he said to the retreating form.

Reb whirled and lashed out, "I'm not a kid, I'm . . ." She hesitated, not willing to reveal her true age lest he judge her by her years. "I'm not a kid," she repeated. "I know more about how to survive out here than a tenderfoot like you, so if you expect to live through this ordeal, I suggest you think twice before you draw any more unfounded conclusions."

Kincaid admired the boy's spunk. "Whoa!" he laughed. "You're a Rebel, all right."

Reb watched the years fall away from the man and was tempted by the change to try once more to help him. "Are you going to cooperate?" she asked testily.

"Sure," the stranger answered. "By the way, where are we?"

"A cabin in the mountains, about fifty miles from Fort Laramie," she replied. "It belongs to a friend of my father's, a trapper named Blue. He should be showing up here any time now."

Damn, Kincaid thought. *Another complication.* He was very tired. Aloud he said, "I could use some sleep," and closed his eyes.

Before she would let him rest, Reb forced the exhausted man to drink some water and provided a pot from under the bed so he could relieve himself. She refused to be embarrassed by the necessity for this assistance, and his lack of knowledge that she was a woman made the duty easier.

The murmur of Reb's voice as she applied the cooling cloths over his upper body and face lulled Kincaid to sleep.

When her patient was resting comfortably, Reb busied herself making a nutritious broth. When she got wood for the stove, she noted the supply was low and decided to take advantage of the respite from her duties with the stranger to split some more logs. The fresh tang of the pine chips assailed her nostrils, replacing the distinctive masculine scent of the stranger that she only now realized she'd been savoring.

When it was nearly noon, she felt the first cold snowflake land on her eyelash. She blinked it away, only to have it replaced by two more on her cheek and upper lip. Licking the snowflake away from her mouth, Reb suddenly became aware of the brisk, icy wind that whirled around her.

She hurried to ensure that her horse, Brandy, and the Indian pony that had carried the injured man had plenty of water and feed, pausing to caress her mount. "What do you think, Brandy?" She slid her fingers across the smooth nose of the mare. "Who is my stranger? A famous hero, or a dastardly villain? He is pleasing to the eye, don't you agree?" The horse nickered softly.

Reb laughed aloud at the fanciful conversation. She gave the horse a final pat on the withers. "Don't worry, Brandy, I won't let him ride you. He's a little large for a dainty lady like yourself."

Reb shivered at the picture of being mounted by the stranger that drifted through her mind. "Although I'm sure he'd be very gentle," she murmured. As she left, she closed the door of the shed to protect the horses from the blowing snow.

Reb gathered a last load of wood to carry to the

cabin and was grateful to be going in out of the cold, which she felt sharply now that she was no longer warmed by the physical exertion of chopping wood.

The stranger was awake again.

"It's snowing," she said, to make conversation.

"Oh," Kincaid replied, unsure what to say. "Is that normal for this time of year?"

"A May blizzard isn't normal, but it's not uncommon either, up here. I hope Adam doesn't get caught in the storm," she worried out loud, catching her lower lip in her teeth.

Kincaid observed the fear in the wide eyes and spoke to calm the urchin. "He's probably halfway down the mountain by now, don't you think?"

Reb regarded him with a tremulous smile. "Yes, you're probably right. I'm worrying for nothing, I know. It's just that Adam and I are very close."

Kincaid envied Adam the apparent devotion of his brother. The love of his parents had alleviated the loneliness of being an only child, but he'd discovered during the war the deep feelings of brothers for each other and the shared camaraderie that was so different from the parent-child relationship.

"He's lucky to have a brother like you," he found himself complimenting the youth, who blushed with pleasure, making him look slightly cherubic.

"I'll get you some broth." Reb moved away to escape the stranger's scrutiny.

Kincaid allowed himself to be spoon-fed to keep the boy's mind off his brother. Somehow the lad appeared younger and younger the more he observed and listened to him. *Pretty soon I'll have him in knee britches*, he mused to himself disgustedly.

The protective instinct that rose sparred with the logical side of Kincaid's mind that told him however young the boy looked, however kindly he acted at the moment, the brat had shot him. Even now, the kid must be thinking up ways to interfere with Dodge's plan.

"Is Adam your only kin?" he asked gruffly, determined to find a subject to dispel the aura of pervasive goodwill in the room.

"No," Reb said. "I have another older brother, Garth, and a younger sister and brother, Dillon and Jesse."

"What about your parents?"

"My father, Matthew Hunter, is alive, as well as my grandmother, the Old One. My mother was killed in the war," she finished bitterly.

Kincaid couldn't imagine how the war had reached out here in the wilderness to snatch this boy's mother.

"The war?"

"You don't remember the war?" Reb wondered what it would be like to have such an earth-shattering event wiped from one's memory. "You were in the war, I think. I've seen your right leg." She paused to watch the stranger massage his thigh for a moment.

Kincaid hadn't realized he was rubbing the pitted scar on his upper leg. It was a habit born of necessity, since without massage or some activity the muscle stiffened and ached. He met the boy's wide eyes, and the two shared a moment of common pathos.

"The war seemed so far from us. It was a fight between Northerners and Southerners. We were no part of it. The only difference out here was that fewer soldiers were stationed at the forts. I had no objection to that. The fewer easterners out here, the better."

Kincaid recognized Reb's attitude toward eastern- ers from her tone of voice. It reminded him of the dis- dainful attitude of Johnny Rebs toward Yankees.

She continued, "My grandfather, my mother's father, who lived in Philadelphia, somehow talked the Yankees into making him an adviser. He wasn't supposed to go near the fighting, but he did, and was hit by cannon fire. We got word that he was dying. My mother hadn't seen him since she married my father, but she insisted on being with him.

"My father couldn't stop her from going, and for some reason he wouldn't go with her. She took a stage until she could catch a train." Reb could barely speak with the strain of holding back unmanly tears.

"You don't have to continue," Kincaid said, empathizing with the boy's loss. It was difficult to imagine people ignoring the war, pretending it wasn't happening. He thought of his own parents, back in their Fifth Avenue brownstone mansion in New York, who'd done a pretty good job of it. Apparently, these people hadn't been entirely successful.

He wasn't prepared for the string of invectives that spewed forth from the youth suddenly, and he was so surprised he only caught the words "filthy Yankees" and "killed by a damned train."

"What?"

"A Yankee train! A Yankee train," she repeated, breathing heavily, barely under control.

"Is it Yankees you have no stomach for, or trains?" Kincaid probed gently, certain now, with the mention of distaste for trains, of his original suspicion that the two brothers hadn't come upon him accidentally.

"Both!" Reb knew she shouldn't be revealing the overwhelming distaste she'd developed for Yankees and the irrational fear she had of trains since her mother's accident. This was one area where knowing she should stay calm and actually accomplishing that goal were two different things. Both her hate and her fear had condensed into dread of the dragon her mother had warned her was coming: civilization.

"You want to talk about it?" Kincaid asked. He didn't wish to upset the now agitated youth any further, but he did want to find out as much as he could to protect his mission and perhaps save his own life.

"My mother is dead because some Yankee was too greedy to spend any money maintaining his train and the track it ran on," Reb accused.

"Men out here aren't guilty of greed?"

"No mountain man could be as greedy as you Yankees."

Kincaid noted his inclusion among the offensive group.

Reb ranted at her captive, "The South only wanted to maintain its way of life. The North wouldn't let go. It destroyed the South rather than give it up. A mountain man would never hang on if doing so would destroy the worth of that which he sought to hold.

"There are rumors the Northerners want to build a railroad out here. That's a perfect example of Yankee thoughtlessness. Did they ask us if we needed it, or even wanted it? No! But they'd put it here, to ruin our way of life without ever considering the consequences. I'll never let that happen if I can help it!"

Reb's statements destroyed any doubt Kincaid had about the reason for his capture. It was difficult to argue that the North hadn't wreaked havoc with the South. Kincaid had seen enough carnage to convince him that the South was close to ruin. For his own reasons, he didn't agree with her comparison between the results of the war and the results of building the railroad.

"Don't you think that's being unfair? What about

the positive things a railroad could provide?" Kincaid argued.

Reb shuddered. "Trains will bring people. We don't need them out here." It was the Old One speaking, through Reb. "It's one thing my father and I agree on."

Kincaid glanced at the fierceness of the kid's countenance as he defended his way of life. Then he amended his impression. *That is no child.*

"What does your father do?" he asked.

"Mostly, he raises cattle. We all help. Adam went to join him for the roundup." Reb gladly left the topic of railroads. It was easy to discuss with the attentive stranger the monotony of herding cattle balanced by the pleasure of hearing newborn calves bawl for their mothers. Before either of them was aware of it, darkness was falling.

"Time to feed you again," Reb said when she noticed the failing light.

At the thought of more broth, Kincaid uttered an "Ugh!" that made Reb laughingly reply, "I never said I could cook."

He watched the boy efficiently stoke the fire and warm the broth left over from lunch. Soon he found himself once more full, sponged down, relieved, and tucked in to sleep.

From the sound of the wind driving the powdery flakes around the outside of the cabin, Reb guessed the storm was abating. She thought how apt was the local saying, "We don't get much snow, but a lot blows through." In acknowledgment of the cold, she quietly stripped off her buckskins and underclothes in the dark to don the full-length nightshirt she kept at Blue's cabin for just such occasions. She gloried in the feel of the soft, warm flannel against her bare skin.

It was a relief to have the stranger asleep, even though his fever remained high and he restlessly tossed in bed. She thought ruefully how wrong Adam had been about the stranger having no bad habits. He was extremely argumentative for someone with no memory. And good at getting me to talk, she thought. Adam probably was wrong about the danger of physical harm, too, she added silently, rubbing her wrist where the stranger had grasped it. Even when he was injured, his strength exceeded that of most men she knew.

She spread a buffalo robe on the floor beside the stove and dropped down to curl up inside it. She wished she hadn't been so glib with the man. Why had she gushed out the story of her mother's death and her aim to fight against the takeover of her wilderness by the Yankees? After all, he was a Yankee, too.

Enough of regrets, she admonished herself. Instead, she should be congratulating herself on how well she'd suppressed even a moment of desire for the stranger throughout the day. "I don't need him, I don't want him, and he won't have me," she pledged as she drifted off to sleep.

The frantic shouts of the stranger woke Reb in the middle of the night. She didn't take time to light the lamp, but bounded over to the thrashing man. Fearing he would further injure himself, she sat on the bucking Yankee to keep him in bed. She pulled her nightshirt up to straddle his waist, quickly placing a knee on each arm to hold them down. She put one palm on the center of his chest and one on his right shoulder, leaning down to his face to talk soothingly to the struggling man, who seemed to be having a nightmare.

"Don't leave me," he pleaded desperately.

"I won't leave you," she reassured him. She laid her cheek next to his to check his temperature. His skin was on fire. When he began to talk again, she decided he must be suffering from delirium caused by the high fever.

"I'm not that rich, arrogant Yankee spy Christopher anymore," he entreated. "I'm just plain Kincaid. I've changed, Laurie. I've changed."

So he was a Yankee spy named Christopher. Or Kincaid. Who was Laurie?

"It's all right, Kincaid," she comforted, hoping to keep him still. "I'm here."

"Let me love you," he urged, his head, the only unpinned portion of his body, coming up from the pillow, seeking contact with the feminine voice in the dark.

"No!" Reb jerked away from the stranger when his mouth found hers, freeing his arms. They came up around her instantly, pulling her down to him, binding them breast to breast, her right hand caught between them.

She could feel the heat from his fevered body through the flannel nightshirt. Amazed and startled at how fast the situation had gotten out of hand, Reb forced herself to remain calm while Kincaid murmured love words in her ear and kissed her tenderly along her jaw and down her neck behind her ear.

She waited, expecting the period of delirium to pass at any moment. She was unprepared for the strange feelings elicited by her close contact with the man's hot skin. She was intensely aware of her bare thighs touching his waist; the constriction of inner muscles warned that Kincaid's affectionate attentions were not without their effect.

She listened to the endearments, anxious for a way to ease the unfamiliar erotic tension mounting moment by moment. She didn't struggle, mistakenly thinking she could ignore the physical sensations generated by the hallucinating man.

"So beautiful," he whispered in her ear. "So soft, so lovely."

Reb closed her eyes and envied Laurie, whoever she was, while she fantasized that Kincaid spoke to her.

"Let me touch you," he implored. One hand forced her upward enough to enable him to cup her breast. She reached up to stop him, but ended by resting her own hand upon his instead, while he gently caressed her nipple until it stood in an excited peak. Without warning, the nightshirt was pulled up and Kincaid's warm, wet mouth replaced his hand and gently tugged on the sensitive point. The whiskers that scratched her delicate skin roused her to action.

Her hands flew to Kincaid's hair, her fingers threading through it. Grasping the silky stuff with both hands, she tried pulling his head away. But it was too late. He increased his hold, swirling his tongue around the responsive tip while his callused fingertips caressed her velvety skin, until at last she abandoned all resistance, pressing him to her and arching backward, offering him freer access to her body.

His tongue titillated first one breast and then the other, while his hands continued their quest over her sleek form. Wrapped in delight, Reb lost track of time until Kincaid slid her down his belly into a prone position so that her most private place made contact with his swollen shaft. She instinctively pressed her body closer to his. He grabbed her naked buttocks to help her in the pleasurable endeavor.

His tongue dipped slowly into her honeyed mouth, then delved deeply, seeking sweeter nectar. Unaccustomed to the intoxicating feelings he generated, Reb relented further to Kincaid's explorations. She could no longer act, she could only react. In a haze of sensation, she felt herself pushed upright to a sitting position once again, as Kincaid's hands set out on a delicious assault of her breasts and belly.

"Perfect," Kincaid praised. "Breasts like ripe fruits, belly so firm, one day to grow large with my seed . . . We'll make beautiful babies."

Bombarded with the satisfaction of itches she hadn't known needed scratching, she didn't resist when he grabbed her waist with both hands, intending to join himself with her. Reb was ready, anxious even, for the consummation of an act she only hours earlier had denied she needed or wanted.

At the last moment, Kincaid placed her back upon his belly, away from the source of satisfaction.

Reb moaned in rebellion, pressing her rosy crests enticingly back down upon his chest and pushing her body back down against him, seeking gratification.

"No, no, love," he said gently in her ear, scraping her sensitive breasts along his chest in sweet pain as he put his hands under her arms and raised her up and away from temptation. "You're right. Must wait, must wait," he chanted, resisting her entreaty with great effort. "Marry me. Be my wife, Laurie," he said, stroking the hair tenderly from her damp forehead.

The shock of being denied brought Reb back to bitter reality. Kincaid was delirious. He was making love to another woman, not her, one he'd wanted to marry and to have his children. Appalled and ashamed at her behavior, and enraged at Kincaid's unknowing callousness to her, she hit out at the source of her humiliation.

"Let go!" she cried, slapping Kincaid and struggling to escape his embrace.

"No, I won't let her go," Kincaid said, lost again in his nightmare. "She's my wife. She's not dead! She's not dead, I tell you. Don't die, Laurie, don't die," he cried in agony. "Don't leave me," he whispered desperately. Kincaid relaxed his hold long enough for Reb to scramble off the bed.

"Don't take her away!" he shouted, arms flailing. One powerful clubbed fist caught Reb in the eye and knocked her across the room, where she stumbled against a chair and fell backward. She hit the door hard enough to knock her unconscious.

Kincaid swung his feet over the side of the bed, but when he tried to rise, he fainted from the effort.

When Reb came to, she found herself slumped in front of the door, one eye swollen shut. Sunlight streamed through the skin window, reflecting off the frigid white snow. Kincaid lay sprawled sideways across the bed, naked and shivering. The fire in the stove had gone out, and she could see her breath in the room.

She rose painfully, stiff from the cold and the fall, and crossed to look down at the man who'd rejected the offer of her virginity.

"How sad," she mused, recognizing in the shivering man symptoms of deadly pneumonia, "for both of us. He's in love with a dead woman, and I'm in love with a dying man."

It's all my fault, she thought guiltily. If I hadn't wanted him to make love to me, I would have been able to control him, to keep him from hurting both of us.

She'd broken her own cardinal rule. She'd gotten involved, and the results had been disastrous. *Well, I won't make that mistake again*, she vowed silently.

She rearranged Kincaid on the bed, covered him with the sheet and blanket, and then added the buffalo robe from the floor as well.

"You're not going to die," she told the unconscious man. "You're going to get well, Kincaid, and then you're going to get out of my life!"

7

"Hey, Blue, wait up," Adam shouted loud enough to be heard across the barren parade ground. He tied his horse and the mules at a nearby hitching rail in front of the officers' quarters and marched diagonally across the length of the austere compound separating him from the mountain man. "Hi there, Trapper," he greeted Blue's wolfish dog. He dropped on his knees to grab the thick, gray fur at the animal's neck, rough-housing playfully with him. "What are you doing here at Fort Laramie, Blue? I thought you never came down here," he said when he stood again.

Blue squinted at Adam, who had his back to the sunset. "Usually I don't," the wiry, long-limbed man replied. "But I was tracking somebody, and this is where he came."

Blue had spent so much time in the sun his face deserved the "beaten" in the word *weatherbeaten*. The unevenly cut black hair that fell into his arched black brows and the several days' growth of black and gray stubble on his face gave him a grizzled look, but the flame in the warm, mahogany eyes testified to the fiery spirit that dwelled within. "I could ask the same about you." He gestured toward the arm Adam still carried in a sling. "You look a little the worse for wear. What happened?"

"It's a long story. Let's go sit where we can talk without being ogled." Adam glanced around at the beardless new recruits lining the barracks wall, who gawked rudely at the two men.

They headed for the sutler's store, which supplied the soldiers with combs, writing paper, thread, sweets, and other sundries not issued by the quartermaster. It was deserted except for the proprietor, a long-toothed man named Sam.

The store was off-limits to the soldiers unless they had money to spend. Fortunately for Adam and Blue, the recruits had long since gambled away the pittance they'd earned, and payday was weeks away. While the Indians usually traded there as well, none were present now.

"Hi, Sam," Adam called to the sutler.

"Jes' make yerselves ta home," the white-bearded coot said from behind the long, waist-high wooden counter cluttered with bolts of cloth, canned goods, tobacco, ribbons, and jars of candy. The old man disappeared through a doorway hung with a tattered red wool blanket, muttering, "Got some unpackin' ta do in the back."

"He's not much for company," Adam excused the old-timer.

When they settled in rickety wooden chairs before the huge black iron stove, Trapper lolling on the uneven dirt floor between Blue's outstretched feet, Adam reached for a peppermint stick from one of the jars on the counter and, while he sucked on it, recounted the events of the previous day.

"That Reb, she's something," he said, finishing his story and the candy at the same time. "Nothing would do but we save that stranger, and we did."

"You left her alone with that man?"

Adam could hear Blue's concern. "We expected you to show up at any minute. I didn't think she'd be alone with him long." He licked his sticky fingers clean, then said, "It's a funny thing. I've never known Reb to show any female interest in a man, but she sure is all-fired attracted to this stranger."

"Mooning over him?"

"Not exactly," Adam replied with a grin. "As a matter of fact, when I left, she was all set to teach him some manners." Adam filled Blue in on the man's amnesia and Reb's pledge to instruct the "mindless Yankee tenderfoot." "I came here to see if I can find out who he is. I don't have any doubt Reb can handle the situation so long as Standing Buffalo doesn't show up."

"You don't have to worry about Standing Buffalo," Blue said, his eyes narrowing.

"What makes you say that?"

"I followed him. He's here at Spotted Tail's camp outside the fort."

"You followed him? From where?"

"From where you ambushed him," Blue said quietly.

"But if you were there . . . ?" Adam couldn't believe that Blue had been there but hadn't made his presence known.

"I guess you're old enough to know the truth and not get huffy," Blue said resignedly. Then, looking into Adam's eyes, man to man, he said, "I've followed you down the mountain from my cabin every year since the first year you came."

"You what?" Adam sprang up in shock at Blue's admission.

"Sit down," Blue said, staring Adam back into his seat. "Hear what I have to say."

Adam sat down, but the tension in his powerful young body belied the blankness of his features.

"I made an agreement with Matt that first year that I'd be sure you and Reb got back down the mountain safely."

Adam's mouth tightened perceptibly at the corners at the thought his father hadn't trusted him.

As if reading his mind, Blue added, "Your father knew a sixteen-year-old boy doesn't want a wet nurse. Anyway, it wasn't you he didn't trust."

"Reb."

"Yes," Blue confirmed. "She had the skills of an adult and the curiosity of a child. She was just as likely to listen to you as to wave your opinion away and do what she wanted. It was only meant to be a precaution, and only the first year," Blue said.

"But you said—"

"I know," he interrupted. "I followed you down after that because I wanted to do it. Once or twice I was glad I was there," he confessed grimly, reflecting back over the years.

"The bear!" Adam recalled the year when Reb had disappeared, making him frantic until she suddenly came up behind him with a black bear cub over her horse's neck, saying it must be an orphan. "You must have provided the distraction that kept that hornet-mad mother from catching up to us."

Blue nodded. Adam could remember as though it were yesterday the cub scampering away after its mother when Reb released it, and their fear the mother bear would come after them.

"And the wolves," Blue said, reminding Adam of the time the pair had been trapped by a blizzard and besieged by a large, hungry pack.

"I'd forgotten that," Adam murmured. "I can be grateful now for the help, although I would have been angry if I'd known about it at the time."

"You've come further than Reb," Blue said. "She still thinks she can handle anything on her own."

"I don't know about that. She's expecting you to show up at your cabin any moment to help her out with the stranger," Adam said.

"I think we should let her stew in her own juices for a while," Blue replied with a conspirational smile.

"Fine by me. So long as she vents her wrath on you and not me," Adam said. "Before you go back up, you might want to ask around and see if anyone can identify that Yankee we rescued."

Blue had seen the captive spread-eagled in the forest and wondered himself where the man had come from. "Be glad to check up on him."

"I'm heading home tomorrow, then." Adam stretched one-armed as he rose. "Think I'll go find a place to bed down and get some sleep."

"I prefer to sleep under the open sky, but if you can stand the stares, there's room in the barracks," Blue offered.

"It beats the ground." Adam took a good look at the awkward youngsters drilling outside. "Pretty green," he said.

"Yeah. They got a new bunch in, fresh from *not* fighting the Civil War, that's supposed to head out tomorrow. They'll escort Spotted Tail and his Sioux to a reservation near the Pawnee. You got a picture of that?"

A frown furrowed Adam's brow. "You're expecting trouble."

"Let's just say I plan to stick around to make sure nobody starts an Indian war," Blue replied.

"Good luck. Send Reb home as soon as you can. We can use her help with the roundup. She's a pretty good roper—for a girl."

"Don't let her hear you say that," Blue said, chuckling.

"I may be crazy, but I'm not *that* crazy."

Blue watched Adam unhitch his animals and head for the stables, then murmured, "Rachel, Rachel, my love, your children are growing up."

The strong smell of bear grease awakened Blue. He slowly opened his eyes to find Spotted Tail squatting next to his head, knife in hand, muscular forearms resting on his knees, his black eyes glittering intently, watching for Blue to become alert.

Without moving, Blue greeted the chief of the Brulé Sioux. "Welcome, my friend."

"You're getting careless in your old age. Were I not a friend, you would be a dead man," Spotted Tail said with a chuckle, setting the point of his knife in the hollow of Blue's throat.

Blue looked around furtively for his dog.

"Your dog has gone to chase a rabbit. You should

not depend on him to be your ears. Someday your ears may not be there when you need to hear."

"I will take your words to my heart," Blue said, gracefully accepting the lesson as Spotted Tail sheathed his knife. "What makes Spotted Tail seek out an old friend in the dark?" Blue rose slowly to a sitting position and crossed his legs Indian fashion.

"Tomorrow the soldiers take us to the land of our enemy, the Pawnee."

"I know."

"My people will not accept the will of the White Father that we live so near our enemy."

"I know," Blue repeated. "My heart is heavy for the people of Spotted Tail."

"Is your grief great enough to help us escape?"

"What can I do for my brother, Spotted Tail?" Blue asked earnestly. "I won't kill the soldiers myself, nor help you kill them."

"We have a way to be free of the Blue Coats without killing. You can help us by keeping them from overtaking us before we reach the Powder River. With the women and children, we cannot travel fast."

"How can I do that?"

"You will find a way," Spotted Tail said confidently, placing the burden squarely in Blue's lap. "Then you can go back to Too-Big-For-Horses."

Blue's eyes hooded.

"Standing Buffalo says his prisoner was stolen by

two young trappers. His picture of them is like that of the two who visit you each new season."

"And if this is true?"

"In return for your help I will keep Standing Buffalo close by my side, and we will not find Too-Big-For-Horses on our journey north."

Blue sat quietly thinking for a moment. "I will do what I can to delay the soldiers because we are old friends. But I make no guarantee."

"That is all I can ask."

"Look well to your path," Blue said. "I wouldn't like it if the young trappers come to harm. Then I might think you no longer value the friendship you gave me in return for saving your life."

"I have not forgotten I owe my life to you, my friend," Spotted Tail replied soberly. "But for you, my scalp would be the prize of a Pawnee warrior."

The men measured each other by the light of the evening stars, pleased with what they found.

"I will keep my part of the bargain," Spotted Tail said, rising to leave.

Blue slowly unfolded from his sitting position and held out his hand. Spotted Tail clasped Blue's arm to his own, so the men were joined elbow to wrist. Blue, a head taller, looked down into the grave eyes of the Brulé chief.

"And I mine." Blue increased the pressure of his grip to seal the agreement. With an understanding reached, they released each other, and Spotted Tail disappeared into the night.

Trapper picked that moment to reappear. "Thanks a lot, pal," Blue said, dropping to his haunches to scratch the animal lovingly under his chin. "That could've turned into more than an embarrassing moment if it hadn't been Spotted Tail. Try to stick around a little closer, will you? You know my hearing's not what it used to be. All right?"

Trapper whined and gave Blue a look of understanding.

"All right," Blue repeated quietly. He pulled the old dog close and gave him a hug. "All right."

8

⟪⟫

Kincaid rolled from his back to his right side on the soft, overstuffed mattress, drawing his bare left leg up and out from under the oppressively warm covers until his knee sank into the ticking at a right angle with his sweat-soaked body. His powerful right arm curled childlike around the matted black curls on his head, protectively cupping the crown. Somewhere, deep in his consciousness, it registered that the pain that resulted from this change in position was located in his left shoulder, not his right thigh.

He opened his eyes and quickly shut them again, then blinked several times to adjust to the daylight streaming in through the opaque window. He waited for the film that blurred his vision to clear.

The first thing he saw was the boy, Reb, sprawled sleeping, legs akimbo, in a chair next to the bed. His head was cradled in his arms on the edge of the mattress. Kincaid touched the youth's frail arm to wake him, but got no reaction.

"Rebel," he managed to whisper, weakly applying more pressure to the boy's arm.

With a languor that bespoke the eight sleepless days and nights Reb had fought death, she gradually raised her tired head to peer half-asleep at the source of the rational baritone voice.

"Kincaid?" She feared she was dreaming, because she wanted so badly to find the fever broken.

Kincaid noted vaguely that she called him by his name. "You look a little under the weather," he said, attempting a grin that caused his dry lips to crack. He licked them with his equally dry tongue, then added, "Where'd you get the shiner?"

Reb heaved a private sigh of relief that Kincaid didn't remember the events leading to her blackened eye. She touched her fingertips to the still tender yellow and purple skin.

"I have you to thank for this," she said.

Kincaid's eyes widened in surprise.

"Delirium," she said.

"Sorry."

It embarrassed her to hear him take responsibility for something she considered her fault. "Are you hungry?" Although she'd force-fed Kincaid regularly, she didn't know when she'd eaten last. She was aware of a gnawing in her stomach that suggested it hadn't been filled recently. She stretched each arm upward from her aching body, palms outward and long fingers outstretched, while a huge yawn forced her mouth to open wide and her eyes to squeeze shut.

"I could eat a horse." Kincaid drew the last word out as his mouth fell open, echoing her yawn.

Reb braced her palms on the sagging mattress and pushed herself up out of the hard, uncomfortable chair, pausing to arch her stiff back and massage her buttocks. She checked Kincaid's brow with her palm and found it cool and moist.

"Fever's broken. Gone," she said. "I'll get your . . . lunch," she finished after checking the angle of the sunlight.

Reb turned quickly to the potbellied stove so he wouldn't see the tears of relief that welled in her eyes. When she'd regained control, she returned to Kincaid and helped him sit up in bed. As she propped the poor excuse for a pillow behind him, the sheet dropped to his hips, barely covering his manhood. Reb hardly noticed the bare flesh, having been on intimate terms with every part of the sick man's body as his physician.

When she spoon-fed him with a variation of the steamy, bouillon-like broth he remembered so well, Kincaid questioned Reb on the details of his bout with pneumonia.

"So I talked while I was delirious," he said with some trepidation. "What did I say?" He had visions of his entire secret mission exposed. With Reb's dislike of Yankees and railroads, there was no telling what the youth would do with such information.

"A lot. And nothing," she replied cryptically. "I know you were a Union spy."

Kincaid's face remained blank.

"I know your name is Kincaid, or Christopher. You seemed to prefer Kincaid," she said, then added, "and you had a wife, Laurie, whom you loved very much, who died."

"You know enough," Kincaid said bitterly, reacting to the grief still evoked by even the mention of Laurie's name.

"You remember?" Reb was so excited that Kincaid's memory might have returned, she spilled a spoonful of breath-cooled soup. It dribbled down the front of his brawny chest, pooled in his navel, and ran down into the line of black curls on his belly.

Reb anxiously sopped up the warm mess with the sweaty sheet. Her efforts took her where the curls thickened to a bush, and she suddenly realized what she was doing. She looked up quickly to find Kincaid staring coldly at her.

"I'll take care of that," he said.

She was so distracted by the unexpected return of her desire that she overreacted to Kincaid's next remark.

"I remember I had a wife who was killed. How I felt about her is none of your damn business!"

His consideration for the dead woman renewed her pique over the events during his delirium, and she abruptly thrust the whole bowl of hot soup upside down in his lap.

"Thanks for saving my life, Reb," she said furiously. "I owe you so much, Reb. I don't know how I'll ever repay you, Reb," she snarled at Kincaid. "You ungrateful bastard." Anger, frustration, fear, and exhaustion had all taken their toll, and the need to remain in control had been dispelled by his recovery. "It's none of my business how you get well, either. You can take care of yourself!"

She was out the door and it had slammed behind her before Kincaid realized she'd dumped the scalding contents of the bowl on his lap. With a nimbleness that left him prostrate afterward, he hopped out of bed and wiped the remains of the disgusting meal off his heat-pinkened skin with the sheet, which he ripped off the bed in his haste.

Reb was still seeing red even after she reached the creek. She followed it quickly to the deep, calm pool hidden in a thick stand of fresh-smelling lodgepole pines that formed an oval at the center so the sun shone through on the sparkling water. She stripped off her filthy, rankly odorous buckskins and stepped across the muddy bank, where the drifted snow of the previous week had only recently melted.

She immersed her long, naked body slowly in the

frigid wetness—toes, ankles, calves, knees, thighs. Shivering, unable to withstand any longer the apprehension of the cold, she plunged in headfirst, diving with fingers delicately forming a V, piercing the small, circular pond without a sound or a splash. Suddenly she simply was no longer there.

Reb held her breath as long as she could, swimming strongly underwater. Finally, she burst upward, breaking the surface with a gush of white spray, enjoying a freedom of spirit she'd missed while nursing Kincaid. Then she dog-paddled in place while her rage cooled.

Whether I like it or not, she concluded after several fatiguing minutes of this exercise, *I'm responsible for this aggravating man. I will mold him into someone capable of surviving in this wilderness, and I won't lose my temper again no matter what the provocation,* she promised herself as she stepped from the water.

Reb dreaded the thought of pulling the crusty, sweat-salty buckskins on over her dewy skin, but having no other clothes that hid her female form so well, she reluctantly put them back on.

She took advantage of the opportunity to walk in the woods after being cooped up for so long, and when she returned to the cabin several hours later, a contrite Kincaid, naked and seated cross-legged on the thoroughly rumpled bed, chin in hands, elbows perched on knees, greeted her warily, "Welcome back."

"Are you ready to behave yourself?" Reb responded frostily, picking up the bowl and spoon from the floor where they'd landed.

"Are you?" he shot back.

Reb gritted her teeth, determined not to allow the stranger to goad her into losing her temper again.

"Get off the bed," she ordered.

"I'm comfortable where I am."

"I have to wash the sheets, unless you want to sleep in this mess."

"Oh." Kincaid moved off the bed and stood wavering barefooted on the cool dirt next to her.

She suddenly became aware of him again as a man—a vulnerable, naked man.

"Wrap yourself in this blanket before you get sick again." She stuffed the red-striped gray wool blanket against his chest and suppressed her disturbingly persistent passion by concentrating on her work.

"Well?" she said when she had the sheets in hand.

"Well?" he repeated expectantly.

"Even for a Yankee tenderfoot, you don't have much common sense. Get back in bed. I'll change the dressing on your wound when I get back."

Kincaid ignored the jibe and gratefully climbed

back into the soft haven. He was asleep almost before Reb left the room.

Reb rinsed the sheets and beat them on flat stones near the creek to clean them, then hung them over the forked branches of a cottonwood to dry in the cool, ever-present breeze. She decided that, having been deprived of lunch, Kincaid should have something more substantial for dinner. By the end of the afternoon she'd snared two rabbits and harvested some wild onions and mushrooms. She returned to the cabin, and a savory rabbit stew soon permeated the cabin with delicious smells.

It was Kincaid's nose that woke him. "Aaaah, ambrosia," he said.

Reb wafted a large bowl of the chunky, mouth-watering concoction under his nose. Kincaid obediently opened wide and waited for Reb to feed him. He ate ravenously, gulping the stew so quickly that he choked at least twice on hunks of meat before Reb insisted that she wouldn't give him any more unless he chewed more thoroughly.

"If you don't slow down, it'll all come back up again," she warned.

"Where'd you get the meat—rabbit, isn't it? I didn't hear a shot," he said, chewing and talking at the same time.

"I used a snare." Reb should have left it at that, but she couldn't resist the urge to begin remaking the man.

"You shouldn't talk with your mouth full. Obviously nobody ever taught you any manners. You're as bad as Adam, and even he knows better."

"What did you expect from someone you've labeled a 'mindless Yankee tenderfoot'?"

"If the shoe fits, wear it."

"Spare me."

"I guess if your mouth is empty enough to talk, it means you're all done eating." Reb said.

"Wait!" He grabbed the fringe on Reb's grimy buckskins. "I could eat a little more." In fact, he only managed another couple of mouthfuls. "Guess my eyes are bigger than my stomach," he conceded.

Reb set the bowl on the table, then came back to change Kincaid's bandage. She carefully unwrapped the torn sheet and was relieved to see the wound scabbed over and healing nicely. "Sore?"

"It doesn't hurt as much as . . . I expected it to." Kincaid had been about to say, "as my leg did," but remembered at the last second he was supposed to have amnesia.

"Just take it easy and rest, and you'll be well before you know it."

Reb slowly poured heated water from the black pot on the stove grate into a large, silvery-colored tin bowl, as she had every evening since Kincaid first evidenced signs of pneumonia. She used a towel as a mitt to carry the bowl over to the chest next to the bed.

As if he were a limp rag doll, Reb began methodically washing Kincaid from head to foot with a soapy rag, starting at the bottom. He struggled like a child as she scrubbed the sole of his foot, and one leg writhed to escape Reb's unmerciful attention while she stubbornly held on to the other ankle and continued the ritual cleansing.

Kincaid endured as long as he could without saying anything, holding in the laughter until it hurt his chest, but finally gasped, "This is torture. What are you doing?"

"Giving you a bath."

Reb dutifully soaped upward from his long foot to the knee, to the deeply scarred right thigh.

The moment Reb touched the scar, Kincaid said, "Leave that alone," and grabbed Reb's hand in a steely grip.

"Ouch!" she yelled, yanking her wrist free. "What's the matter with you?"

"Don't touch that scar."

"I've been washing that scar for eight days, and I see no reason to stop now," she said, nostrils flaring dangerously.

"Eight days?" Kincaid bunched his brows in consternation. He calculated the days and realized he'd missed the meeting with Dodge. He felt a pang of sympathy for his parents, who would surely worry when they got a telegram from Dodge saying that he hadn't shown up.

"Why do you think the leg's not stiff? Just who do you think has been massaging it all this time? Little green elves?" Reb hissed sarcastically. "Now sit back, get your hands out of the way, and let me finish so I can eat. I'm hungry and tired, and I've had just about all I'm going to take from you today!"

She soaped the pitted scar, then set the warm, wet rag on the opposite thigh while she used all her strength to firmly and thoroughly work the muscles of the right thigh from knee to groin until they were supple. She found the area near the groin less pliant than usual and worked until the muscle yielded.

When Kincaid had been unconscious, Reb had deemed the job a labor of love. Now that he was awake, she was embarrassed to be manhandling him so familiarly. Actually, she would have been perfectly comfortable performing the service if only she weren't so conscious of the deception she practiced on him regarding her sex. She shuddered to think what the arrogant Yankee would do if he knew she was a girl. Her recent experiences with him had convinced her that the last thing she should do was reveal her female nature.

"Thanks, Rebel," Kincaid said as Reb finished.

She stared into his fathomless gray eyes. "That's

the second time you've called me that. My name is Reb."

It irked him to have the brat return his thank-you with a complaint, but it made his explanation all the more fitting. "You remind me of a Rebel." He gazed away, lost in memories, then turned granite-gray eyes back on Reb. "By the end of the war most of them weren't much older than you."

Reb snorted.

"But they had lots of the same kind of misguided fighting spirit. Which are you denying—that you're young or that you've got spirit?"

"I ain't—I'm not denying nothing—anything," Reb gritted out between clenched teeth. She could feel herself flushing from the roots of her hair. She hadn't made a slip in grammar like that since she'd been six! How could he rattle her so successfully?

Kincaid noticed the embarrassed blush and thought it couldn't do the boy any harm to learn a little more politeness to his company. "So, Rebel, if the shoe fits, wear it."

Reb finished rewrapping the wound in furious silence as quickly as she could. She got the pot out from under the bed, practically threw it at him, and left to eat her own meal alone outside. There she contemplated just what it was about Kincaid's comments that had upset her so much. She realized it was his attitude more than the words themselves that galled her. The man assumed from his lofty male perch an "I know best" tone that he probably used for all women and children. And although he didn't know she was a woman, he'd apparently categorized her as a child. She hadn't thought of herself as a child since she was eleven and first came up here to Blue's cabin with Adam. She reminded herself that she'd vowed to create a "new man" out of this Yankee.

Well, he could certainly use a new outlook toward women and children. And this was one young female who could teach him a few things!

Her self-confidence restored, she returned to take the pot out to empty it, then came back with the sheets. "Up, so I can make the bed."

Kincaid leaned against the log wall wrapped in a blanket while Reb quickly and efficiently made up the bed.

"Get in," she said when she was done. It made her feel immensely better to add under her breath, "You mindless Yankee tenderfoot."

When she had Kincaid tucked in, Reb crossed to the stove, banked it for the night, and lay down on the buffalo robe in front of it.

"Wait," Kincaid said, disturbing her. "Are you planning to sleep on the floor?"

"I have for the past week," Reb answered antagonistically, "when I wasn't unlucky enough to be sitting in that chair next to the bed."

"There's more than enough room in this bed for the two of us," he said, shifting over to leave space for her.

"You're hurt. I might roll over on you in my sleep," Reb countered. God forbid Kincaid should discover she was not the boy he thought she was.

"Either you sleep here with me, or I join you on the floor," he said, throwing his feet out to the side of the bed.

"Fine," Reb said, rising from her spot on the floor. "If it'll keep you from making yourself sick again, I'll share the bed. Anything to get you well and out of here!"

She stalked around the foot of the bed and sat cautiously on the edge opposite from Kincaid. But when she glanced over her shoulder at him, he'd already lain down again to sleep.

She pulled off her moccasins and removed her belt and sheath, but left on the stinking buckskins, figuring that the smell would wake him if he got too close. She lay stiffly on her side, as far as possible from the man who'd aroused in her an unaccountable curiosity, along with a totally accountable ire.

"Rebel?" Kincaid said a few minutes later.

"What?"

"You need a bath."

Reb smiled to herself, and closed her eyes to sleep.

9

They called an uneasy truce that lasted three days, while Kincaid mended. Just after supper on the evening of the fourth day, while he lay naked on the bed after his daily sponge bath, Reb began the questioning that would be the basis of her education of the tenderfoot.

"You can start by telling me everything you can remember. That'll give me some idea of how much I need to teach you," she said.

She pushed the chair far enough back from the disheveled bed to plop into it and extended her moccasined heels up onto the dirty sheets, rationalizing that she would wash them again tomorrow. Slouching down a little more comfortably, she crossed her arms and waited patiently for her patient to speak.

Kincaid cocked a skeptical eyebrow. He passed through a number of reactions to her command, from incredulity, to chagrin, to stubborn refusal. Finally, not unmindful that Reb had saved his life, he grudgingly offered, "I remember several events surrounding the things you've reminded me about, nothing more."

"Perhaps if we talk about those things, you'll recall other facts about your life."

"Don't be so sure," Kincaid muttered.

"What was that?" Reb leaned forward at the waist to hear better.

"I said 'Sure,'" he replied, recovering quickly. "Where would you like to start?"

Reb thought for a moment, then said deliberately, "With spying for the Union."

Kincaid could imagine how that sort of intrigue would appeal to the boy. He'd never spoken to anyone about the events during the war, but hesitated only a moment before he started talking.

"It all began one warm, moonlit summer night— the night I first met my wife."

Reb could see his tension in the tic in his cheek and the white knuckles of the clenched fists lying on the sheets beside him. She immediately pictured a long white front porch with two lovers reclining on a squeaky wooden swing, baby-pink roses on a nearby trellis cloying the still air with their perfume.

"On my ship," he continued, breaking her reverie and forcing her to refocus her thoughts.

"Your ship?" she asked, jaw dropping.

"My cover as a spy was as a ship's captain smuggling goods past the Yankee blockade." He reached over to push Reb's mouth closed with his forefinger.

"Laurie Simmons was, believe it or not, my Confederate contact to move the smuggled goods inland to Atlanta. I knew I was to meet a woman, but I had no idea she'd be so beautiful."

Reb had to bite her lower lip hard to avoid a jealousy-provoked comment about the dead woman. She spied the whiskey bottle on the cupboard shelf and crossed to pour herself a stiff drink to anesthetize her raw, sensitive feelings against the coming revelations.

"That's hardly medicine I would have thought you'd prescribe, but if it's what the doctor orders—" Kincaid held his hand out for the full glass.

Reb hesitated only a second before extending the drink. Then she poured another for herself.

"Are you sure you're old enough for that?" Kincaid asked with a raised brow.

"Plenty old," Reb retorted, taking a big gulp. She immediately gasped and put her hand to her throat, trying desperately to breathe. She managed to wheeze a breath of air, then bent over in a fit of coughing. When the coughing subsided, she looked up at Kincaid through watery eyes.

"To old friends—and new," he said, toasting her and taking a sip of whiskey.

Reb watched with satisfaction as Kincaid's eyes widened ever so slightly when the whiskey hit his stomach.

He sipped in silence, apparently waiting for some indication that he should continue.

Reb was warmed and more lightheaded than she had expected to be from the whiskey. She could only guess the effect the spirits would have on the sick and injured man. At least he would keep talking about himself, she thought. When she could speak again, Reb rasped, "You were saying?"

"She was only eighteen," he said as though there had been no interruption. "My job was to get close to her, make love to her, whatever was necessary to gain her confidence and obtain the list of men working with her. The Union wanted to shut down Atlanta's supply channels."

"Didn't it bother you to use her like that?" Reb asked, her disgust at the assignment plain in her voice.

"War is hell," Kincaid said. "Anyway, you're not giving the lady enough credit if you think the job was easy. She had me pegged as a rich, arrogant Yankee profiteer within minutes of our first meeting, and I had my work cut out for me."

"Is that when you changed your name from Christopher to Kincaid?"

"I didn't change my name. I merely resorted to using my last name for my first."

Reb's face mirrored her confusion. "Your full name is Christopher . . . Kincaid?" She tried out the name, rolled it around on her tongue with a sip of whiskey, and decided she liked it.

"Yes."

It occurred to Reb in her alcoholic euphoria, looking at Kincaid sitting stark naked on the bed, black stubble on his face, hair askew, eyes bleary, that learning his name was not the momentous occasion she'd imagined it would be. Her feelings for the stranger hadn't miraculously disappeared when she learned his name. Nor had she suspected the jealousy she would suffer on account of a dead woman—one who could get a man to change his name.

A touch of her incredulity, mixed with a dab of envy, came through as she voiced her thought aloud. "I didn't give Miss Simmons enough credit, if she managed to get you to change your name."

"It was my idea," he said, "but it came after I'd completed my mission."

"After?"

"She took me into her proper southern home in Atlanta, I got the names of her supply network, and I gave them to the army," he said without apparent pride in his accomplishment, eyes focused into the empty whiskey glass. "Another," he demanded, and passed the glass to Reb for a refill.

If her own senses had not been so dulled by strong spirits, Reb wouldn't have allowed it. Instead, she rose unsteadily and poured him a second cup—to the brim.

Kincaid took the cup from her carefully and drained an inch of it. They both sat in moody silence for several minutes until Kincaid added softly, "And I fell in love with her."

"But she didn't love you." The words came slowly and were somewhat slurred.

"Not at first. Especially when she found out what I'd done. It would be more accurate to say she hated me."

Reb was surprised at the personal information Kincaid was revealing. Maybe his amnesia wasn't permanent after all.

"I changed my name because I wanted Laurie to know I was different," he continued. "I wasn't the Union spy Christopher anymore. I was just plain Kincaid . . . and I loved her."

Reb's eyes sought the ground guiltily as she recalled Kincaid's prayer to Laurie in his delirium.

"She didn't believe it would work," she whispered, not meeting Kincaid's gaze.

"How did you know?"

"Lucky guess." Between sips of whiskey Reb murmured, "She knew you loved her . . . but that you hadn't really changed who you were."

"Maybe you're right." Kincaid scratched the whiskers on his chin. "I persisted in my pursuit until I caught her," he said wryly. "She married me, but she was such an unbroken filly, even then there was no tying her down. That's what I loved most about her . . . and what killed her."

"Killed her?"

"We both knew it was the end for Atlanta. Everyone was fleeing. I begged her to leave with her family. I even ordered her to go, but she wouldn't. She insisted on being there to help the Confederacy to the last. There was an ambush. She was where she didn't belong," he said bitterly, "and a stray cannon fragment killed her."

"Where she didn't belong?" Reb asked somewhat confused, the whiskey having dulled her senses. "Working for what she believed in was where she didn't belong? I don't understand. It wasn't wrong for you. Why was it wrong for her?"

"She was a woman," Kincaid argued, "trying to do a man's job."

"What?" Reb found herself ominously close to anger. "And I suppose I'm a *boy* trying to do a man's job," she challenged.

"You did childishly lose your temper earlier," Kincaid chided, tenderly touching his scalded skin where Reb had dumped the hot soup in his lap several days before.

"You think *that* was losing my temper?" Reb jumped up to pose feet apart, hands defiantly on hips, swaying slightly from lack of equilibrium. "Where is it written that women can't think or feel or be dedicated to a cause? Your wife was fighting for the South the same way you were fighting for the North—only a whole sight more honorably, from the sound of things. If you'd really loved her, you would have understood that!"

"I *did* love her," he said. "And I still do!"

Reb flinched openly at Kincaid's ardent declaration and staggered back a step.

"I loved her enough to let her have her own way even though I thought she was wrong," he said angrily. "She died because I allowed her to do what she wasn't capable of doing."

"Wasn't capable of doing?" Reb sputtered furiously. "A woman can do anything a man can do, and she can do a whole passel of things better!" Perilously near to revealing herself, Reb amended, "And so can a boy like me."

"I'll believe that when I see it," he retorted.

"You will. Tomorrow morning, bright and early, we begin your lessons. We'll see just how capable a Yankee tenderfoot like yourself is in areas that matter out here."

"Such as?"

"Shooting, riding, roping, and tracking," she spat.

"Fine," he said, handing her his empty glass. "Now, if you'll excuse me, I need to rest."

Reb stood aghast as he lay down and turned his back on her to sleep.

"Tomorrow," she grumbled to herself. "Tomorrow the tables will be turned."

Because of his recurring mild fever, however, almost a week passed before Reb allowed Kincaid to venture beyond the cabin door. Keeping him in bed resting challenged the patience of both to the utmost. Reb had long since given up hope of relief from Blue.

"I think this is the day," Reb said when she placed a hand on Kincaid's forehead and found his temperature normal. "Time to go to work."

"Hallelujah!" Kincaid snapped a sharp salute. "General, suh," he drawled. "Private Kincaid reporting for duty, suh!"

Reb couldn't help laughing at the contrast between Kincaid's precise, square-shouldered salute and his lazy imitation of southern speech. She spunkily returned his salute, falling in with his silliness. "At ease, soldier. We have some unfinished business to attend to. There's the matter of your frontier education, Private."

"Aw, General, ya know us sturdy, pink-cheeked plowboys is too dumb to l'arn new regulations, suh," he mocked, eyes twinkling.

"Well, we'll start with something as simple as your mind, then," Reb said teasingly. "First you need to get dressed."

Kincaid jumped out of bed to stand magnificently

naked before her. "Ya mean I get a real uniform, General?"

"What you're wearing now is hardly sufficient, Private." Reb covered her rising blush with a smirk as she casually pitched him his Union pants and one of Blue's dark blue wool shirts she'd found in the chest. Inside she felt anything but casual. Her heart pounded as she stood and watched, fascinated at the magical transformation from "patient" to "person."

Kincaid shimmied into long johns before adding the tight, yellow-striped navy britches, tugged on socks and his tall black boots, finally donned the worn shirt, which fit snugly across his broad shoulders. He brushed his hand back and forth across his thick beard. "Now all I need is a shave to feel human."

"That can be arranged." Giving in to the desire to attract his attention, she flipped her razor-sharp bowie knife across the room so it stuck in the bedstead an inch from Kincaid's right hand.

He slowly and carefully worked the large knife free. "I've only got ten fingers, and I'd like to keep them all," he said sharply.

"No problem," Reb replied. "I never miss. Want some soap and water?"

"Not if they're delivered the same way," Kincaid replied dryly.

Reb chuckled. "They're not." She poured some

warm water from the pot on the stove and gave the chary man water, a towel, and a precious cake of soap. Then she returned to the table and sat, prepared to ogle Kincaid's toilette.

He took two strokes, then frowned. "You wouldn't have a mirror handy, by any chance?"

"No, but if you like, I can play barber for you." She'd observed his grimace of pain as he lifted his left hand to hold the skin on his neck firm for the knife and had surmised that his left arm pained him when he lifted it.

"Just remember you're *shaving*, not *skinning*," he said. He wiped the knife clean, balanced it momentarily in his palm, and then threw it with a dexterity equal to Reb's, embedding it in the log wall an inch above her head.

"Not bad," Reb replied somewhat shakily, eyes wide in alarm as she felt the shaft of the knife caress her hair when she turned to pry it free. She noted the depth to which the blade had penetrated and thanked whatever lucky stars had made his throw accurate.

She sat Kincaid in the chair by the bed and tilted his chin up to make his neck accessible.

"Careful with that thing," he said, eyeing her warily.

"Look who's talking," she muttered. She grabbed her lower lip in her teeth and resisted the temptation to nick him on purpose. She was already regretting her impetuous offer, as she realized just how close she needed to be to this infuriating man to remove his soap-lathered beard. She'd shaved her father and brothers on several occasions, and she knew very well what she was doing. She was amazed, however, at what a different pleasure she derived from performing the service for Kincaid. It gave her a possessive feeling that wasn't at all appropriate under the circumstances.

"What other hidden talents do you have?" Reb asked as she worked.

"I don't know. What did you have in mind?"

"Marksmanship."

"You mean like with bow and arrows?" he asked.

"No. I mean like with swords and battle axes!" Reb glared in irritated exasperation at Kincaid as she wiped the last of the soap and whiskers from the knife to the towel and replaced her knife in its sheath. When Kincaid didn't respond to her taunt, Reb forced herself to explain in a civil tongue. "I mean like marksmanship with a rifle."

"Oh, that." Kincaid smiled as he felt his face with his hands. "I have absolutely no idea."

Kincaid had to marvel at the boy's skill with the knife. Considering the kid's smooth face, he couldn't have had much practice doing this job for himself. "Close shave," he commended. "Thanks."

Reb rolled her eyes to the ceiling helplessly, then forgot her question, forgot everything, as Kincaid stood. Reb looked up at her stranger and gaped in awe. Her heart hammered in her throat, and she felt a tightening in her belly. She found that she wanted more than anything to touch the firm jaw that had been shielded first by stubble, then by beard.

Kincaid, puzzled at Reb's glazed stare, looked for something amiss in his appearance. "Something wrong?"

"Absolutely nothing," Reb whispered, jaws now clenched tight, as she stared hard at his face. She abruptly turned, picked up her Spencer from where it stood next to the door, plucked her hat from its peg, and escaped outside into the glaring sunlight.

It had been difficult before to withstand her eager appetite for the stranger. She now discovered it was even more difficult to repress her ravenous craving to touch Kincaid. She needed some time alone to think.

And Kincaid gave it to her. He followed on her heels, but not too close, since as a form of self-protection Reb had refused to clean her buckskins. The pungent garments did their job, keeping Kincaid at least three feet away at all times.

Kincaid couldn't help noticing the boy's pungent odor. He'd held his breath through most of the shave in the interest of self-preservation.

"You know, you could use a bath," he said when he caught another good whiff of Reb during their march into the forest.

"I haven't had time," Reb said, she changed the subject quickly, assuming the role of teacher. "Knowing how to use a rifle can mean the difference between life and death." She stopped and turned to Kincaid as they reached a grassy clearing. "It's important not only for self-defense, but also for putting food on the table. Are you familiar with the Spencer rifle?" She held it before her for his examination.

"No," Kincaid replied honestly. The Spencer was an out-of-date weapon, usually carried only by the enlisted man. The more modern Henry rifle was purchased by the officers who could afford them, including Kincaid. So while he might claim expertise with the Henry, he could plead comparative ignorance of the Spencer.

"I thought not," Reb said smugly, misunderstanding his answer to mean he had no experience with rifles at all. "This is a .52 caliber weapon with seven shots, loaded here in the tubular magazine in the butt."

Kincaid listened with rapt attention and watched closely while Reb demonstrated how to load the weapon and sight down the barrel.

"We've had a lot of trouble with the Sioux the past few months."

"Really?"

Reb shuddered. "I've seen some sights I'd rather not have seen. It gave me a little more incentive to see you rescued. Now Red Cloud has retreated with his braves to the Powder River up in the Black Hills to spend the summer hunting, and General Dodge is moving the Brulés to a reservation. Adam and I are hoping Dad can talk some sense into Dodge and change his mind about sending the Brulés away. At least he should reconsider sending them to Pawnee territory."

"So Dodge has got to be controlled . . . ," Kincaid mused quietly.

"Exactly," Reb replied.

Kincaid shook his head in disgust as he realized how he'd misconstrued the exchanges between Adam and Reb after his rescue. Apparently, the boy only coincidentally disliked Yankees and railroads. He and his family would obviously be concerned with Dodge's handling of the Indian situation. Well, that certainly wouldn't interfere with his assignment. To reassure himself of this new view of things, he asked, "What would you like to have Dodge do?"

"I haven't really thought too much about it. I guess I've had too much happening in my own life to think about trying to run somebody else's."

"Except mine."

"I haven't—"

"I forgive you under the circumstances," he interrupted with a laugh that cleared the tension he could see building in Reb's body. "Now, what did you want to teach me?" Fully relaxed for the first time since his rescue, he suspected his memory was going to return with amazing rapidity from this point forward.

"Let's start with standing targets," she began, eyeing his boldly grinning face warily. "See those four pines over there, the ones evenly spaced about two feet apart? You'll notice they each have the bark scraped off in a small circle about five feet up. The center of that circle is your target."

Reb shouldered the rifle, took a quarter turn from the targets, aimed, and fired four quick rounds. Kincaid could see from where he stood that each bullet had found the bull's-eye.

"Your turn," she said as she handed him the rifle and some bullets. "You'll need to reload."

"You're a pretty good shot."

"I never miss."

"Only 'miscalculate'?" Kincaid taunted. He put the stock to his right shoulder and aimed, having some difficulty balancing the gun with his left arm, which was uncomfortably stiff from the recent injury. His first shot went far to the left, missing the tree entirely.

Reb smirked at Kincaid's obvious lack of skill, so typical of a tenderfoot, but inside felt a stab of disappointment. For some reason she'd hoped he would do better.

The recoil on the gun surprised Kincaid, jarring

his wound enough to make him tighten his jaws to avoid groaning aloud. He braced the gun more effectively to absorb the shock, gritting his teeth at the stress this put on the knitting skin and bone of his left shoulder. The second shot hit the next tree, but at least a foot high of the mark.

"Take your time. There's no rush. This usually takes a little practice," Reb said.

Kincaid examined the rifle sight, noticing that it was bent slightly. He grunted to himself, then aimed the gun again. He hit dead center of the circles on the next two trees.

It was Reb's turn to cock an eyebrow and speculatively observe the stranger. "I thought you said you'd never shot a rifle before?"

"I said I wasn't familiar with the Spencer," he replied. "I did most of my shooting with a Henry."

"Your memory is making remarkable strides," she said suspiciously.

"Your sight is crooked," he answered, ignoring her suspicion. "It marks the target wide and to the left."

Reb had the good grace to look abashed. The sight had gotten bent years ago, and she hadn't thought to advise Kincaid of the problem, since she automatically compensated for it herself.

"How are you with a moving target?" she asked to cover her dismay at her oversight.

"Fair."

He was more than fair. Kincaid never missed the wood chips she threw as high and as far and as fast as she could.

"I guess I'm not going to teach you anything you don't already know," she said, not sure whether that pleased or infuriated her.

He reloaded, then handed the boy the rifle and picked up a handful of wood chips. "You haven't had your turn."

Mesmerized by his steady gaze, Reb waited too late to take aim after he threw the first chip, and to her intense embarrassment, she missed.

"Never miss?" Kincaid badgered mercilessly. He suddenly threw three chips at once.

She hit all three before they reached the ground. He immediately threw three more, and she hit those as well.

"Bravo!" he said, patting Reb heartily on the back, impressed by the youth's obvious capability.

"The lesson's over," Reb said irritably as she moved away from Kincaid's touch. "I hesitate to ask. How are you at tracking game?"

"Passable."

"We'll see. Follow me."

Kincaid turned out to be as skilled in the forest as he was with a gun. For every sign that Reb showed him, Kincaid responded with one for her throughout the afternoon.

"Because of the cottonwood and willow, this is a good habitat for beaver," she instructed.

"There are some signs one has passed," Kincaid said, pointing to the spot where a beaver had dragged a felled tree. "That must mean there's a creek around here somewhere, right?"

"Yes."

"A deep creek?" Kincaid inquired with a grin.

"Not very."

"Deep enough to rinse off the dust of the day?"

Reb realized now where the conversation was headed. As a matter of fact, they were not very far from her hidden pond. However, she had no intention of letting Kincaid know where she'd been taking secret baths. Although her buckskins might be filthy, the skin underneath was not. She had daily stolen away to bathe in her reclusive spot.

"How about a swim?" Kincaid urged.

"The creek's too shallow. Besides, we're out here so you can learn to survive in the wilderness, not so I can take a bath," Reb said acidly. "Shall we continue, or would you rather return to the cabin?"

"By all means, continue. I want to learn how to survive in your wilderness, although with the Yankee railroad coming through, I don't expect it to be 'wild' much longer."

Reb flushed, but led Kincaid away from the pond without saying anything. She pointed out a rabbit burrow. He found some day-old deer spoor. She discovered the feeding place of a black bear. He located a tree where they could count on finding honey later in the summer. She led him to the wild onions and mushrooms she'd used in the stew. He instructed on herbs that were useful for medicinal purposes.

As the afternoon drew to a close, Reb circled back toward Blue's cabin. They were very near the pond again when she noticed that Kincaid's limp was more pronounced, his hand massaging the leg as they walked, his shoulders not as square as they had been earlier in the afternoon.

"How about a rest?" she suggested.

"I could use a break," Kincaid admitted. He lowered himself wearily to sit against a tall pine, his long legs stretched out in front of him. He closed his eyes and laid his head back against the rough bark. Reb squatted beside him. She was in no hurry to return to the confines of the cabin.

Kincaid spoke with his eyes closed while he massaged his thigh. "The rustle of these pines is as rhythmic as the sound of hooves on cobblestones. That sound lulled me to sleep more than once when I was flat on my back in New York with this leg wound."

Reb didn't answer, merely watched as Kincaid's face relaxed into sleep. She realized guiltily that she'd pushed him too hard, too soon after his illness. She sat, her chin on her knees, prepared to wait for him to awake. However, her nose wrinkled with disgust when she smelled the trousers she wore. She was as offensive to herself as she was to Kincaid. The pond was so close, she probably could bathe and be back before he ever knew she had been gone. She quietly abandoned her watch over Kincaid for the icy water.

Reb had been gone only a few minutes when Kincaid knew something was wrong. Without opening his eyes, he bunched his muscles and quickly rolled away from the tree, coming up in a huddle behind a nearby outcropping of rock. Senses alert, he looked and listened for the danger he thought was near.

At the same time he conceded there was no threat, he discovered Reb was nowhere to be seen. Unable to believe the boy intended him harm, but nevertheless cautious, he set out to track the youth down. He was indeed as practiced in wood lore as Reb had suspected, but the task turned out to be surprisingly easy. Apparently the boy hadn't expected to be followed, since he left a clear path.

As Kincaid neared a stand of scented pines and heard the sound of splashing water, he slowed his approach. He moved stealthily among the trees, approaching an open glade with a pool of glistening water in the center. Standing at the edge of the pool, back to him, was the curvaceous, peach-skinned form of a long-legged female.

The small waist would almost have fit the span of his large hands, but the hips were developed for childbearing, the buttocks enticing in their firm roundness. The statuesque legs went on forever, disappearing at the calf into the depths of the pond.

Kincaid stood stunned at his discovery. All thoughts of the missing boy were gone, his eyes riveted on the beautiful sight of the softer sex before him. His passion rose unbidden in response to this totally unexpected delight. Abruptly, he turned his head to determine the source of a noise in the undergrowth nearby. Satisfied that it was only a small animal, he returned his attention to the pond.

The woman had disappeared. Kincaid searched the glen anxiously with his eyes. Just as he was ready to conclude that he'd suffered a hallucination, the apparition reappeared before him. She emerged from the water like a sleek crystal goddess, light-refracting droplets of water clinging to her small, firm breasts, her flat stomach, and to the long stemlike legs that made her so tall. She shook her glossy hair as a dog shakes its pelt, whipping it back to expose the clean lines of her softly feminine profile.

Kincaid couldn't believe his eyes. It was Reb! The boy Reb was a girl! No, he said to himself, taking a closer, longer, lingering look. Not a girl, a woman.

10

Kincaid's unbridled lust waged war with his reason. His gray eyes were dilated with avidity, his face frozen rigid with desire. He licked his lips unconsciously and, like a hungry puma, took two long, graceful strides toward his prey. Then he paused, tantalized by the beads of water surrounding Reb's mouth. He imagined the tip of his tongue flicking each drop away, finally lodging itself between her full lips in the deep recesses of that honeyed cavern.

In the months since Laurie's death, he'd endured a self-enforced celibacy. To seek another woman for his needs had seemed a betrayal of his wife, and he'd felt guilty whenever the persistent reminder of his virility made itself known. He felt no guilt now, only the pulsing insistence of his manhood that he slake its thirst.

Innocent of Kincaid's private battle, Reb titillated his senses by cavorting playfully in the shallow pond. The cold hardened her nipples into coral buds and tinged her skin rosy pink. She crossed her arms under her breasts to hug herself in an attempt to get warm, inadvertently lifting the tips so that they jutted out in an invitation to be kissed.

Kincaid swallowed the saliva that had accumulated in his mouth, and held his body rigidly in check.

Rubbing her hands up and down along her body to flick off the icy drops, Reb moved completely out of the water. Once on the muddy bank, she looked around warily and then yanked on her buckskins.

Kincaid watched her slim waist and rounded hips disappear under the blousy leather shirt that made her the same width from chest to thigh. A row of bright beadwork camouflaged her pert breasts, while her shapely limbs vanished in the wide, fringed leggings. She added the loose-fitting belt that held her knife sheath, then hopped on opposite feet as she tugged on her moccasins.

Kincaid had already slipped away by the time Reb grabbed her rifle, pulled her flat-brimmed hat down low on her brow, and moved quickly but carefully back through the forest to where she'd left the sleeping man.

A peaceful scene greeted her. Kincaid's head lolled back against the rugged bark of the spruce, his eyes closed, the long, inky black lashes lying peacefully on his tanned face, his breathing even and slow. In a moment of tenderness at his seeming childlike helplessness, she brushed back an unruly curl from his forehead. She jumped back as Kincaid woke from his torpor. He stretched in a leisurely way and slowly blinked his eyes open.

Reb couldn't know the effort Kincaid exerted to give the lazy appearance of a waking sleeper. It had taken all his willpower not to confront her when she brushed the lock of hair from his forehead. *How could I have been so blind?* he wondered as he stared into Reb's smiling freckled face.

"Have a good rest?"

Kincaid analyzed the voice that had deceived him so well. It was husky, mellow like good brandy, and now that he knew Reb was a female, seductive as hell.

"Kincaid?"

"What?" He stared at her with a glazed, unblinking look.

Reb tilted her head quizzically at his expression. "Are you all right?"

Kincaid nonchalantly waved away her question to cover the frantic scurrying of his mind. He was glad he hadn't revealed himself to her at the pond, since fast on the heels of his lust was the nagging suspicion that he'd somehow been made a fool. With that suspicion rose an equally strong desire to repay Reb in full measure for her deception.

"I'm fine, really. I just wasn't quite awake," he said, yawning broadly.

"We should be getting back. Are you sure you're all right?" Reb asked with a nervous laugh.

"Your hair is wet."

Kincaid's stare stripped away at her veils of deceit until Reb dropped her eyes to avoid his penetrating gaze. "I . . . I took your advice and . . . and rinsed off," she stuttered. "But we were talking about you."

"I'm fine. Just a little tired," he said. "I guess it would be a good idea to get back to the cabin so I can rest."

He rose in one powerful, fluid movement. If Reb had been paying attention, she would have questioned the limberness of his scarred leg. Instead, she hurried away to avoid Kincaid's steely gray eyes and missed this clue to his newfound knowledge.

This time, when Kincaid followed, he held his breath and stayed close, looking for signs of femininity. And he found them. Her hips swayed ever so slightly from side to side. The steps he'd thought so sure he now decided were delicately placed. The leanness of youth was the fragility of woman.

With his eyes opened to the truth, her womanhood seemed blatantly apparent, and Kincaid's disgust with himself increased. He pushed down the admiration for Reb that kept rearing its ugly head. What was there to admire in a woman who hid her charms in filthy buckskins?

His chagrin grew into anger as he thought back on

Reb providing a pot so he could relieve himself, washing him like a baby, and changing the bed while he stood by like a naked idiot. That inspired the memory of the scalding soup dumped in his lap. *That* was something a spiteful woman would do, all right.

And the confessions about Laurie! That was none of her business. The foibles he was willing to overlook in the "boy" he found intolerable in the girl. Without taking time to fully analyze why he felt the need for it, Kincaid began to plan his revenge.

His jaw tightened in determination as he mulled over the best way to show Reb the error of aspiring to a man's role. He wondered that she hadn't seemed affected by his nakedness. But she did have brothers. Kincaid was willing to believe anything of a hoyden who could outshoot anyone he'd seen and nurse a sick man back to health in the bargain.

He winced as he thought of the black eye he'd given her in his delirium. For that he was truly sorry. He'd never hit a woman before—but he'd already apologized for that.

Surely she must realize how ridiculous this pretense was. If not, he would have to give her a little help. But how? Kincaid's lips quirked into a sly grin as he hit upon the perfect solution—physical contact. Surely she couldn't ignore that. He'd never met a woman who could.

He hadn't forgotten how to arouse a woman, and

this one would probably take all his expertise and then some. He had the perfect excuse to force her to touch him—his leg—his shoulder, too, for that matter. They both needed massage. She had admitted that herself.

Yet Reb hadn't seemed affected by touching in the past. After all, she'd given him a bath every day without so much as a rosy blush. Or had she? He hadn't been watching for her reactions in the past. Perhaps she hadn't been as unmoved as he'd imagined. His stride lengthening, he caught up with Reb and walked beside her the rest of the short distance to the cabin.

When they arrived, Kincaid immediately collapsed on the bed as though exhausted.

"Reb, can you help me?" he asked as he extended a booted foot toward her.

"Sure." She straddled his leg with her back to him and grasped the heel of the boot to pull it off. Kincaid placed his other foot on her rear and shoved hard just as the boot came free. Reb sprawled forward awkwardly on the dirt floor.

Why didn't seeing her on the floor like that feel more satisfying? Kincaid's contrition was genuine, and he cursed himself for his weakness as he admitted, "Sorry. Guess I gave it a little too much."

Unaware that Kincaid knew her to be female, it was easy for Reb to dust herself off without embarrassment and come back for more.

"No problem," she assured with a grin. "Just take it a little easier this time."

She assumed her position over the other boot while Kincaid placed his socked foot on her fanny, thinking to himself how lusciously soft it was. Again, at the most vulnerable moment, he couldn't keep himself from giving a hefty push that sent Reb flying with the boot in hand.

"That isn't funny!" She came up sputtering, red-faced.

"I don't know how that happened. I didn't do it on purpose," he said between gritted teeth. Kincaid couldn't explain to himself why he'd done such a despicable thing to a young lady. How could he begin to explain it to her?

Kincaid pulled his scarred leg up onto the bed with both hands. "I guess I must have had a muscle spasm." He groaned piteously and clutched his leg, looking up sideways from under hooded eyes to see the effect his performance was having on Reb.

He thought he saw something like disgust, a moue of distaste around her mouth as she chewed her lip with sharp white teeth, but then sympathy replaced that expression, and she shoved him down flat on the bed.

"Let me see."

Before he could protest, Reb placed her hands on his leg in the area of the scar and let her fingers do the looking. Coming so soon after his recent perusal of her unclothed loveliness, Reb's manual investigation was nearly Kincaid's undoing. Her fingertips massaged his inner thigh and moved upward toward the groin. Kincaid closed his eyes and breathed deeply to dampen the fire growing in his loins.

"There does seem to be a great deal of tension in the leg," Reb said.

Kincaid almost choked, trying to hold back the burble of laughter in his throat. There was tension, all right, but she needed to look just a little higher for the source.

"Lie still a moment and I'll try to work it out," she said.

Totally oblivious to the reason for the tensed muscles, Reb continued her massage. She worked her thumb into the muscle on top of his leg while her fingers pressed, then released, the sinewy thigh.

As she worked her way upward, Kincaid's breathing became ragged, and his forehead and upper lip beaded with sweat. He could feel the evidence of his desire rising in his tight pants and thought surely Reb couldn't miss it either.

Reb noticed Kincaid's difficulty breathing and paused in what she was doing to glance at his face. She took one look at the strained features covered with sweat, then placed her hands on her hips and glared at him.

"You lied to me!" she accused.

Kincaid opened his eyes in alarm, wondering how he'd revealed he knew her secret.

"You aren't fine at all. In fact, you look positively *ill!*"

Kincaid's face contorted again. He truly was suffering—from the inability to release the explosive guffaw that grew deep in his chest. "Can't fool the doctor, can I?" he managed to gasp, freeing a silly grin.

"No, you can't," she responded, unable to resist meeting his grin with a relieved grin of her own. Then she chided good-naturedly, "I expect you wouldn't have had this problem with your leg if you'd just admitted when you were tired. You should rest. I'll get us some dinner. We'll take it a little easier tomorrow."

Kincaid laid his head back on the pillow and stared moodily at the pine rafters in the ceiling. His revenge wasn't working out exactly as he'd planned. She was unaware that he knew she was a female, so of course she wouldn't act any differently around him than she always had.

He'd had no idea his body would behave so traitorously, either. After all, there was absolutely nothing appealing about Reb in buckskins. She smelled! He decided to wait until bedtime to renew his attack. Surely in that confined environment she couldn't dismiss his attentions so easily.

Kincaid was wrong about Reb's lack of reaction to him. She'd noticed his rising passion but had attributed it to thoughts of Laurie she assumed her massage of his war wound must be provoking. What else could it be? She tried to ignore the ache that invaded her chest when she admitted to herself that he still loved his wife enough to become physically aroused just by her memory.

For the first time in days, Reb wondered what had happened to Blue. She needed rescue from this man who was no longer a stranger. Immersed in her thoughts, she ladled up some leftover stew and absently handed the bowl and a spoon to Kincaid.

"Something troubling you?" he asked when he saw she wasn't paying attention to what she was doing.

"Huh? What?"

"What are you thinking?" Kincaid asked.

"I was just thinking how little I taught you today," Reb admitted irritably. She served herself a bowl of stew and shoved his legs over to sit down next to him on the bed.

She'd sat next to him to eat at this same spot for many days, but this was the first time Kincaid was aware she encroached on his space. He edged his thigh farther away so it didn't rest against her buttocks. After all, he was the one who was going to make the advances. He peered over his bowl of stew into her wide, innocent brown eyes, then focused again on the chunk of rabbit he pushed around with his spoon.

"I wish I knew what brought you out here," Reb said.

Kincaid wanted to say, "I'm here on a mission for the Union Pacific railroad. It's my job to survey two alternate routes and report to General Dodge which is better. One goes through Denver. The other goes across the base of these beloved mountains of yours." Instead, he sighed and said, "I do, too."

Silence enveloped the room.

"Well, you're certainly no tenderfoot. You probably ride and rope as well as you track and shoot," Reb said disgustedly.

Kincaid couldn't keep his lips from quirking, but brought his hand up to cover his amusement. "I never said I was a tenderfoot. You did." He continued in spite of her wince. "I merely agreed to let you give me a frontier education. You're a very good teacher."

"I'm tired." She lowered her eyes dejectedly, crossed to the chair, and sat with her clenched hands pressed into her face.

Kincaid felt a tenderness well inside him, a desire to alleviate her misery. He opened his mouth, then abruptly clamped it shut. The best thing he could do for her was make her see how wrong she was to play this unnatural role. As a woman, she deserved to be coddled, and when she admitted she was a woman, he would do so. Posing as a ragamuffin lad, she was not entitled to the same deference. He had to make her acknowledge the advantages of her femininity for her own good.

Armed with his good intentions, Kincaid boldly unbuttoned his shirt and pulled it off. He then unbuttoned his trousers and peeled out of them as well. Determined to arouse a response from her, he called to her when he was naked. "Come to bed."

His gruff voice startled Reb out of her reverie.

As she passed him on her way to her side of the bed, Reb shuddered slightly, but otherwise Kincaid noticed no outward reaction to his state of undress. Eliciting a response from her became not only a duty for her own good, but a challenge.

Reb perched on the bed to remove her moccasins as though she were on the edge of a high cliff, then raised the covers and scooted underneath. An unshaven and unconscious Kincaid Reb found enticing. An unclothed Kincaid provided a formidable temptation. Turning away from him, she pulled the blanket over her shoulder like a woolen shield.

So she was not unaware of him, Kincaid mused, only purposefully ignoring him. Slowly and carefully he lifted the covers and moved himself underneath to join the brat. He crossed his arms behind his head, causing a twinge of discomfort in his wounded shoulder.

He smiled grimly and launched the next phase of his attack. "Reb, my shoulder aches. If you could rub a little of the stiffness out, maybe I could sleep better."

"I'm not your servant." She couldn't touch him now, Reb thought. She couldn't handle much more of the kind of strain Kincaid was imposing on her self-control. She wanted to unashamedly look her fill and to touch what was forbidden. The possible results of succumbing to that desire, given her current pose as a young man, almost made her giggle in hysteria.

"I know. I know," he responded glibly. "But you are my doctor, and as a patient I'm asking for your services."

"I'm done for the day."

"And of course this particular ache is one that you inflicted," he added relentlessly.

"Oh, all right," Reb said, sitting upright in the moonlit dark that had fallen around them. *Why not?* she thought to herself. He believed she was a boy. What did she have to lose? "Turn over on your stomach."

Kincaid obeyed instantly.

Reb crossed to him on her knees and adjusted the sheet and blanket over him so that he was exposed only from the waist up. She rose on her knees to gain leverage for the job, then leaned over to place her palms on the taut muscles of his left shoulder. Kincaid shivered under her fingertips.

"I'm sorry. My hands are cold," she apologized, curling them against her chest.

"Please," Kincaid said tightly, more affected than he cared to admit, "go ahead."

A moment later Reb obeyed his command. She closed her eyes and devoted herself to easing his pain. She marveled at the corded muscles along the back of his neck, then smoothed the rippling flesh across his broad back to his shoulder and down the knotted left arm.

Kincaid knew Reb had been reluctant to come into physical contact with him. Her touch, however, was decidedly caressing. He closed his eyes and allowed her fingers to work their magic. The next thing he was aware of was Reb's voice in the dark.

"Turn over."

Incredibly, he'd fallen asleep! Kincaid damned the illness that had left him so fatigued. Then, determined not to lose the effect of this lesson on Reb, he interrupted her by marching away from the bed to the table.

"Wait a minute."

He fumbled around in the dark. He scratched a match against wood, there was the smell of sulphur, and a brief red flare merged into a golden glow on his body as he lit the lamp. He carried the light with him over to the chest next to the bed and treated Reb to a view of the stalking lion. When he held the lamp up to her face, her eyes were huge mahogany pools in a visage blanched white. She stared at him like a rabbit trapped by a wolf. He kept his eyes locked on hers as he placed the lamp on the chest and sat on the bed. He lifted the covers and slid under, laying his head down on the pillow, his arms relaxed at his sides.

"I'm ready."

He waited patiently for Reb to begin.

As if in a trance Reb raised her hands to his bared chest. Gently, lovingly, she fondled the warm, smooth skin beneath her fingertips, living the fantasy she had imagined the first day she saw him.

Kincaid watched for her reaction. His eyes hooded slightly and his lips pressed into a grim line.

Reb worked away from the healing bullet wound toward the enticing bare skin in the center of his chest, then spread her hands outward toward each turgid nipple, skimming the hardened tips. Her fingertips slid down along the muscled ribs she could see as well as feel, coming to rest in the line of curls at his navel.

Kincaid knew desire in a woman's face when he saw it, and the bright shine in Reb's eyes, the soft, full, partly opened lips that she wet occasionally with her tongue, convinced him that she was not immune to his masculinity. He decided to move on to the next step in his plan.

Slowly, so as not to frighten her, he reached up to

stop her hands on his abdomen. He was well pleased with the avid look he found on her face. "Thank you, Reb. That feels much better. Good night now."

Reb stared at him as though he'd told her she could leave for the moon now, and removed her hands as though they belonged to someone else. A blush rose on her cheeks when he had to nudge her back to her own side of the bed. She jerked the sheet and blanket up over her shoulder, then breathed deeply to avoid crying out loud with mortification.

Kincaid listened to the muffled sobbing with only a small pang of regret. He was doing this for her own good, he reminded himself. He raised himself enough to blow out the lamp. He'd proved he could—what—disturb her? Certainly *arouse* was not the proper description for the sounds he was hearing from the other side of the bed. No, arousal would come later. With a fleeting smile that belied his own uncomfortable state, he closed his eyes in satisfaction and slept.

11

Reb snuggled against the warmth that enfolded her, relishing the feeling of comfort. Soft lips caressed her forehead, then moved down her temple to kiss each closed eyelid. The endearments continued along her cheek toward her mouth, which she raised slightly in anticipation of the coming touch. Gently as a butterfly, two lips brushed across her own, hesitated, then briefly lit again. She shivered when callused fingertips lifted her short locks away from her nape. That touch was followed by warm, wet lips, causing another shiver. The tantalizing caress worked its way up her slender neck to her shell-shaped ear, leaving behind a trail of tingling flesh. *If this is a dream*, Reb thought, *I don't want to wake up*.

"Laurie," a husky voice breathed in her ear.

Reb groaned inwardly as her heart sank to her toes. Kincaid dreaming! She couldn't let this farce continue. She wouldn't let it continue. She began the delicate process of extricating herself from his grasp. How in the world had they gotten so tangled up? she wondered. When she tried to edge backward, his hands increased their splayed hold on her bare ribs, thumbs resting under her breasts.

"Come, love," he coaxed, "give me a kiss."

Reb's first reaction was to press her lips tight in refusal and pull away from the strong hands that had slipped under her buckskin shirt. When he stirred restlessly, she began to have second thoughts. What if her refusal caused him to wake up?

Aside from the loss of pride she would suffer from being caught in such a compromising situation, she was not altogether sure she was ready to deal with Kincaid woman to man. Perhaps if she assuaged his desire for a kiss, she could escape from this predicament without discovery. Then she would make sure they headed down the mountain tomorrow, whether Blue had returned or not.

Never having taken the initiative, she was unsure how to proceed. She moved her head closer to Kincaid and tilted it slightly so their noses wouldn't collide. Her eyes were open, but the moonlit shadows were deceptive. She edged closer until her lips touched lightly stubbled skin. She'd kissed his chin! Now what?

A voice sighed, "Again," and she could tell from the sound and the exhaled breath where to move her mouth to make contact with his. She inched her lips upward until she met the warm lips waiting for her.

At the same time their lips met, his thumbs reached up to brush her nipples, which hardened into coral pebbles under his caress.

Reb almost gasped at the concurrent tightening in her belly, but the surge of desire that rose in her center only made her more anxious to get away. She took advantage of his concentration on one part of her body to try to extricate her legs from under the powerful thigh he'd thrown over them, but without much success.

Reb didn't panic, although the urge to do something desperate was great. With reluctance, she admitted that until Kincaid was satiated, she was stuck. Well, there was more than one way to skin a cat. She would tame the beast by feeding its hunger. When she had taken the edge off its appetite, she would make her escape.

Kincaid was delighted with the success of his plan. The greatest danger had been at the time of Reb's awakening. Apparently her fear of confronting him had been sufficient to make her compliant. As long as Reb thought he mistook her for Laurie, she would do nothing to resist his advances, and he would be satisfied with nothing less than total capitulation.

The next step was to get her out of those smelly clothes.

With no more effort than it took to tear an autumn leaf from a limb, he pulled Reb's shirt up over her head. She immediately rolled away from him. He flung the shirt away and reached for her shoulders, bringing her bare breasts, now protected by her hands, against his chest and sliding his arms around her.

He could feel her trembling, her breath shallow. He ran the fingers of one hand through her hair, smoothing it away from her ear so he could nibble on it. Light pressure applied to her elbows brought her arms up and around his neck.

Then he set about calming her obvious fear by running his hands up and down along her spine and across her shoulders, pressing her breasts flat against his broad chest.

Frightened as she was of discovery, Reb never questioned the vigor of Kincaid's actions. How should she know what a man might be capable of in his sleep? All she had for comparison was the episode when he was delirious. This activity seemed in total keeping with that. She was determined that her responses would be so compliant as to put him off guard. Then she could withdraw without waking him.

They were pressed together now, nose to nose and toe to toe, and Reb knew once again the warmth and strength of his desire against her flushed skin. The demands he made with his mouth she responded to as gentle, unspoken requests. She was surprised at her body's languid acquiescence to Kincaid's possession. She felt safe in his arms.

It was time to feed the beast.

She threaded her fingers through his hair and arched her head sideways, offering her willowy neck for his kisses. She pressed her loins against his belly and slipped her knee between his legs. Her breasts she slid teasingly back and forth across his own. She shivered in pleasure when he kissed a path down her neck and throat to her shoulders.

Then she put her own mouth to good use, tasting his salty brow with the tip of her tongue and bringing his head up with her hands, her tongue gliding down his temple. She tenderly kissed each closed eyelid, and the tip of his Grecian nose. She felt his strong jaw with her hands, celebrating the memory of her first touch of his mobile lips with another visit from her fingertips. Her tongue found the scar under his eye, and she nipped it with her teeth.

She could do all these things without self-consciousness because Kincaid would never know. He was asleep and thought she was Laurie. Her soul cried with wanting it otherwise. When she realized Kincaid was releasing his hold, she tensed in preparation for the move away from him.

The wanton sensuality of the woman in his arms surprised and confused Kincaid. She was supposed to resist his advances so he could overcome her objections, then expose her for the female she was. Instead, he felt a fierce protectiveness for the innocent abandon of her response, while his body raged with a need that only she could fulfill.

The next thing Kincaid knew, he'd landed on the floor, his head striking a flour barrel with enough force to stun him.

"What the hell is going on here?" a voice bellowed.

"Blue!" Reb shrieked in joy. She threw herself into the mountain man's arms, oblivious to her state of undress. While she was hugging him, the realization dawned that she was naked from the waist up—not that she was embarrassed to be so unclothed before Blue, but it exposed more fully the nature of the activity she'd been involved in when he'd entered the room.

He put his hands on her bare shoulders and pushed her away. "Put your shirt on."

Reb skittered to obey.

"Do you mind telling me what's going on?" Blue growled, glaring at the naked man he'd laid out flat on the dirt floor.

Reb had to light the lantern in order to find where Kincaid had thrown her shirt. The dark frown she saw on Blue's face when she picked up the garment from the floor in the corner made her hasten to explain.

"He thinks I'm a boy," she began hesitantly.

"Then he must be blind!"

Reb blushed and crossed her arms to hide her breasts. She turned around and yanked her shirt down over her head. "He thought I was his wife," she blurted over her shoulder.

"Well, which is it? Does he think you're a boy, or does he think you're his wife?"

Kincaid controlled his twitching lips, which kept threatening to grin at Reb's discomfiture. However, not knowing the limits of Blue's anger, and, after all, discretion being the better part of valor, he bit the inside of his cheek and remained still.

"Both!" Reb snapped in reply to Blue's question, her temper now a match for his. After all, he wasn't her father, and besides, she hadn't done anything wrong. "He mistook me for Adam's *brother*, and I saw no reason to disenchant him," she spat. "As for tonight, he was dreaming and thought I was . . . another woman. If you hadn't interrupted us, I would have soothed him and managed to disengage myself before he woke up, and he'd never have been the wiser."

So that's what she was doing! Kincaid marveled at her ingenuity, even while he rued his own willingness to once again be duped.

Blue glanced at Kincaid, who still appeared to be out cold, then back at Reb. No matter what she said, there was a whole lot more going on between these two than she was telling.

"I'd appreciate it if you'd help me get him back on the bed," she said. "It took a lot to get him well, and I'd just as soon not go through that again."

Kincaid grunted when Blue easily picked him up and threw him over his shoulder. When the mountain man dropped him on the bed, he opened his eyes to stare into two startlingly similar faces—bright mahogany eyes framed by arched black brows, shaggy, midnight black hair, prominent cheekbones, full mouths, and stubborn chins. One was an older man he'd never seen before. He shook his head groggily. No wonder the man had laid him out. He was lucky nothing worse had happened.

"Your father?" he questioned Reb.

Kincaid watched the man flush and a curious expression flicker across his face as Reb answered with a smile, "No, this is Blue."

"What happened?" Kincaid asked, pretending ignorance while rubbing the knot on his head.

Reb and Blue exchanged looks, and she put a hand on Blue's arm before she answered, "You were dreaming, and you fell out of bed. Go back to sleep. Blue and I have some things to discuss. You two can talk in the morning."

Why, the little liar! Kincaid thought. Well, he had a few lies of his own to set straight. "Reb, I remember everything," he improvised quickly. "Must have been that knock on the head. My memory is back."

She quickly hid the pain in her eyes, but couldn't suppress a sigh. "Good. Get some rest, and tomorrow we can think about sending you on your way." It didn't matter anymore who he was, or what he was doing out here. She already knew all she needed to know about him—she loved him.

"Reb." He called her back to the bed and pulled her down to whisper in her ear so Blue couldn't hear. "I can ride, but I don't know a blame thing about roping." He grinned. She chuckled, then laughed aloud. He joined her, and soon the two of them were laughing so hard Reb had to wipe the tears from her eyes. Blue just watched them like they were crazy.

"Private joke," she giggled, then gave an unmaidenly guffaw and slapped her knee.

Kincaid was glad to see the pain gone from her face. Tomorrow was soon enough for pain.

12

Seated across from each other at the timeworn table, Reb and Blue talked quietly to avoid disturbing Kincaid, who had finally relented to Reb's pleas and turned over to sleep.

"Why can't you tell him you're a woman?" Blue demanded.

"It would be very . . . awkward to admit it now," Reb replied. "Anyway, what purpose would it serve? You've just told me that I have to take him down the mountain alone, and it would only complicate things if he knew the truth."

Blue didn't argue, just shook his head. "When do you plan to leave?"

"Tomorrow, I guess, if Kincaid hasn't suffered any lasting effects from your overenthusiastic greeting."

Blue scowled. "My greeting was damned appropriate."

Reb laid a hand on Blue's sleeve, and she concentrated on her fingers as she toyed with a snag in the navy colored wool. "Thank you for caring, but things were not as they probably seemed."

"I know what I saw," he said brusquely.

Her deep brown eyes peered up into the matching orbs that were sunk deep in Blue's rugged face. "It was dark, Blue. What did you see?"

Blue recalled the scene to mind, and a frown wrinkled his brow. His reflex action on finding the two in bed together had been to save Reb from the unwanted attentions of that rutting rogue. It dawned on him now that it was Reb who'd been caressing Kincaid when he'd interrupted them.

It was hard for Blue to imagine his Reb desiring any man, but if his recollection was accurate, he must be mistaken.

When Blue looked at her, the question was plain in his eyes, but Reb waited for him to voice it aloud.

"You were the one kissing him?"

Reb flinched, even though she'd known the query was coming. It was true, though. She had been the one kissing Kincaid, not the other way around. What was wrong with her? Her throat closed on the admission she was about to make. She tightened her jaws to stop the trembling in her chin and took a deep breath before plunging into her confession.

"He was dreaming and asked for a kiss from his wife—she was killed during the war—and I guess I got carried away by my feelings." She swallowed painfully over the lump in her throat before finishing in a frightened and confused whisper, "I can't seem to keep myself from wanting to touch him."

Blue watched the tears of frustration gather in Reb's eyes, and as a giant teardrop slid down the side of her freckled nose, he asked bluntly, "Do you love him?"

"I think so," she choked out.

"You think so?" Blue snorted and muttered in exasperation. "All this moaning and groaning, and you *think* so?"

Reb laid her head down on her arms to muffle her gulping sobs as the vulnerable child in her wailed, "He thinks I'm just a smelly, bratty boy!"

Reb's tears tore at Blue's heartstrings; he couldn't remember anything in the past that had reduced her to such a womanish display of emotion, not even Rachel's death. His knuckles whitened in clenched fists as he controlled the furious desire to strangle Kincaid for being the cause of Reb's unhappiness.

At the same time, he was not able to hide his exasperation with Reb for acting so out of character. His mind racing for a solution that would resolve Reb's dilemma, he quickly concluded that, whether she liked it or not, the first step out of this pile of buffalo flop was to tell Kincaid that Reb was female.

When he came to this conclusion, he was aware of

a sinking feeling in the pit of his stomach. His face took on a pinched, grim look as he admitted to himself the source of his distress. The Reb that had giggled in pleasure and wide-eyed adoration when he had dandled her on his knee had grown up. What she wanted—what she needed now—were the attentions of another man.

It startled and pained Blue to realize he was jealous of the love Reb had bestowed on the unknowing Kincaid. He wasn't going to stand by and see that precious blessing go to waste.

"Dammit, Reb," Blue said angrily, "tell the man you're a woman. Tell him how you feel."

"No!" She grabbed his arm, and her magnificent fiery eyes, glistening with tears, locked with his. At a stirring from the bed, she checked over her shoulder anxiously to make sure she hadn't wakened Kincaid. While she waited for the sleeping man to finish shifting his position, she wiped her eyes with her dirty sleeve, leaving childlike smudges across her cheeks.

When Kincaid quieted, she confronted Blue once again. "You don't understand," she said. "His wife was killed, but he hasn't stopped loving her. There's no room in his life for anyone else."

Blue tugged his bottom lip in thought. Perhaps Reb was right. There had only been one woman for him. Even though they hadn't been destined to share their lives together, he'd never desired another. But he well knew that not all men were so constant. "How do you know unless you ask?" he said.

Reb was reluctant to disclose everything she'd learned about Kincaid over the past weeks, not to mention the episode during his feverish delirium. "I just know," she said miserably. She tipped her chin up in a way that made it clear this was not a subject she wished to discuss any further.

Blue knew better than to argue with her. When Reb's mind was made up, it was made up. As he'd taught Reb, however, there was more than one way to skin a cat. He would just have to talk with Kincaid himself.

"All right," he said, rising from his seat at the table, "we might as well get some rest if you're going to leave tomorrow."

Reb sat forlornly watching the lantern flicker. *It wouldn't make any difference,* she kept repeating to herself. *There's no way Kincaid could feel anything for me at all. He thinks I'm a boy, for heaven's sake!*

She laid her head back down on one arm, and her eyelids drooped further closed with each twist of the lantern flame. Her other hand dropped down to scratch Trapper's head as Blue's dog lay down across her feet.

"Reb."

Drowsily, she responded to the parental tone of Blue's voice and slid from the chair onto the buffalo

robe he'd spread on the floor next to the stove. She
tossed and turned like a cat in a basket until she'd
achieved a comfortable fetal curl inside the robe,
then mumbled, "Good night, Blue."

Trapper waited for her to quiet, then chose a spot
as close as possible to Reb and, after a canine version
of Reb's nesting efforts, settled himself on top of the
buffalo robe next to her.

Blue bent to one knee next to Reb. Parting the hair
on her forehead, he brushed it back to each side with
his forefinger to make a place for the soft kiss he
pressed on the center of her brow.

"Good night, Rebecca," he whispered.

⚬

After breakfast the next morning, it was Kincaid who
first brought up the subject of leaving the cabin.

"Now that you're here, perhaps you can help me
get to my destination," he said to Blue.

"Just where is it you're going?" Blue asked.

"The second Overland Stage station west of the
Laramie Mountains."

Blue and Reb exchanged surprised glances. Seth
Barker's stage station, where Kincaid would have met
his party, was one stop beyond Matt's ranch. If
Kincaid had completed his original journey, Reb
observed with unaccustomed green-eyed jealousy, he

would have eaten a meal in her home served by her sister Dillon. Reb, being a part of the roundup crew, would have known about Kincaid only through her sister's glowing reports. Reb bit her lower lip to control the smug satisfaction that she experienced because she'd met Kincaid first.

Reb loved her sister, but Dillon tended to sweep most men off their feet with her beauty. She didn't relish the idea of facing Dillon's competition where the tall Yankee was concerned.

Blue interrupted her train of thought. "I'll be glad to get you started on your way," he said to Kincaid. "I should tell you first that I asked some questions about you at Fort Laramie, and apparently there was quite a stir at your disappearance. A Corporal Jennings reported that everyone on the stage he was guarding had been killed.

"Of course, when they went to retrieve your body for your folks, it wasn't there. General Dodge left word with the commander of the fort, Colonel Moonlight, to send word to him immediately if you were found.

"When I informed the army that Adam and Reb had rescued you and that you were safe, but had lost your memory, they provided a horse for you and instructions where you were to be taken. Moonlight wired your parents to advise them you're alive."

"Thank God for that," Kincaid said quietly.

"I've brought the horse, but I can't be your guide. I have some unfinished business with Chief Spotted Tail," Blue said.

"Wasn't he being sent to a reservation?" Kincaid asked, recalling his discussion with Reb.

"He was." Blue grinned. "He changed his mind."

Blue explained how the cavalry had considered itself more an escort than a guard and, unsuspecting that there was any resistance to moving to the reservation on the part of the Sioux, had marched in front of the Indians rather than following them. The troops hadn't even been issued ammunition.

Three days away from the fort, the Sioux had slipped away from their camp before dawn to cross the Platte River, heading north for the Powder River region west of the Black Hills. It was a while before the soldiers even realized the Indians weren't asleep in their tepees. By that time, most of the Sioux women and children had crossed the Platte.

"Although the Indians' ponies were trained to ford rivers, the army horses weren't," Blue said, "and most of the soldiers couldn't swim. Besides, there were only a hundred and forty soldiers against nearly four hundred armed warriors. You see, they never thought to take the Indians' weapons from them, either."

Blue scratched the stubble on his jaw, then shook his head in disbelief. "Sometimes the stupidity of the U.S. Army amazes me."

"You won't get any argument on that from me," Kincaid said ruefully, recalling his own disastrous encounter with the army's protection.

Blue continued, "The Sioux harassed the soldiers just long enough to allow their women and children to escape. When the braves quit chasing them, those army boys raced for home. That's where I came in.

"When Colonel Moonlight heard what had happened, he sounded boots and saddles and lit out from the fort with over two hundred men. I volunteered to act as scout.

I suggested to Moonlight that we pace ourselves, but he was so anxious to catch Spotted Tail and his Sioux that we rode a hundred and twenty miles in two days. Of course that ruined a lot of horseflesh, and about half the men had to go back.

"We stopped for breakfast the third day along Deadman Creek. We unsaddled the horses to let them graze between the walls of the narrow canyon there. I warned Moonlight we should hobble the animals, but it seems every suggestion I made on that trip, he did the exact opposite." A wry smile lit Blue's face when he remembered how easy it had been to manipulate the bullheaded colonel.

"He insisted the horses were too tired to move very far on their own. Unfortunately"—(or fortunately, Blue thought to himself, depending on whose side you were on)—"there was a surprise attack by Spotted

Tail. He and his braves came down into the canyon, shooting and yelling and waving blankets. Scared a year's life out of those fledgling recruits and sent the horses flying.

"I tried to explain to the good colonel that I was shooting my gun to try to head off a few of our mounts, but it seems he saw it otherwise. He accused me of being in cahoots with those Indians. We did manage to catch about twenty-five horses, but Spotted Tail's Sioux got clean away with the rest."

"You lost all but twenty-five horses?" Reb repeated in awe.

"Unbelievable," Kincaid murmured.

"Moonlight was furious. He burned the extra saddles and all the tack and supplies we couldn't carry, and we walked back. It was a long, thirsty four days for those young boys. When we arrived at the fort, the colonel threw me in the stockade. Nobody thought about me again until Moonlight got relieved of his command. I remembered to inquire about you then," Blue said to Kincaid. "You know the rest."

"Oh, Blue, you've been in jail!" Reb exclaimed. "I've been thinking so much of myself, I never wondered what could have kept you away so long."

Kincaid ignored Reb's outburst, more intent on the other information Blue had revealed regarding his relationship with the Indians. If the mountain man did have some connections with the Sioux, it might be a good thing for the railroad to know about. "Were you working with the Indians?" Kincaid inquired innocently.

"Not exactly," Blue hedged. "You could say I helped make an opportunity that the Sioux took advantage of. I'd promised an old acquaintance of mine I'd do what I could to slow the army down."

"An old acquaintance?" Kincaid prodded.

"Spotted Tail."

"The chief of the Brulé Sioux is a *friend* of yours?" Kincaid said incredulously.

"I saved his life once."

Reb was also startled at Blue's revelation. If Spotted Tail was his friend, might not Standing Buffalo be a friend as well? For a horrified moment, Reb feared she and Adam might have killed someone close to Blue in their slaughter at the renegade camp. "Standing Buffalo isn't—"

"Standing Buffalo and his braves are murdering renegades and deserve whatever happens to them," Blue said.

"You never told me you were friends with any Indians," Reb accused, still shocked at the idea of Blue sitting down peacefully with the same Indians who scalped and murdered the white man with such violent ease.

"You never asked," he answered simply. "General Connor was the one who urged General Dodge to

relieve Moonlight of his command. He convinced
Dodge at the same time to let him lead his own expe-
dition to the Powder River to solve this Indian situation. Blast the army for its ignorant generals! I owe it
to Spotted Tail to warn him things are bound to heat
up for the Sioux."

"Owe it to him? I thought you said you saved his
life, not the other way around," Kincaid said.

"He did save my life." Blue let the sentence hang
in the ensuing silence without offering further explanation before he added firmly, "I only came by to
bring you that big-devil black horse the army sent—
Satan, I think the hostler called him—and to tell you
where to meet your people. Reb'll have to lead you
back down the mountain."

"Reb?" Kincaid asked skeptically.

Reb immediately flared up at this uncalled-for
questioning of her capabilities, especially since the
insult had occurred in Blue's presence.

"Any objections?" she snapped.

"Would it matter if I did have any?" he retorted.

"No," Blue said quietly, causing them both to turn
and stare at him. "You're stuck with Reb, like it or
not. And damned lucky to have such a good guide."

Blue watched the tension sparking between the
two pairs of flashing eyes, and wished he knew more
about what had happened between them before his
arrival.

"Do I meet my party at the same place as before?" Kincaid asked.

"Yes, it's one stage station after Reb's place."

"Reb's place?"

"My father's ranch is also a rest stop for the Overland Stage," Reb said.

Kincaid went through practically the same speculation as Reb had, mistakenly concluding, because he wasn't aware she would have been gone on the roundup, that if things had gone as initially planned, he would have met Reb when he stopped at her father's way station.

He eyed her surreptitiously. Would she have been wearing a form-fitting print calico dress like the farmer's daughters he'd seen back east? Probably not. He corrected his image of her, mentally redressing her in a pair of sturdy, *clean* buckskins.

He rubbed his thigh to still its aching, but didn't repress the smile that flickered across his face. "When do we leave?" he asked Reb almost jovially.

"After lunch," she replied. "That'll give us plenty of time to get down the mountain to camp before dark. We'll arrive at your point of rendezvous tomorrow."

Reb couldn't believe they were calmly planning Kincaid's departure from her life. Although once she'd wished fervently for just such an eventuality, that was no longer true.

Kincaid was also reluctant to part from Reb. There was unfinished business between them. She still hadn't paid for her deceit. Perhaps an opportunity would present itself on the way down the mountain. He would have to make sure one did.

Blue sent Reb out to feed and curry the horses to give him an opportunity to speak with Kincaid alone, warning her to take care with the mount he'd brought for the tall Yankee.

Reb looked back and forth between the two of them seated at the table and grumbled something about child labor, but did as she was bid.

Blue leaned back in his chair and took a sip of coffee. "You know, the army never did say what you're doing out here."

Kincaid had expected Blue's question. He had no particular reason to trust the man, yet he did. If the mountain man had intended to do him deadly physical harm, he'd already passed up the perfect opportunity, and words alone wouldn't deter Kincaid from his mission. He decided to take the grizzled character into his confidence.

"That's because the army, except for Grenville Dodge and a few generals in Washington, doesn't know what I'm doing out here," Kincaid admitted.

Blue raised a quizzical eyebrow that encouraged Kincaid to elaborate.

"The Union Pacific is trying to determine the best

route for their half of the transcontinental railroad. The businessmen in Denver have been trying to convince railroad officials that south through Denver is the way to go.

"Grenville Dodge is a qualified engineer himself, and when he got a look at the terrain out here, he suggested that my father privately check it out. I studied engineering at Harvard, and that made me a logical choice to survey the mountainous grades in this area. So here I am."

"What about the uniform?"

"That was to get me in and out of my meetings with Dodge without raising questions," Kincaid acknowledged.

"Your father's a railroad man, then."

"That and several other things—banker, financier, industrialist. You name it, he has a probing finger in the pie."

"You'll be going back east then when your job is done, I expect," Blue said, trying to determine where Reb might fit into this blueleg's plans.

"No," Kincaid replied pensively, "I don't think so. There's nothing for me back there now." He massaged his thigh, which seemed to ache more than normal this morning, perhaps as a result of his trip to the floor the previous night, and maybe because the past few hours had stirred up distressing memories that had only begun to soften their grip on his heart.

"Sorry about your wife," Blue said.

The grizzled man's sympathy surprised Kincaid. He replied with a gruff curtness intended to cover his feelings, "I'll get over it."

Blue didn't miss the regret that crossed Kincaid's face. He knew the emotion well. He also knew from his own experience that regretting something didn't change the fact that it had happened. It was time, if not more than time, that this young man got on with his life. Reb loved Kincaid. Blue set his mind to determining whether there was a way in his power to have this providential stranger recognize and return that love.

"Reb's quite a . . . boy," Blue began.

"Yes, he is," Kincaid readily agreed. That was an understatement.

"You don't have to worry about getting down the mountain safely. Reb's one of the best trackers I know."

"A crack shot, too," Kincaid muttered.

"Yes. How did you know?"

"She gave me some lessons," he said, smiling at the recollection of Reb's reaction to her one missed shot. It wasn't until he had the sentence out that Kincaid realized what he'd said. The smile faded, and he looked quickly at Blue to see if he'd noticed the slip.

He had.

"How long have you known?" Blue asked ominously. This was a twist in the trail he hadn't counted on, and he hoped that what he found around the corner wouldn't be a polecat.

"I just found out yesterday," Kincaid admitted reluctantly. "She's played her role very well."

Blue gave an inaudible sigh of relief but remained tense, searching Kincaid's face for any indication of his feelings for Reb. What he encountered was a stony visage to outmatch anything he'd ever seen, even on the close-faced Matt Hunter. He had to find a way to crack that facade and make this Yankee reveal his intentions toward Reb.

"Are you going to tell her you know?" Blue demanded in an icy voice.

"Why should I?" Kincaid retorted. "We've managed very well up to now. She seems perfectly happy with the current arrangement. There's certainly no modesty on my part," he sneered. "I'm perfectly happy to parade around naked while she plays doctor. She's even welcome to bathe me when I'm bare as a babe!" Kincaid snarled furiously.

A throaty growl drew his attention to the corner of the room. What he saw there would have terrified a lesser man. Trapper crouched with fangs bared and silvery gray hackles raised on the scruff of his neck, ready to spring at the man whose tone of voice threatened Blue. Kincaid was certain that any movement from him would precipitate an attack by the wolflike animal.

"He belong to you?" Kincaid asked without taking his eyes off the dog.

"Friend, Trapper," Blue commanded.

The dog immediately relaxed and came over to investigate Kincaid, who held his hand out tentatively for the canine to nuzzle. When Trapper had satisfied his curiosity, he dropped to the floor and rested his head on Blue's foot.

Blue was somewhat surprised by his own tolerant patience with the younger man's challenging response, but when he put himself in Kincaid's place, the attitude was pretty understandable. Kincaid's belated awareness that it had been no ragged lad that had attended him, and the stinging knowledge of Reb's highly successful pretense, had injured this proud man's pride.

On the other hand, it had been Kincaid who'd asked Reb for a kiss. Blue was not at all fooled by the nonsense about a "dream." He was sure Kincaid had known exactly what he was doing.

Surely the request for a kiss meant he was interested in the woman beneath the rags she wore? Apparently, taking advantage of Reb's naïveté was part of some plan of Kincaid's to get back at Reb for her breach of feminine conduct. It was necessary, then, to make it clear to the angry man that, if Reb were hurt, Kincaid would have to answer to Blue.

Blue sat forward and braced his palms on the

table before him. "If you're offended by Reb's lack of modesty, then I suggest you don't have any more 'dreams' that require her to administer immodest attentions."

Blue spoke so softly Kincaid barely heard him, but he couldn't misinterpret Blue's aggressive posture, his narrowed eyes, and the iron in his voice. It was obvious that Blue saw through the ploy he'd used with Reb. It was equally obvious that the older man was setting himself up as Reb's champion.

"This matter is between Reb and me," Kincaid said, with a steel in his voice that parried the iron in Blue's.

"I don't want her hurt."

Kincaid bristled at Blue's commanding tone and answered angrily, "Reb started this game, and she set the rules. I don't intend to throw in my hand just when the pot has gotten interesting."

"Reb isn't playing a game with you," Blue replied.

"Then what do you call it when a beautiful woman pretends to be a dirty, stinking ragamuffin boy?" Kincaid raged, rising so violently that his chair fell with the crash of splintering wood behind him. He towered menacingly over Blue, letting his full height intimidate if it would.

At Trapper's warning rumble, Blue laid his hand calmly on the dog's head and ran it down his back to soothe the raised, black-tipped gray hackles. Blue was amazed at Kincaid's vehemence and the all too obvious resentment manifested at Reb's ruse, but he was more sure than ever that all was not lost. In fact, he had to tense his jaw to keep from smiling ear to ear.

Perhaps he could help these two find each other before it was too late. Kincaid's fury at the tack Reb had taken would have to be soothed. Thanks to the Yankee's most recent outburst, however, Blue was confident that his job wasn't going to be as difficult as he'd thought at first.

What virile man, and Blue had no qualms about Kincaid on that count, wouldn't want to be persuaded that the "beautiful woman" who'd masqueraded as a "dirty, stinking ragamuffin boy" had done so because she was afraid she wouldn't be able to resist his masculine charms?

"Reb wasn't raised to play coy games," Blue said. "Her father . . ." He stumbled over the word, then continued, "Her father saw fit to teach her things a girl wouldn't normally learn. Reb was a good pupil, and what seemed strange at first became pretty normal over the years. She's only doing what's natural for her. Reb is an innocent where men are concerned," he finished pointedly.

Kincaid snorted his disbelief. He walked in a limping circle in the small room, glad for the opportunity to exercise the cramped muscle in his leg and to observe Blue from behind without being subject to the same scrutiny.

He found it hard to connect Reb's wanton sensuality with inexperience. Yet she had been shy at first when responding to him. That kiss on the chin was certainly not the work of a practiced lover!

"At least, she was innocent before she met you," Blue turned and added probingly.

Kincaid stopped and glared at Blue. He found the insinuation that he regularly deflowered helpless virgins repugnant. He also couldn't help a twinge of guilt when he acknowledged at the same time that he'd set Reb's virtue as the price she must pay for her masquerade.

"I've never known Reb to treat any man as other than a friendly competitor," Blue continued, undeterred.

"Friendly competition? That's what you call the way she's been leading me around by the nose?"

Blue had to struggle against a guffaw at Kincaid's indignant question. He managed to control himself and replied, "I'm sure Reb used her best judgment under the circumstances. You can hardly blame her for not admitting she's female—alone with you, not knowing what kind of man you are . . ." Blue let his voice trail off significantly.

Kincaid's brow arched in thought. "I wouldn't have hurt her." Although it was true that, had he known sooner that Reb was a woman, events might very well have led him to bed her. He couldn't deny the heat in his loins when he remembered her striking appearance in the pond.

Blue couldn't resist forcing the issue. "Do you find Reb attractive?"

Disconcerted by the question that followed so closely his own train of thought, Kincaid paced away from the older man. "What's attractive about a woman in filthy buckskins?"

However, to be perfectly honest, he'd admired many facets of the woman beneath the clothes. Capable, competent, caring Reb. Beautiful, enticing, lusciously soft Reb.

Kincaid turned back to Blue with a troubled look that caused the mountain man to adopt his severest expression to hide his inward satisfaction. Clearly this was a subject Kincaid had never examined closely. Good. Let him think.

"I do admire her . . . capabilities," Kincaid grudgingly admitted. "Are you going to tell her I know?"

Blue made a tepee of his hands in front of his pursed lips, trying to decide what would be best for Reb. She hadn't wanted to tell Kincaid she was female. It could only cause pain for her to know she'd been discovered, especially when Kincaid didn't yet acknowledge that he returned Reb's feelings.

Blue had warned Kincaid there would be consequences if he hurt Reb heedlessly. He could only conclude it was best to let them work this out on their own.

"No," Blue sighed, resigning the outcome to fate. "I won't tell her you know she's a woman."

13

The sounds of creaking saddle leather and the muffled crunch of horses' hooves on the thick layers of dead brown pine needles imposed upon the quiet dignity of the mountains. An occasional warble or chirrup issued from nests hidden in the towering trees. The mournful wail of the wind through the thousands upon thousands of pine branchlets raised goose bumps on Reb's skin, which were smoothed by the wafting currents of billowing air that surrounded her like a comforting bath of whirling warm water. She could almost forget that Kincaid followed close on her trail.

A small doe and its dappled fawn paused curiously as she and Kincaid rode by them, but didn't flee. It was unusual to find such fearlessness in the forest creatures anymore, and Reb knew that the days of seeing such a rare occurrence were numbered. Even dumb beasts learned quickly that death followed when men invaded their sanctuary.

She and Kincaid had made steady progress since

leaving Blue's cabin after lunch and had just emerged from a narrow, shadowy path through a stand of blue spruce into a small, sunny open meadow that sloped sharply downhill. With her eyes receptive to the wonders around her, Reb couldn't help admiring Kincaid's mount when he rode up beside her.

The glossy, coal-black animal stood seventeen and a half hands high at the withers, so tall that even the willowy Reb had been forced to stand on tiptoe to see over his back when she'd brushed him down earlier in the day. Satan hadn't lived up to his name, quietly tolerating the strokes of the currycomb through his inordinately long mane and tail without biting at her or trying to kick. Nor had he yet this afternoon proved to be the devil on hooves. Kincaid hadn't had any trouble controlling him. In fact, the two seemed to go together like a pair of well-made buckskin riding gloves.

"That's a beautiful stallion," Reb said.

"My father bought Satan for me as a gift on my twenty-first birthday," Kincaid replied.

"He's your horse? I thought the army sent him."

"I've owned Satan for about five years, but I had no chance to ride him during the war. I only started working with him again after I'd recovered from my leg wound. Guess my father wanted to surprise me by having him brought out here."

"You could have bought a horse for a lot less than it probably cost your father to do that."

"He can afford it."

Reb had discounted Kincaid's reference to being rich made during his delirium, since he'd so obviously appeared to be a soldier. Soldiers weren't rich. If you were rich, you paid someone to fight in your stead.

Reb had never really considered what her competition would be for Kincaid's attention once they left the mountains. Suddenly it dawned on her that not only could she not compete with the feminine wiles of the women she felt sure must be attracted to Kincaid's masculine charms, but as a rancher's daughter, she might not meet the social criteria that a rich man expected from his wife.

"Are you rich?" she couldn't help asking.

Kincaid cocked his head at the question. "Does it really matter?"

"I'd like to know."

"I have money enough for my needs."

"But are you rich?" Reb insisted.

Kincaid laughed. "Yes. Does it show?"

Reb looked Kincaid over seriously. His black leather boots were standard army issue. He'd donned one of Blue's shirts, which pulled tightly across the shoulders. He'd needed to roll the sleeves up to the elbow to disguise the fact that they were too short, revealing his muscular forearms. He wore no hat, and the wind teased the black curls that fell across his tanned brow and down over his collar. The yellow-striped pants seemed indecently snug across his flat belly and along the steel-thewed legs that gripped the huge stallion. No, there was nothing in his appearance to indicate that he was wealthy.

Reb also felt somewhat comforted by the fact Kincaid had never evidenced the pomposity she automatically associated with the very wealthy. A few of that breed had passed through on the stage, and she'd observed their ostentatious displays with an odd mixture of disgust and humor. Never in all the time they'd been together, however, had she ever detected the slightest sign of such behavior from Kincaid.

It left her reassured as to the unimportance of his wealth in their relationship, however mistaken that impression might be. She had no inkling of how different her behavior seemed from that of the women Kincaid knew.

"I guess you don't look rich," she said finally. What she meant was that he didn't *act* as though he were rich, but of course she couldn't say that aloud.

"I take it that's a compliment?"

"Could be."

They headed into a copse of pine, and Kincaid fell back to follow Reb's winding path through the trees. It occurred to him that he could now safely inquire about his missing gold pocket watch. He'd noticed the loss immediately upon waking in Blue's cabin, but had been constrained by his ruse of amnesia from asking about it.

"Did you by any chance find a gold watch at Standing Buffalo's camp, or in my clothing when you rescued me?"

"Another gift from your father?"

"It was a wedding present from Laurie. It's very special to me."

"Don't you think I would have returned it to you by now if I had found it?" Reb asked icily, bristling at the insinuation that she would have kept the object, but even more upset that Kincaid treasured the gift because it had come from his wife. Then shame washed over her at the selfishness that could make her jealous of a dead woman.

"I guess you would have returned it if you'd had it," Kincaid said, eyeing her askance. "You've always been so scrupulously honest with me in every way in the past."

Reb blanched. His words hinted at knowing so much more than they said.

Kincaid had registered Blue's warning about hurting Reb, but there had been nothing in their discussion to dissuade him from making her pose as an unwashed lad as uncomfortable as possible. He thought he knew just the way to set a prickly burr under her saddle for the rest of the ride down the mountain.

"I'm looking forward to seeing your brother Adam again," Kincaid said.

"Adam?" Reb swallowed the fear that rose in her throat.

"Sure. From what you and Blue have told me, it sounds as though we have to go right by your ranch to get to my rendezvous. I'd like to thank Adam for his part in my escape from the Sioux. You were planning to stop by and introduce me to your family, weren't you?"

Reb thought fast. She was horrified at the thought of the humiliation she would suffer if she and Kincaid rode up to the ranch together and her family greeted her as she knew they would, with questions and comments that would quickly free Kincaid of any notions he had that she was a lad.

Even if she could somehow get there ahead of Kincaid, she wasn't sure she could convince her family to keep her secret. The Old One and Garth would go along. Dillon would, too, if only for the chance to flirt with Kincaid.

But not Adam. Adam would think it great fun to blab everything. Then, too, Jesse was so young he would likely let the cat out of the bag without knowing it had escaped.

Reb was uncertain what her father's reaction

would be, but she strongly suspected he would insist she square with Kincaid. It was better not to tempt fate.

"I hadn't planned to go by the ranch," she said. "I didn't want to hold you up."

"No problem," Kincaid assured her. "I'm anxious to meet everyone, especially your sister Dillon. Is she pretty?"

"My sister?" Reb said dumbly.

"Now that I'm a widower, I need to keep my eyes open for a suitable new wife."

"New wife?" The hairs on the back of Reb's neck stood up in warning, and she turned around in the saddle to watch in astonished silence the performance that followed.

Kincaid wrapped the reins around the saddle horn so he'd have his hands free to emphasize his words. "I'm looking for a petite woman, but with a respectable bosom." Grinning lasciviously, Kincaid gestured crudely with both hands. His idea of "respectable" was clearly larger than what could be considered adequate, and unquestionably more generous than those modest crests with which God had seen fit to bless Reb.

"She should have long, copper-colored hair that curls around her face, like so," he continued, making circular motions at his temples with his forefingers. "Let's see. Green eyes would be nice, and an alabaster complexion. No freckles. Can't *stand* freckles on a woman's face. She should be the kind of woman who needs a man to take care of her. *All* of her, if you get my drift," he said, winking slyly at Reb.

Kincaid had intentionally described a woman as far removed from Reb as possible, thereby suggesting that she was not his type. He watched Reb's face redden in what he expected was embarrassment and was well satisfied with the result of his pointed teasing.

If he'd been thinking rationally, however, he would have realized that for Reb to be offended or even more than perturbed by his graphic presentation, aside from its crudeness, she would first have to be attracted to him herself.

Unfortunately, the significance of Reb's blush was lost on Kincaid because he was fighting so hard to deny his own attraction to her. Also, unfortunately, he had unknowingly described a woman who bore a striking resemblance to Dillon.

Reb felt sick to her stomach. Here she'd believed Kincaid so filled with remorse at the loss of Laurie that he couldn't think of another woman, and he'd just lecherously described the kind of feminine pulchritude he had in mind to take his wife's place—her sister Dillon!

Kincaid's big black stud reached over to nip Reb's mare Brandy on the neck for the second time in the space of a few minutes. Brandy whickered in pain and excitement at the stallion's sexual foreplay and danced away from the overbearing animal, so that Reb's leg was crushed against a pine.

"Can't you control that beast?" Reb snapped.

Kincaid reined Satan away from the mare. "He wouldn't be so tempted if you didn't keep putting her pretty tail in his face. We're alike that way. Neither of us can resist an obvious invitation."

Reb turned around quickly enough to catch the mischievous grin that showed off Kincaid's sparkling white teeth, then whipped her head forward when she felt the second furious blush rising on her cheeks in the space of a few minutes. She was grateful that Kincaid was behind her and couldn't see. "That wasn't . . . I didn't . . . I wouldn't . . . Oh!"

Reb was totally tongue-tied. The rider *was* just like his mount, she agreed furiously, always trying to prove his superiority by dominating some female! She couldn't understand why she cared for such a lop-eared mule of a man. It wouldn't break her heart if she never exchanged another word with that arrogant bully.

Content that he'd come away as victor, Kincaid peacefully followed Reb's squared shoulders down the mountain. With his vision focused on Reb, Kincaid's thoughts drifted to her as well. Tonight would probably be his last chance to teach her a good lesson.

Then Blue's speech about Reb's unusual upbringing repeated itself to him. Perhaps he was being unfair. He tried to think of a single occasion when Reb had purposely demeaned him and had to admit there was none. On the other hand, he'd done his best to humble her at Blue's cabin on at least two occasions that he could remember, and she had cleverly managed to turn the tables on him both times.

He realized what he found most irritating was that a mere girl had been able to handle everything he'd thrown at her and come up smelling like a rose. Well, she didn't smell *exactly* like a rose, he admitted. His nose wrinkled at the thought of Reb's pungent buckskins.

Her skin was as soft and pink as rose petals, though. He recalled the velvety smoothness of her small, rounded breasts under his callused fingertips, and the rosy pink tips of those luscious mounds as they hardened in response to his caress.

Kincaid shifted in the saddle, seeking a way to accommodate his uncomfortable state of arousal. Reb rode blithely before him, totally unaware of his frustration. Damn! She'd done it to him again!

He'd be glad to get out of these mountains. Reb was in her element here, more so than he. He wondered whether she'd seen the world beyond the Laramie Mountains, beyond her father's ranch.

He tried to picture Reb dancing gracefully in his

arms at a grand ball, clothed in an elegant ruby red satin evening gown, her raven black hair perfectly coifed. He felt genuine regret for her hacked-off tresses. What would Reb have looked like with long ebony hair falling forward teasingly over her satin-clad shoulders?

He could see Reb in buckskins, and he could visualize her naked, but he simply couldn't imagine her clothed for a role in polite New York society.

Kincaid startled Reb when he broke the silence that had reigned for several hours. "Have you ever been back east?"

Reb hesitated warily before answering, trying to gauge whether Kincaid intended to bring her down a peg once again. He'd pulled abreast of her as they moved completely out of the low brush to the beginning of the open grass. She noted the earnest expression in his eyes and decided his question was sincere.

"Only as far as Fort Laramie," she replied.

"How about south?"

"Adam has been to Denver with Daddy, but I've never gone along. Garth's been talking about going to Texas to pick up some longhorns now that the war is over. I've thought about going with him, just to see what it's like, but I've very happily lived my whole life between these mountains and our road ranch."

When Kincaid's brow arched disdainfully, Reb added defensively, "Of course, I've seen pictures in books of New York and Philadelphia. It looks too crowded to me." She sniffed disdainfully. "People living practically on top of one another. Is it as bad as it seems in pictures?"

"Worse in some places, better in others. New York is never peaceful and quiet like this, that's for sure. It bustles. It hurries. People have places to go, things to do. Everyone's trying to get the most out of life they can."

"Trying to grab what they can from those too weak to protect themselves, you mean."

"Don't start with me, Rebel," Kincaid said abruptly, sitting up straighter in the saddle.

Reb should have been warned, but she couldn't help herself. He was leaving her forever. She needed to hear his voice, to store the timbre of the sound so she could draw on it when he was gone. Even arguing with him would be better than a return to the silence of the past few hours.

"You can't tell me they aren't greedy," she said. "They want to take away the wilderness. They want to claim it for their damned Yankee train."

"Who is 'they,' Reb?" Kincaid asked antagonistically.

"The Yankees."

"I'm a Yankee," he said dryly.

"I didn't mean you. I know you're not like that."

Reb's naive trust in him angered Kincaid. Such

trust had no place in a world that let brothers fight and kill brothers in a war that just as senselessly took sons from mothers and husbands from wives . . . and wives from husbands. Such faith in the goodness of a man who was a virtual stranger was dangerous. Moreover, it was an anachronism, just like those stupid trusting deer that were going to get shot for somebody's supper if they didn't wise up fast.

"I never told you why I came out here, did I?" he said.

"It isn't important," Reb said. They weren't even going to be in each other's company very much longer. What difference could it possibly make?

"Even if the reason I came was to pave the way for a Yankee train through these mountains?"

Kincaid's statement didn't register immediately. When it did, Reb stopped Brandy dead in her tracks. She laid the reins on the left side of Brandy's neck to turn her mount so she faced Kincaid head-on. "You haven't. You wouldn't!" Reb gasped, appalled.

"Oh, but I have and I will. Not 'they,' Reb. Me. By the way, while I'm making a clean breast of things, I never lost my memory. I only pretended to have amnesia because I didn't want some unwashed mountain brat interfering with my work for the Union Pacific."

Reb felt a lump form in her throat. A pain, like a heavy weight, pressed on her chest, and her vision blurred with tears that she struggled to restrain. She wavered in the saddle and grabbed the horn with trembling hands to steady herself. Reb forced her next words out in a hoarse whisper.

"You know how I feel about trains—and any low-down Yankee who would bring them here where they're not wanted. I trusted you."

Kincaid winced at the ferocity of the quiet statement, and cursed his self-righteous arrogance under his breath. Maybe she needed to learn to be more cautious with strangers, but there were certainly less cruel ways of making his point.

Then he hardened himself to her agony. Not any way so sure, he said to himself. She wouldn't soon forget this betrayal, and if it saved her greater pain later, then it was worth it to endure the role of bastard now.

He'd learned a lot from his experience with Laurie. His wife had also been innocently sure that no stranger would ever purposely and unjustifiably harm her. He'd tried to warn her of the danger of such blind trust, but she'd laughingly kissed his concern away, until he'd relented to her soft, sweet persuasion. If he'd been strong and firm with Laurie when he'd had the chance, she might still be alive today.

"Mindless Yankee tenderfoot," Reb said bitterly. "You were neither first nor last of those names, only the most hated one in between." Reb's heart hardened against Kincaid to keep from being crushed by his revelation.

They'd reached the base of the mountains, and a bright green rolling plain dotted with sagebrush and wildflowers stretched out endlessly in the distance. There was no visible shelter. The ball of orange sun was dropping quickly, painting the white clouds along the base of the azure sky in beautiful diagonal stripes of pink. The full moon had already come up and sat incongruously in the bright blue sky.

Neither Reb nor Kincaid appreciated the beauty of the sunset.

"We'll make camp here," Reb announced.

Reb stepped down from the saddle and began efficiently gathering buffalo chips for the fire. By the time she had the fire started, Kincaid had unsaddled both horses and hobbled them nearby. He set the saddles near the fire for future use as pillows and unrolled their blankets to make pallets.

Meanwhile, Reb had unwrapped the cold cornbread and jerky she'd packed for their dinner. There would be no cooking. The fire was strictly for warmth. She concentrated on the food in her hands and ignored Kincaid.

Kincaid didn't think he'd ever seen anybody look so tired and desolate as Reb did now. He leaned back against his saddle with his long legs stretched out before him and gazed pensively into the fire while he chewed the dried beef.

"You know," he said, trying to ease the blow of his confession to Reb, "it isn't a sure thing that the railroad will come through here. In fact, the reason I'm here is to determine whether the tracks should be laid along the base of the southern Rockies or down by Denver."

He might as well have been speaking to a stone wall. Reb didn't exhibit the slightest interest in what he was saying, just took a bite of cornbread and stared blankly into the growing dusk beyond the fire.

The movement of a large grasshopper caught Reb's eye, and she watched mesmerized as the insect gobbled down small blue wildflowers, chewing furiously as he stuffed each petal into his mouth with his spiny forelegs, then moved rapidly on to the next.

What Kincaid wanted, without admitting it to himself, was Reb's forgiveness for hurting her. It was a sign of how much he cared that Kincaid contemplated excusing the harshness of his actions by telling Reb the awful truth about how Laurie had died. "You really should be more careful who you take into your confidence," he said. "When I first married . . ."

Reb watched the grasshopper stop chewing in mid-petal and suddenly take flight. She looked overhead but didn't see any sign of a bird or other natural enemy. "Shut up!" she snapped.

Astonished at her brusque interruption, Kincaid was even more bewildered by Reb's next actions. She pitched the rest of her cornbread over her shoulder and laid her hands flat on the ground on either side of her crossed legs to intercept the growing vibrations from the earth. Then she bent sideways to lay her ear next to the ground.

"Get saddled up quick!" she ordered.

Kincaid obeyed the urgency and something else he'd never heard in Reb's voice—fear.

They hastily kicked the fire out, mounted, and galloped north. The moon lit up the plains like daylight, revealing to Kincaid a dark mass closing fast. He could hear a distant rumble that sounded vaguely like thunder and imagined some sort of prairie tornado descending upon them.

"What is it?" he shouted to Reb.

"Buffalo stampede," she called back. "Ride!"

Kincaid didn't understand how the lumbering herd could threaten two riders he believed could easily outrun them on horseback, but he deferred to Reb's superior plains knowledge. He kicked Satan in the ribs, and the giant animal surged ahead of Reb's bay mare.

Reb urged her horse to keep up with the racing stallion. Without warning, Brandy's left foreleg dropped into an unseen hole, and at the speed she was moving, the bone snapped like a dry stick. Reb flew over Brandy's head as the horse rolled forward.

Kincaid turned his stallion at the mare's screams, and saw Reb on the ground, staring at her horse in shock. As he watched, she sank to her knees to cradle the mare's head in her lap. The animal quieted as Reb's husky voice crooned comfort.

Kincaid dismounted in a rush to stand at Reb's side. He glanced away quickly at the oncoming buffalo, then laid his hand gently on Reb's shoulder.

Reb raised her eyes to Kincaid, pleading for a miracle to save her horse.

Nothing had prepared Kincaid for the gut-wrenching pain he experienced when Reb turned to him for help it wasn't in his power to give. Kincaid gladly would have martyred himself to spare Reb the distress he saw on her face, but he was no saint, and there was no way he knew to make the mare whole.

"Her leg is broken," he said, his voice throaty with emotion. "We have to go."

He reached down to loosen Reb's Colt from her belt. She put her hand over his to keep him from taking the gun and met his questioning gaze with stone-dry eyes.

"She's my horse. I'll do it."

Reb gently laid the mare's head down and slid her hand comfortingly down the slick, lathered neck one last time. She leaned over to nuzzle the still-bellowing silky nose, her own nostrils flaring as she inhaled the familiar musky smell of her sweaty horse. Then she slowly rose on her knees, pulled her razor-sharp knife from its beaded sheath and quickly slit Brandy's throat. The mare jerked once before she shuddered and died.

Kincaid held his breath, waiting for Reb to move away from the dark red blood that began pooling in rivulets around her, but she remained in her prayer-ful pose with the knife hanging slack in her hand.

"Reb."

"Go away," she answered dully.

The buffalo still barreled toward them, and Kincaid knew there was no time to let Reb grieve. He grabbed her around the waist and hauled her away from the dead animal, twisting the knife from her hand as he rose.

Reb fought him like a wild woman, tooth and nail. He suffered her abuse, understanding the loss that precipitated her attack, until at last he had manhandled her stomach-first onto Satan's neck.

Over the top of Satan's back, he could see the ghostly whites of the giant humped creatures' eyes reflecting the moonlight. Their labored breathing whooshed in and out like the rhythmic straining of a mighty steam engine. With the foreknowledge of certain death if he didn't turn and run, Kincaid vaulted into the saddle and yelled a command to his horse. The sound was lost in the deafening roar of thousands of cloven hooves trampling everything in their path.

Satan needed no urging. The stallion bolted away from the mystical shadowy shapes pressing down from behind.

If Reb and Kincaid had been caught by such a stampede even ten years before, their hopes of survival would have been slim. In years past, the buffalo had run in herds of tens of thousands, stretching as far as the eye could see across the plains. Trapped in the center of such a maelstrom, they would have had little chance of escape.

But the white man had killed so many of the beasts that this buffalo herd was not even a thousand strong. It was no wonder that the Sioux, who depended on the buffalo for their livelihood, were bitter and angry.

Kincaid was able to move steadily across the herd until he reached the edge of it and safety. He dismounted after the last of the buffalo had thundered by, pulling the lifeless Reb down before him. Her legs buckled at the knees when her feet hit the ground. As she started to fall, Kincaid picked her up and held her in his arms like a child. Her glazed eyes stared up at him without seeing him.

Kincaid's heart went out to her.

"My valiant Rebel," he murmured. He clutched her still form to his strong, warm body, then pressed a chaste kiss to her brow, but it wasn't enough comfort for him or for her. He kissed each side of her mouth, then urgently sought her full, parted lips, driving his tongue between her teeth to the solace deep within.

Reb's soul, so chilled first by Kincaid's bitter betrayal and then by Brandy's violent death, reached out desperately toward the fiery blaze Kincaid had ignited. Her eyes fell closed, and she entwined her hands in his hair, desperately pulling his mouth down to hers and battling his tongue with her own.

Their close brush with death had left Kincaid vibrantly alive, and Reb's frenzied response inflamed his passion. He laid her down upon the verdant sea of grass. With nothing but the starry, moonlit sky above them, each found in the other's arms a balm for his loss.

Kincaid released Reb's belt and pulled her shirt up from the waist, breaking her hold on him long enough to strip the garment from her.

Reb arched her back away from the fringes of cool grass beneath her so that her breasts flattened against Kincaid's rough wool shirt. Her hands groped blindly at the cold, sharp buttons, trying vainly to tear them free.

When he heard her cry of frustration. Kincaid ripped the shirt off himself and flung it away.

Reb's hands sought his hot flesh, roaming hungrily across his chest, grazing his flat nipples as she felt her way up and across his broad, sinewy shoulders. She raked her nails down his muscular back, demanding closer contact.

Her whimper of desire drove Kincaid beyond the bounds of sane consideration for her untried state. Her shoulders gleamed like mother-of-pearl in the moonlight, and Kincaid craved the sight of all of her. He yanked at the thong that held her buckskin leggings in place, then tore it when it would not yield. He freed her long, slender legs and leaned back to look at Reb, who lay panting, wild-eyed beneath him.

"God," he whispered, "you're beautiful."

"Love me," she implored.

14

Kincaid felt as though Reb's soulful plea to be loved had cast a spell upon him, for now everything seemed to move in slow motion. He was entranced by the sensual fire he saw in Reb's eyes. Her pupils had dilated until the black centers were enormous, and he couldn't resist their siren's call. He held himself motionless when Reb reached up to trace his lips with the pad of her finger. Her touch was soft as corn-silk.

The wonder of lying beneath Kincaid, awaiting the fulfillment of every fantasy her vivid imagination had conjured over the past weeks with this powerful man, left Reb breathless. Her entire body quivered with anticipation.

Kincaid, feeling Reb tremble beneath him, attributed her reaction to fear. He sought to calm her, much as he would any frightened thing, with gentle stroking and soft words, but soon he'd forgotten why he was touching, aware only of the desperate need to possess this bewitching woman. His hands caressed her ribs and narrow waist. For a time that seemed endless, his fingertips teased the rosy nipples that he'd remembered so vividly from the day at the pond. He marveled at the rounded crests made opalescent by moonbeams when she strained upward toward the tingling stimulation.

Kincaid skimmed his hand downward slowly along her silky skin until he reached Reb's inner thigh. She opened herself to him, and his caresses moved steadily upward until he met the proof of her innocence. When Reb stiffened, Kincaid withdrew.

"Let me love you," he breathed in her ear, searching her face for signs that she was willing.

Never before had Reb wanted so much to please another. Always before she'd carefully run her life to satisfy her own need for independence and control of her destiny. Her eyes slowly closed in surrender to the smoldering passion she saw in Kincaid's darkening, smoky gray eyes, breaking the straining tether on Kincaid's barely leashed desire.

Reb knew at last what it meant to give herself up totally to another human being. She shuddered in pleasure as Kincaid's lips pressed hers once possessively in acceptance of her gift, then roamed across the petal-soft skin of her shoulders, lingering when they reached the racing pulse at her throat. His mouth and tongue suckled her sweet flesh, while his hands moved downward to grasp her soft buttocks.

Feeling her acquiescence in his arms, Kincaid once again coaxed Reb's thighs open to him. He paused when she struggled in his arms, until he realized she was only arching her loins, urging him onward.

He kept himself turned away from her so she couldn't incite him to take her before he was sure she was ready. When he did bring her close, she bucked against him.

Kincaid groaned his delight at the challenge of subduing Reb's writhing body. Her lips clung to Kincaid's, her mouth seeking more, needing more, the liquid fire inside her eager to join the burning flame with which Kincaid threatened to consume her. The pressure of Kincaid's shaft intensified what was by now an unsatiated craving. Her hands raced down Kincaid's spine to his strong, muscled flanks, achingly aware that once again cloth separated her from the fiery flesh she sought. She made her dissatisfaction known to Kincaid, and he remedied the problem, leaving Reb momentarily bereft while he stripped off pants and boots.

While she lay there naked and panting, the night breeze whirled mysteriously around her, cooling the lover's sweat that covered her from head to foot. Before she could descend from her euphoria to rational thought, Kincaid mantled her chilled body with his own.

He sheathed himself immediately, pressing with certainty beyond the slight impediment to his passage that signaled Reb's virginity. Reb gasped at the surprising but not painful intrusion.

Kincaid held his desire in abeyance while her body accommodated him. Slowly, ever so slowly and deliciously, he began to move.

Reb was delighted with the sensation. She responded with small, throaty animal sounds of pleasure to the crescendo of heat growing within her as Kincaid's thrusting shaft impaled her again and again.

Somewhere, just beyond her reach, lurked fulfillment of a need she couldn't identify. She instinctively wrapped her legs around Kincaid's waist and grasped with inner muscles to hold him within, soaring ever higher toward the elusive satisfaction that stayed just beyond her reach.

Kincaid suddenly drove his tongue deep into Reb's honeyed mouth. His kiss smothered her anxious cry as she rushed to meet the final savage explosion of passion that threatened to overwhelm them both. Reb felt herself suspended amidst the beauty of moon and stars. She grabbed Kincaid's shoulders and held on tight, not wanting to fall, not wanting to ever come down among mortals again. Someone called to her.

"Lovely Rebel. My beautiful Rebel," a husky voice murmured.

Reb reached out to the voice with all her being and found the fulfillment she'd been seeking. Shattering into a million sparkling pieces, she willingly fell from the heavens and drifted languorously back to earth.

Matt Hunter observed through narrowed eyes the angelic halo of pink dawn light encircling his sleeping daughter's head. Stretched out next to her, though wrapped in a separate blanket, an impressively large man slept, the same halo of pink crowning his raven black hair. Reb was obviously naked beneath the wool covering, for Matt could see her buckskins crumpled carelessly near the cold campfire.

If he'd been an impulsive man, the stranger lying in the dewy grass next to his child with his hand laid possessively across her hip would be dead now, but no one could accuse Matt Hunter of not being fair. It didn't make sense that the man was fully dressed down to his boots if he and Reb had spent a night of passion together.

He would listen to what this Yankee rogue had to say in defense of himself before he acted.

"Wake him up, Adam," Matt said quietly.

Adam could hear his father's controlled fury in the

command and regretted for the umpteenth time his mischievous decision to leave Reb alone with the stranger. Adam hadn't been overly concerned at first by Reb's delay in returning home, since Blue had suggested he would wait a while before returning to his cabin.

However, when Reb still hadn't shown up after the roundup was completed, Adam had finally admitted to his father his fear that the stranger could have harmed Reb or Blue or both. Matt had sent Garth to drive the cattle back out to pasture, and they'd set out to find Reb.

Adam vowed he would kill this stranger himself if Reb had suffered at the sleeping man's hands. He kicked Kincaid in the ribs with the toe of his boot a little harder than was truly necessary to wake him.

Neither Matt nor Adam was prepared for Kincaid's attack. Waked from a sound sleep, he reacted with instincts honed sharp by four years of war. He rolled to the left, sweeping Adam off his feet, and slammed his massive fist into Adam's jaw before he heard Matt cock his rifle.

"Hold it right there," Matt shouted angrily.

"Daddy, stop!" Reb screamed.

All three men froze. Awakened by Kincaid's first movements, Reb stood clutching the blanket draped provocatively across one shoulder and down around her waist like a statue of some goddess. The top of one creamy breast was exposed, and her arms and the greatest part of her long legs as well. Her hair fell across her large, frightened mahogany eyes, giving her a vulnerable, wanton look that each man reacted to from his own perspective as father, brother, or lover.

Both Kincaid and Adam scrambled to their feet. Kincaid froze again when Matt swung the gun up at him.

"No, Daddy," Reb cried. She reached out to knock the barrel of the rifle down to the ground, causing the blanket to drop so that an entire breast was exposed. At Kincaid's audible intake of breath, Reb scooped up the rough cloth to cover herself, although the blanket did nothing to hide the rosy blush on her face and neck.

"Why aren't you dressed?" Matt questioned severely. One of the first things he'd taught Reb was the need for readiness on the trail. That meant denying oneself the luxury of removing clothing at night for greater comfort. The fact that Reb had disregarded this rule was significant, and her state of undress in Kincaid's presence made Matt doubly suspicious.

It was only when her father spoke that Reb realized she was the only one unclothed in the group. Kincaid was fully dressed, as though last night had never happened. Could she have been having some fantastic dream? Her nakedness convinced her otherwise.

Reb wasn't at all cowed by her father's stern face and would have been tempted to respond less seriously, except she was afraid he would make Kincaid suffer if she didn't come up with some plausible excuse for why she was sleeping nude—other than the truth.

"I ran into a polecat. My clothes smelled so rank, I couldn't stand to sleep in them," she replied. Her breathlessness was the only sign of her anxiety.

Reb's reason for being unclothed made sense, yet she'd been known to stretch the facts. Matt would have believed the evidence before his eyes—that the two had been intimate—if he hadn't known Reb's strong aversion to physical relationships with men. And if Kincaid had forced her, there would be no reason for her to say otherwise now.

He looked from Reb's proudly defiant stance to Kincaid. The tall man's stony face gave no hint as to what he thought of Reb's explanation, but to Matt's way of thinking, Kincaid's powerful frame, tensed for action, told a story fraught with guilty knowledge.

That, added to the tales Adam had told about Reb's attraction to the stranger, left Matt unconvinced that the situation was as innocent as Reb had suggested.

Matt let his gaze wander up and down the side of Kincaid's Union Army britches before he asked Reb sardonically, "It wasn't a yellow-striped polecat you tangled with by any chance, was it?"

Out of the corner of his eye Matt thought he saw the edges of Kincaid's mouth tilt in the whisper of a smile, but it vanished when Matt shifted his position to confront the imposing man.

Reb found herself in a highly uncomfortable situation. What was her father trying to prove? She had half a mind to announce that she and Kincaid had spent the night in reckless passion, just to see what he would do.

She was furious with her father for prying into something that was none of his business, and just as furious with Kincaid for taking the whole thing so lightly. She hadn't missed the telltale hint of a smirk on his face. Her father was a dangerous man when crossed, and Kincaid was foolish to underestimate him.

Sometime, somehow, Kincaid had obviously discovered she was female. The question was, when? And why hadn't he admitted he had found out her secret?

She turned her gaze on Kincaid. How did he feel about her? Was he angry at her deceit? He had lied so cunningly about losing his memory. Had the endearments he'd whispered last night also been a lie? Did he care for her, or had she merely been a convenient female body?

This time his face didn't give her any clues to what he was thinking. She wanted to ask him some pointed questions, but not here and now. That meant curtailing her father's persistent curiosity in a way that would get both her and Kincaid out of this gracefully.

When all else fails, she thought, tell the truth—or as much of it as will get the job done.

"This man is Kincaid," she said, using her head to gesture. "I'm sure Adam told you he couldn't remember anything when we found him."

"Adam told me a lot of things about you and your stranger," Matt said insinuatingly.

Reb ignored the provoking statement but was pleased to see Kincaid squirm. "When he regained his memory, it turned out he's supposed to meet some people at Seth Barker's station," she continued, undeterred. "I was taking him there. Last night a herd of buffalo stampeded and almost caught us. Brandy fell, and I was thrown. Kincaid saved my life."

Matt could picture the stampede all too vividly. He was so thankful that someone had been there to help that whatever animosity he might have had for Kincaid was immediately dispelled. He just thanked God—and Kincaid—that Reb had survived.

He relaxed his hold on his rifle and thanked Kincaid. He turned to Reb and asked, "Where's Brandy now?"

The pain of that loss was still too new. Reb's eyes

misted, and she reached up with her free hand to run her fingers agitatedly through her hair, sending it into even wilder disarray. She had to clear her throat before she could answer, and even then there was a strained quality to her voice that she couldn't control. "Brandy's dead. She broke her leg, and I had to kill her.

"I went a little crazy afterward, I guess. Brandy was Blue's last gift to me when we left the mountains, and when I lost her, it was one more part of that life torn from me against my will. If Kincaid hadn't been there, I . . ."

Up to this point Reb had been speaking to her father, but she missed the anguish that darkened Matt's eyes at her troubled admission, because she turned to Kincaid and continued, "But we escaped, and then we . . . then I was so cold, so cold that . . . and Kincaid . . . my clothes . . ."

Reb's voice had drifted off in a whisper. She felt for the first time the shame of having given herself to a man she hardly knew, who had no commitment to her and who had promised nothing.

The stricken look on her face evidenced the even more frightening realization that if he came to her again, she wouldn't deny him.

Kincaid thought what he saw on Reb's face was fear that her father would deduce from what she'd said that they'd been lovers, so he made no move toward Reb that would deny her innocence. He knew that if she wanted the events between them disclosed, she would do so herself. Therefore he stood immovable as a stone, even though he yearned to give her solace.

In fact, what Reb dearly wanted from Kincaid was some sign that he really cared for her, an acknowledgment of the love she believed they'd shared. His features betrayed so little emotion, they could have been carved in granite.

Reb was shrouded suddenly by the awful fear that he'd used her body merely for his pleasure, and that she'd been no more than a willing receptable for his passion.

Reb's quivering chin fell to her chest, and a single tear made its way down her cheek. Unconsciously Kincaid took a step toward her, but was drawn up short when Matt angrily jerked his rifle up to aim it at Kincaid's chest.

Matt's thankfulness to Kincaid had found its Waterloo in Reb's tears. Adam moved past Kincaid and took Reb in his arms to comfort her.

When he did, Reb began to sob in earnest. She hadn't seen that her father had stopped Kincaid, only that it was Adam who held her. Kincaid didn't care! The proof lay in the fact that it was Adam's possessive hands on her bare shoulders, not Kincaid's, Adam's chest against which her face lay buried, Adam's strong arms in which she stood protected. She wanted Kincaid! She cried harder.

Kincaid's lips thinned to a grim line, and his fists alternately clenched and unclenched in frustration at not having had the opportunity to talk with Reb about what had happened between them before they were confronted by her father and brother. He should be the one holding her now, not Adam.

No doubt remained in Matt's mind about what had transpired here last night. His eyes hooded in hostile speculation. Kincaid had apparently already rewarded himself handsomely for Reb's rescue, but Matt couldn't very well kill him for that.

Actually, he didn't blame either Reb or Kincaid for what had happened. They were both young and had allowed their passions to rule when their minds should have. Nor did he blame Adam, although his son had set this chain of events in motion.

No, the real culprit here was Blue. Adam was too inexperienced to know better, but Blue, of all people, should have used sounder judgment than to leave Reb alone with a virile young man any longer than was absolutely necessary.

Matt swore under his breath, then vowed silently that Blue would never get another chance to interfere with his family. He would make sure Reb didn't visit the mountain man again, even if it meant he had to tell her about Rachel and Blue.

It was just as well Kincaid didn't see the seething hatred on Matt's countenance, but his eyes had never left Reb, so he was startled when Matt spoke.

"I'll take you wherever it is you're headed, stranger. Adam, you take Reb home."

Matt had expected some sort of protest from Reb, but she continued to stare mutely at Kincaid until Adam picked up her buckskins and handed them to her.

Reb turned her back on the men to pull on her shirt and used the blanket to shield herself from view, even though the soreness between her legs reminded her uncomfortably that there was no part of her Kincaid hadn't already seen. Of course, Adam and her father didn't know anything for sure, she thought, even though she'd fueled their suspicion by putting on such a disgusting show of tears.

Devastated as she was by Kincaid's unfeeling actions, she determined not to let him know how much he'd hurt her.

A perplexed frown creased Kincaid's brow as he watched Reb dress. Could he let her walk out of his life now, perhaps never to see her again? She was a woman to satisfy a man's every desire, generous with her passion, capable in her caring. Any man would jump at a chance to call such a woman his own.

Yet Kincaid knew he was asking for trouble if he gave his heart to a woman of such boundless independence. He'd made that mistake once before, and he always learned from his mistakes.

Loving Reb, who spurned danger like some courageous lioness, meant certain heartbreak when some catastrophe befell her, as it eventually would in this wilderness. In this primitive environment she was prey to marauding Indians, to buffalo stampedes, to killing winter storms, even to violent death in childbirth.

He wanted her desperately, but not out here. Not where she wasn't safe.

When Reb pulled up her buckskin pants, she saw that sometime during the night Kincaid had replaced the broken thong with a piece of rope. That little bit of thoughtfulness took away what little composure she'd managed to regain, and she couldn't keep the tears from filling her eyes.

"Let's get out of here," she said bitterly to Adam, "before I make an even bigger fool of myself."

"Rebel."

Reb stiffened at Kincaid's call, but didn't turn around.

"Sir, I'd like to speak to your daughter alone."

Surprisingly, Matt agreed, and Kincaid suddenly found himself alone with Reb. Matt and Adam moved just beyond earshot but didn't take their eyes off the pair left standing by the cold ashes of the campfire.

Kincaid massaged the ache in his wounded thigh as though by doing so he could wipe away the horrible scars the war had left on his leg and on his life. Then he stepped up behind Reb, who stood taut as a bowstring. When he put his hand on her shoulder, she flinched. He didn't try to touch her again.

"Rebel, come away with me," he coaxed softly.

Reb exhaled the deep breath she'd been holding. Not "Reb, I love you." Not "Reb, marry me and have my children." Not nearly so much as he'd offered Laurie.

Reb couldn't keep the bitterness from pressing her mouth into a flat line and pinching her eyes at the corners. She closed her eyes and recalled the feel of Kincaid's strong, supple body pressed against her own, the demanding passion of his kiss. She wanted to say yes anyway, but her pride wouldn't allow it. She deserved a mate who loved and respected her. Desire alone was not enough on which to build a life.

She turned to tell Kincaid no and was brought up short by the unexpected love she saw blazing in his eyes. "I . . . I . . ."

Encouraged by her hesitation, Kincaid grasped both Reb's hands in his to urgently plead his cause. "You'll love New York. I know you will. It's only because you've never been anywhere but the mountains that you think you won't like it. I'll make it right for you."

Reb's eyes widened in horror. Kincaid couldn't be asking her to choose between a life with him and a life in the mountains! How could she make such a choice? After everything she'd told him, he must understand how she felt.

"I can't!" She jerked herself from Kincaid's grasp and cried, "Can't you take the wilderness away fast enough with your damned Yankee train? I'll never leave. Never!"

"Hang on tight to the past, Reb," Kincaid said angrily. "You wouldn't want anything as rotten as change to worm its way into your life. But don't expect the world to stand still around you, because it won't!

"I just spent four years watching half this nation destroy the other half to force them to change their way of life. I won't force you, Reb. You have to make up your mind that this is right for you. Change is coming. You can choose to ride the crest of the tide or be crushed by it, but you can't ignore it.

"Come with me, Reb!" He held out his open palm to her, asking her to share his life.

So violent was the battle between fear and desire within her breast that Reb began to quake. Kincaid made it sound so easy. Reb need only say yes, and she would be absorbed into his regimented world. Yet leaving the mountains had killed her mother.

Reb was terrified, certain that trying to fit in where

she didn't belong, even for Kincaid, would just as surely kill her. The tug of war went on for breathless moments longer before Reb's fear won. "I can't!"

"You're a coldhearted woman. Rebel Hunter," Kincaid snarled. "I hope your precious mountains keep you warm at night, because it's damn certain no man ever will!"

15

Even if she lived to be a very old woman, Reb thought, she would never forget that dawn conversation with Kincaid. Often over the past month since she and Kincaid had parted ways, the nightmarish scene had plagued her in her sleep.

It replayed vividly in her dreams, and lately, whenever she got to the part where she'd refused the handsome Yankee's offer, she awoke with a jolt to find hot tears streaming down her face, her balled fists pounding the mattress, and her teeth gritting so hard her jaw ached. Then she would stifle her sobs in her soft feather pillow.

Reb didn't know how to handle the emotional free-for-all wreaking havoc with her life. Falling in love with Kincaid had meant putting chinks in the safe wall behind which she'd contained her emotions. She'd tried to fill those gaping holes, tried not to feel anything, but the anger and regret and love and fear broke through in torrents.

Regret stood first and foremost among her cascading emotions, and Reb wasn't coping well with it. Within a week after their confrontation, she'd decided to go after Kincaid, only to realize in dismay she had no idea how to find him.

Then she remembered that he wanted to take her away from the life she knew, and panic rose to grip her heart. The whole experience was too painful to discuss without crying, so Reb, ashamed to admit her weakness to her family, remained silent.

She found a balm in having the warm sun upon her face and the stiff breeze cooling the damp hairs on the back of her neck. She rose before dawn each day to ride out and check on the cattle and came back after dark, so tired that she sat in a daze at the supper table. Then she retired to her room, dreading the time she would have to close her eyes and sleep. For then the real battle began. Unhampered by her conscious will, the love and regret fought the terror, leaving her ravaged when she awoke.

Lying awake in the dark on her narrow bed, Reb admitted that saying no to Kincaid had been a terrible mistake. Too much had happened in too short a time, and she'd acted impulsively, rather than thinking it through.

If only she had it all to do over again, she would find a way to convince Kincaid to stay here in the wilderness with her. She conceded the wishfulness of such thinking, but indulged herself because it kept the tears at bay.

In her bed across the room, Reb's younger sister Dillon waited for the sounds of distress that had become an almost nightly occurrence. Dillon had garnered enough information from her father and Adam to know that Reb and Kincaid had argued, and that neither was speaking to the other when it was all over.

Matt had taken the angry man on to his destination, leaving Reb in Adam's care. Adam had managed to pry most of the story of what had happened at the cabin out of a distraught Reb on the way home. Once home, however, she'd retreated inside herself as a turtle crawls inside its shell.

Adam was convinced that Reb pined for her stranger, but he could come up with no suggestions as to what he and Dillon could do to help. Reb encouraged no sympathy, hiding her tears under cover of darkness.

It was fortunate that Adam had gotten Reb to tell him Kincaid's full name, and that the Yankee worked for the Union Pacific railroad, because that information had put Dillon in a position to offer an end to her sister's misery.

"Reb, I know you're awake," Dillon said. "I've been wanting to talk to you about an article in the *Rocky Mountain News* that a passenger on the stage left here. I kept thinking you'd get over this Yankee, but you're worse now than ever."

Reb pushed her face into the pillow to prevent the sob that arose from getting past the lump in her throat.

"Garth keeps telling Daddy he should have killed Kincaid, but that's just his temper talking. Just yesterday Jesse asked Daddy why your eyes are always so red these days. Daddy told him, you're spending too much time eating cattle dust."

"Daddy's against your ever seeing this Yankee fellow again, but Adam and I think that you and Kincaid should get a chance to work things out." Dillon paused and noticed that the room was deathly quiet. "Reb, are you listening?"

When Reb didn't answer, Dillon sat up to light the lantern on the small table near her bed. She kept the flame low so it wouldn't spill through the small stepladder opening in the pine floor planking at the far end of the room that led down to Matt's bedroom. She didn't want her father waking up and asking what was wrong.

The dim light revealed the embracing eaves of the loft bedroom. A window had been cut in the triangular wall at either end of the room to catch the breeze, but no wisp of air relieved the oppressive heat.

As she rose, Dillon automatically checked her appearance in the small, gilt-edged oval mirror that hung at the head of her bed. The sultry look in her green eyes and the kissable pout of her mouth were natural feminine assets that she didn't have to practice, but Dillon had spent hours learning the coquettish tilt of her head that she used when she perused herself.

Too bad Kincaid hadn't asked *her* to go away with him. From Adam's description of the man, she wouldn't have hesitated to give the proper answer. Poor Reb had said no once too often, and look where it had gotten her.

Dillon nodded determinedly at herself in the mirror when she picked up the muffled sounds from Reb's side of the room. She was going to help Reb get her man if she had to hog-tie Kincaid herself to do it!

Dillon marched to the foot of her bed and rummaged through the cedar hope chest full of the quilts, tablecloths, and embroidered pillowcases she'd made, looking forward to the day when she would marry. At the very bottom she found the folded newspaper article she'd carefully hidden there. She flounced over and pulled her thin flowered cotton nightgown up to her thighs before she sat down cross-legged on the foot of Reb's bed. She leaned back until her elbows rested on Reb's hope chest.

The contents of that cedar box testified to how unprepared Reb was for the role of wife, Dillon thought. Instead of the necessities of a frontier home,

it contained such memorabilia as the fur of the first
beaver Reb had trapped, some stones with fish fossils
in them, a switch of hair from Brandy's tail, a blue-
and-white beaded Indian parfleche the Old One had
made to hold the berries Reb collected on the trail,
and a copy of Shakespeare's *Taming of the Shrew* that
their mother had given Reb for her sixteenth birthday. No wonder Reb had given Kincaid the wrong
answer!

"I know you're listening, so don't say anything
until I'm through," Dillon said to Reb in a conspiratorial whisper. "How would you like another chance
to talk to Kincaid?"

Dillon had no way of knowing she'd caught Reb at
such a receptive moment. Reb sat bolt upright, but
was cut off before she could answer when Dillon continued, "There's going to be a railroad meeting in
Denver City on the Fourth of July. The *Rocky
Mountain News* says that officials of the Union
Pacific will be meeting with Denver City merchants
to discuss the proposed route for the railroad west of
Nebraska. It specifically mentions that a Mr.
Christopher Kincaid, who's a major stockholder of
the railroad, will be there.

"Here's the part I thought might interest you. The
article says, 'Mr. Kincaid is one of the official hosts for
a grand ball being sponsored by the railroad at the
Broadwell House at 16th and Larimer Streets begin-

ning at eight o'clock on the evening of July Fourth. All of Denver is invited to the ball, which will culminate with a special fireworks display at midnight in front of the hotel.' Well, would you like to go to the ball?"

Before Reb could get a word in edgewise, Dillon added, "If you say no, I will personally smother you with your own feather pillow!"

"Yes, yes, yes," Reb cried, grabbing Dillon and hugging her. "I do want to see Kincaid and talk to him. But I don't see how I can dance with him at the ball," she added breathlessly.

"Why not?" Dillon thought perhaps Kincaid's limp was worse than she'd been led to believe.

"Because I haven't anything to wear!"

"You sound like Cinderella," Dillon said, giggling in relieved satisfaction. "If that's the only thing stopping you, let me help. I've always wanted to play fairy godmother. This looks like the best chance I'll ever get. I have some material that ought to be perfect for a new gown."

Dillon hopped off Reb's bed, heading for her own hope chest. Reaching within, she pulled out a length of crimson satin.

Reb gasped at the beauty of the vibrant red cloth. "Where did you ever get anything so magnificent, Dillon?"

"I found it in Mama's things after she died. I know

I should have told you about it, but you never seemed very interested in this sort of thing." She laid the satin in Reb's outstretched hands.

Dillon was right, of course. Before Reb had met Kincaid, she couldn't have cared less how she looked in a dress made of satin. The feel of the satin in her hands was wonderfully sensual. "Shall we see how it looks?" Reb suggested.

When the two girls had stripped Reb's nightgown away and draped her in folds of the cool satin, Dillon pulled Reb over to stand in front of the mirror.

"Look at you. You're gorgeous!" Dillon said in surprise.

Reb could hardly believe what she saw in the mirror. The crimson satin heightened the beauty of her opalescent skin and brought out the sparkle in her mahogany eyes. "It is amazing, isn't it?" she said uncertainly.

"Your hair is long enough now for a curling iron to do some good, and a little kohl would emphasize your eyes. We'll use some powder to cover your freckles and, of course, lip rouge."

"I can't believe this is happening," Reb said. "How did you know I wanted to see Kincaid again?"

"When you nearly snapped my head off after I called him a 'dirty bluebelly pig,' I got the hint," Dillon replied, grinning. Neither girl mentioned the nightly tears, but both thought of them.

Dillon's features sobered. "Reb, do you think he might have changed his mind about whatever he said that's been making you cry?"

Having been given a second chance, Reb was determined to work things out with Kincaid. "If he hasn't changed his mind, he will."

Dillon sighed. *Please, God, let Reb be successful.* It wouldn't be easy for her to hog-tie someone as big as Kincaid was reported to be.

"Now we just have to figure out how to get you from here to there, which won't be easy, considering the way Daddy feels about letting you anywhere near Kincaid. Adam said he'd be willing to help, if we can just come up with a good idea."

Eventually, it was Adam who came up with the plan to convince their father that what Reb needed to bring her back to her old self was a trip somewhere away from the mountains. Dillon refused to be left out, so Adam suggested that he, Reb, and Dillon go to Denver to pick up a hay rake Matt needed.

Matt received Adam's suggestion enthusiastically. In fact, he thought it so good an idea that he insisted on coming along himself to observe its success. Garth and Jesse would stay with the Old One to care for the ranch and maintain the stage station.

Although Matt would never have admitted it to Reb, he was concerned about the unhappiness in his eldest daughter's eyes. It reminded him of a similar look he'd seen in Rachel's eyes, but had ignored until it was too late. Matt had surmised that it was more than a moment's passion that bound Reb and Kincaid. He wasn't sure which of the two had denied loving the other, but he knew Reb had taken their separation hard.

If Adam thought this trip would heal Reb's wounds, he was more than willing to give it a try. Matt was pleasantly surprised by Reb's acquiescence to the journey. He had stayed at the Broadwell House in the past, so it wasn't difficult for Adam to get him to agree to stay there again.

Reb and Dillon pushed and prodded their father as much as they dared without making it seem as though they had a reason to hurry.

He kept delaying, though, until Adam decided it made more sense to encourage him to attend the Fourth of July fireworks display, so they would be sure to arrive in Denver on time.

However, because Dillon had waited so long before suggesting the trip to Reb, the foursome didn't arrive in Denver until almost noon on the Fourth.

Everything in the city was new to Reb. She was agog at the rows and rows of buildings they passed, many more than she'd expected to find. Larimer Street was wide, with hard-packed dirt streets lined with wooden sidewalks.

They had to maneuver their wagon among the

oxcarts, people on horseback, and coaches that crowded the streets. All of the buildings on the block had been rebuilt in brick after the fire that had destroyed the city in April two years ago. Then, just last May, Cherry Creek, which ran through the city, had flooded its banks and made it necessary to rebuild again.

Among the many structures they passed on Larimer Street while wending their way toward the hotel were the Emporium of Fashion, Marx's Bakery, Peabody's Dry Goods and Drug Store, A. E. Cresswell, Photographer, the First Methodist Church, and the noisy construction on the Central National Bank.

Reb decided that when she and Kincaid had reconciled, they would visit the photographer straightaway. She wanted to have a remembrance of her first trip to Denver.

The red, white, and blue pennants hanging across the street evidenced that the Fourth of July celebration was in full swing, and Matt was delighted to discover from numerous posters they passed that there was a horse race scheduled in just an hour at the edge of the city.

Several dandified gentlemen in fawn trousers and broadcloth coats, sporting low-crowned, round-brimmed felt hats, leaned against the white-painted wooden posts that held up the balcony porch of the Broadwell House. Older men, less fashionably dressed in dark trousers and plain white shirts topped by variously hued vests, took their ease in wooden chairs that lined the porch next to the windows.

According to the painted sign in the large picture window, the massive two-story Broadwell House, the one wooden structure on the whole street, provided the best hotel accommodations in Denver.

Reb jumped down from the wagon while Adam dismounted and helped Dillon down. Reb had worn her buckskins for the trip, insisting that it made no sense to put on a dress to impress the jackrabbits and deer. She could have passed for a young man, and apparently did, for it wasn't until Dillon stepped up onto the porch in her lace-trimmed yellow cotton day dress, with her matching parasol perched daintily over her shoulder, that the male whistles of appreciation for feminine face and form began.

Seeing the doffed hats and courtly bows for her sister brought a flush to Reb's face. Would she ever learn what it meant to be a woman at all times? How did she expect to make a good wife for Kincaid if she couldn't even manage to wear the proper clothing for the occasion?

Her father and brother hurried Reb and Dillon into the spacious lobby of the hotel, where Reb stood gaping at the appointments in admiration. While their father registered for two rooms, Reb and

Dillon perused the crystal chandelier and examined the gold-brocade-covered couches set along the wall.

They could hear the tinkling piano and the clink of beer and whiskey glasses from a saloon that was separated from the lobby only by a doorway set with a pair of short, slatted wooden swinging doors. A steady stream of male customers moved through the lobby to the bar.

As Reb's father signed the register, he spoke over his shoulder. "It appears we made it here in plenty of time for the Independence Day celebration. I think I'd like to take in that race at one, then go see if I can find a hay rake. How about the rest of you?"

The bespectacled clerk handed a key to her father and one to Reb after he checked the register. "That'll be the last two rooms upstairs on the left at the end of the hall," he said.

Dillon exchanged a surreptitious glance with Adam. She'd expected to spend the entire day getting Reb bathed and gussied up to meet with Kincaid. They'd prearranged for Adam to keep Matt occupied so there would be no chance of his last-minute interference.

"Reb and I want to freshen up and then go look around the stores," Dillon replied.

"I'd like to go with you, Dad," Adam said. "Reb and Dillon will be fine on their own. We can all meet here at midnight to watch the fireworks I told you about."

"Reb and I will probably have dinner at the hotel restaurant, so you two just enjoy yourselves and don't worry about us," Dillon said.

"We can all meet here at midnight," Reb said.

"Enjoy yourselves," her father said. When he turned away from the registration desk, he faced a hulking brute dressed in a filthy green-and-yellow plaid shirt and fringed buckskin trousers. A luxurious raccoon cap topped the trapper's greasy, untrimmed red hair. A long red beard and shaggy mustache covered his face and chin so completely that the only skin visible was a bulbous nose and two wide-set light blue eyes framed by almost white eyelashes. Gargantuan arms circled her father's chest, and the redheaded behemoth began to squeeze.

Matt bent his arms at the elbows to try to get his hands up to save his ribs, but it quickly became evident there was nothing to prevent the redheaded man from cracking him like a hazelnut.

At first, Reb thought the aggressive man must be an old friend, since her father hadn't made a sound. Then she began to fear that her father's stubborn pride was keeping him silent. Adam seemed unperturbed, and while Dillon shared Reb's agitation, she seemed uninclined to act.

In the next moment, Reb had pulled her bowie and held it at the giant's ribs near his heart.

"Be this yer whelp, Matthew?" the man said calmly.

"Uh," her father grunted, having no air left to say more.

"Tell 'em I only crush ants 'n' spiders," the burly redhead chortled. As he released her father, the mountain man whipped an arm down, intending to disarm Reb. Instead, he found an eight-inch slit in his arm, and Reb standing next to her father facing him, knife poised for action.

Reb was astonished when, instead of attacking her, the bear of a man laughed out loud. "Be ye Garth?" he asked Reb.

"This is my *daughter* Reb," her father said, grinning. "Garth's at home minding the ranch with his younger brother Jesse."

"Well, I'll be a three-legged buffalo," the man guffawed. The giant pulled the dingy yellow kerchief from around his neck and wrapped it around the cut on his arm. "I'll take her! She'd make a grrreat lassie to have 'rrround in them mountains," he bellowed, rolling his r's with Irish gusto.

Reb reared back when a ham-fisted paw reached for her.

"Hang on, Breck. This isn't some Sioux squaw

you can buy," her father said. "This is my daughter Rebecca."

By now, the piano in the bar had stopped playing, and a growing crowd of men and women were gawking at Reb, waiting to see the end of the scene unfolding before them. It was only too apparent to Reb now that her father knew this unsavory character, and she'd foolishly interfered where she didn't belong.

More than anything else, Reb was concerned that word of this awful incident would get back to Kincaid. She searched the room for a way out.

Fortunately her sister seemed to recognize her plight and provided a diversion that allowed Reb to escape, taking the stairs two at a time on her way up to their room.

"Daddy," Dillon said, "could this possibly be *the* Breck O'Hanlan that saved your life when he killed a grizzly bear with his Green River skinning knife back in '46?"

A murmur ran through the crowd as the famous mountain man acknowledged he was the same. Then O'Hanlan turned toward Dillon and stood speechless for a moment, gazing at her, before he turned back to her father. When her father nodded, the repulsively hirsute man walked up to Dillon and worshipfully lifted a copper curl. He watched, mesmerized, as it drifted silkily through his fingertips.

Dillon stood motionless, letting the blue-eyed man drink his fill.

"She be real purty, Matthew. Just like Rachel."

"I'd like you to meet my daughter Dillon," her father said. "Standing next to her is my son Adam."

"Ye look like yer pa, boy."

"Thank you, sir," Adam replied. He was awed by the sight of Breck O'Hanlan; he and his brothers and sisters had grown up with bedtime stories of the legendary mountain man. Somehow there was nothing insulting about having a legend call you "boy."

"Adam and I are planning to take in the nag race at one o'clock. Care to join us?" Matt asked.

"Need ye ask?" O'Hanlan replied with a grin that showed only in his twinkling eyes. "I heard tell some of these city fellers might have a job fer me to do fer them in the mountains, so I've made up me mind to wager a mite of those earnin's on the outcome of the race. We might's well catch up on old times while I double me money. Boy, did yer pa ever tell ye 'bout the night we was charged by a white buffalo?"

The three men were so engrossed in each other that Dillon was left standing, forgotten, as Rachel also must have been once upon a time.

Dillon was not alone long, however, for the men standing at the swinging doors of the saloon recognized beauty when they saw it, and without her male protectors, she seemed like fair game.

The boldest of the bunch quickly made his way forward. His hair was parted in the middle and slicked down on either side with some kind of perfumed oil that wrinkled Dillon's sensitive nose even at a distance. His chocolate brown suit was too wide for his narrow shoulders, and his orange checked shirt pulled apart over the rotund belly that preceded him as he advanced across the room. An untrimmed mustache drooped onto crooked, tobacco-stained teeth as the self-important man greeted Dillon with an ingratiating smile.

"Clemens Fremont at your service, Miss Dillon." The man bowed smoothly, then stood with palm outstretched, waiting for Dillon to supply her hand.

"Excuse me, please, Mr. Fremont," Dillon said primly. "I believe my sister is waiting for me." As she turned toward the stairs, pudgy fingers gripped her arm and turned her around.

"Not so fast, young lady. You haven't allowed me to greet you properly." Fremont held on to Dillon's arm while he tried to bring her hand up to his lips.

Dillon's struggle to free herself was greeted by jeers from the remaining men standing bunched at the saloon door and spilling into the room.

"Hey, Clem," one shouted, "why don't you give her a real big-city welcome right on the mouth!"

"That's good advice Frank give ya', Clem," another echoed.

The ladies of the night employed by the saloon remained aloof, waiting disdainfully to see how the country girl would handle herself.

The hotel clerk pushed his spectacles up his nose agitatedly before he spoke from behind his polished cherry wood counter. "Mr. Fremont, the lady would like to be allowed to proceed to her room."

Fremont hardly gave the timid man a glance. "Back off, Otto. The lady can speak for herself."

"I certainly can. I would appreciate it, sir, if you would kindly let go of my arm," Dillon said firmly.

Her statement was greeted by encouraging shouts from the onlookers. "I think I'll take Frank's advice instead," Fremont said, leering down into Dillon's face. Catching sight of a pearl-studded white shirt and black frock coat over Dillon's shoulder, he looked up to see who had had the temerity to intrude on his fun.

Dillon had her sharp-tipped parasol poised and ready to strike where it would do the most good (on his instep, of course) when the disgusting man released his hold.

"I don't believe the young lady desires the pleasure of your company."

The commanding baritone sent shivers down Dillon's spine. It also obviously had an unsettling effect on Clemens Fremont, for the fat man stepped back so hastily that Dillon lost her balance and would have fallen except for the firm hands that caught her around the waist from behind.

She could feel the muscled wall of a chest against her back but was far too amused by the pasty white face of Clemens Fremont to do more than smile in kittenish smugness at his cowardly retreat.

She waited a moment more, expecting the firm hands to release her, but they didn't. As the men made way for Fremont, Dillon could see her reflection in the huge mirror that filled the wall on the opposite side of the room.

She stared into the mirror at the striking man who was studying her features so carefully in the same glass. He turned Dillon in his arms so she found herself looking up into a pair of sad gray eyes.

Suddenly, Dillon knew the identity of the gallant, raven-haired man who'd rescued her.

16

Kincaid couldn't help seeing the irony of the situation. He'd lost the wife he wanted and found the wife he'd dreamed up in his imagination. In his arms stood the very image of the flawless woman he'd teased Reb that he would marry, right down to the copper curls, green eyes, and full bosom.

He'd spent the past month telling himself he could live his life without Reb, but he hadn't been very successful in getting the thought of her out of his mind. This encounter was a perfect example. He should be calculating how to entice this young lady into his bed, not remembering that she epitomized a woman with whom he'd taunted Reb.

A grin broke out on Kincaid's face. He did have one thing to thank Reb for. He no longer reacted to women as a celibate. His thumbs rested just under this wonder's ample breasts, and his body had responded with astonishing speed to that simple stimulation. *Oh, Reb, where are you when I need you?* Kincaid thought. Although the physical evidence of desire was there, the woman he really wanted to bury himself in had short black hair and freckles.

Dillon could see why Reb had gone crazy. This man had to be Kincaid. There couldn't be two men this good-looking in the territory. Imagine letting him get away!

What on earth had prompted the silly grin on his face? she wondered. She'd just opened her mouth to ask what was so funny when Kincaid dropped his hands as though he'd been holding a hot potato.

"Excuse me, miss. I'm late for a meeting, but can I escort you somewhere?"

"I'm registered here at the hotel. If you'll just walk me as far as the stairs, I'm sure I'll be fine." Dillon linked her arm in Kincaid's and walked the few steps to the winding staircase that led to the second floor. She gave Kincaid her most inviting smile and tilted her head so that she looked upward through feathery eyelashes as she'd practiced hour after endless hour in the mirror at home.

Kincaid seemed impervious to her charms. In fact, he seemed downright anxious to be rid of her. Dillon had to exert some effort not to be miffed, but decided the least she could do was make sure for Reb that he planned to attend the ball.

"Are you going to the dance tonight?" she asked, glancing up through demurely lowered eyelashes as she ascended the first step.

"I hadn't planned to, no," Kincaid replied. His father, who was here to speak to the Denver businessmen, might owe attendance at the ball to the railroad, but he did not. He was here only to make his report.

"Oh." Dillon let her disappointment show. "I thought you—" Dillon bit her tongue. She'd almost let it slip that she knew Kincaid was a railroad official and had supposed he, as a sponsor of the ball, would attend.

It was important to Reb that he be there, so Dillon tried a different tack. "Is there any chance you might change your mind? You see, I have a friend that I think you might like to meet."

Kincaid was intrigued. He'd seen enough coquettish flirting to recognize the signs, yet now the girl professed to want him to attend the dance to meet a friend.

"A friend?" he questioned, an eyebrow cocked in tolerant amusement.

"Yes, well, you see her mother died recently, and she's been very sad lately, and it seemed to me that seeing you might cheer her up."

"Why is that?" Kincaid asked.

Dillon gulped, crossed her fingers behind her back, and launched into a whopper. What else could a fifteen-year-old fairy godmother do if the prince wasn't going to cooperate and come to the ball?

"Right after her mother died, her fiancé was wounded in the war. He looked a lot like you."

Kincaid let his disbelief out in a small smile.

"Except he was shorter. And had lighter hair. And of course his eyes were hazel." Dillon rushed on in spite of Kincaid's skeptical features. "His leg was so devastated that it never healed, and he finally died. If you could just take pity on her and be there, I know it would help her to overcome her grief."

Dillon really thought she'd overdone it when Kincaid frowned, but she waited patiently while the man who could make her sister happy pondered her fantastic story.

It was the mention of the leg wound that made up Kincaid's mind. Here was one more soul robbed by the war that had so unrelentingly killed so many young men. Kincaid felt a kinship for the girl, whoever she was. Her story was not unlike his own, only he'd lost a wife, not a fiancée. If a simple dance or two would cheer her, why not?

"I think I could manage a waltz," he finally said. "I'll be there at nine tonight. See you then."

Dillon heaved a great sigh of relief, and then had to suppress a whoop of excitement. *Wait until Reb hears this*, she thought. She tucked her parasol under her arm and gathered her skirt in her hands in great bunches to race up the stairs, but was stopped by that familiar baritone voice.

"What's her name?" Kincaid called to Dillon from halfway across the room.

"Rebecca," she replied with a grin. Then she turned and ran up the stairs before he could ask more.

Kincaid briskly crossed the lobby, heading for the private dining room at the back of the hotel restaurant. When he arrived, his father greeted him at the door.

Christopher Lyle Kincaid stood several inches shorter than the son he'd named after himself, but was no less imposing. The full head of snow-white hair testified to his patriarchal role, but there was nothing old about the lean, hard body inside the dark gray, vested suit. Lyle Kincaid was all business, his rigid stance a clear spokesman for his unyielding nature.

"I'm glad you could make it, son. We've been waiting for you." There was a trace of irritation in his father's voice. Lyle Kincaid believed in punctuality.

Kincaid turned to the assembly gathered at the table. He greeted Grenville Dodge with a quick, firm handshake, then eyed the twenty or so Denver businessmen who'd assembled to hear his report. They weren't going to like what he had to say.

"Gentlemen." He nodded to them as a group. "Shall we eat first?" he inquired of his father.

"Good idea. You may serve now, Mr. Potts," Lyle Kincaid said to the obsequious bald-headed waiter.

They dined on oxtail soup, followed by a thick steak and fried potatoes, and finished up with apple pie for dessert. Strong black coffee accompanied the meal, since Lyle Kincaid believed liquor and business didn't mix. When a second cup of coffee had been poured, and the cigars that Lyle had so graciously provided to his guests had been lit, the entrepreneur gestured to his scion to begin.

"Gentlemen, let's get down to business," Kincaid said. "We know you want the Union Pacific to run its tracks far enough south to be able to service Denver. However, as much as we would like to accommodate your needs, it isn't practical to do so. The grades through the mountains down here are too steep in an east-west direction for the construction to be done without a great deal more time and expense than is justified.

"There are more gentle grades running east-west about a hundred miles north of here, just across the base of the Laramie Mountains, and that's where I would recommend laying the tracks."

Angry shouts of disagreement came from every direction. All Kincaid could hear in his mind were Reb's pleas to spare her wilderness. It was some time before Kincaid had answered all the arguments against bypassing Denver, and it was a disgruntled group of merchants who left the room in grumbling pairs and griping trios. Finally, only Kincaid's father and Grenville Dodge remained at the table.

Lyle Kincaid puffed steadily on his cigar while he evaluated the success of the luncheon. "Do you think they'll go crying to the Republicans in Washington?" he asked Dodge.

"I suspect so. But we've done our homework, lobbied hard. We should have the vote to hold them off. At any rate, I'll start them talking about a spur from Denver directly north to connect with the Union Pacific. That ought to hold off the worst of the complainers until we finish what we have to do."

Kincaid had wondered how the nondescript Dodge, with his plain features and neatly trimmed, sandy-colored muttonchop whiskers, had worked his way so far up in the army. Now the general's canny political maneuvering made the answer to that question clear.

Dodge convinced Kincaid of his astuteness when he asked, "What do you plan to do about the Sioux, Lyle? You know they've been cheated by the Indian agents and had so many treaties broken that you can expect real problems with your track gangs unless something is done."

"Do you have any suggestions?"

"I allowed General Connor to maintain a campaign against the Sioux at the Powder River this past month. But he's been something less than gloriously successful. I've never accepted the idea anyway that annihilating the problem is a viable solution.

"That leaves the option of another treaty. Unfortunately, I don't believe the Indians will be willing to listen."

"I think I know someone who may be able to help," Kincaid said. "When I was recuperating in the mountains, I met a trapper who's a good friend of the chief of the Brulés. Perhaps he could be persuaded to speak on our behalf."

"That sounds like our best bet. Are you volunteering to be our emissary to him?" Dodge asked.

"I'd be willing to give it a try." Kincaid could barely contain his enthusiasm for the trip. Blue would know how to convince Reb that she should come back east with him. She might even be there visiting when he arrived.

Their discussion was interrupted by a plate clattering against a cup. "I'll be finished here in a minute. Just clearing the table." The portly waiter had entered through the dark green velour curtains at the far end of the room sometime during their conversation.

"Thank you, Mr. Potts, but you can do that later," Lyle said sharply.

"Certainly, sir. Anything else I can do for you?"

"No, thank you." Lyle Kincaid didn't believe in servants listening in on business conversations.

When the waiter had gone, Dodge stood and paced from one end of the long table to the other.

"You can be sure the Denver businessmen will know we're concerned about the Indians."

"They can't make the savages any more savage than they already are," Lyle said.

"They can supply them with guns and bullets. You give them the ammunition, and those Sioux can lift so much hair we won't be able to get a track gang to go near there."

"The Indians won't raise hell if we can promise them enough food and supplies that they don't have to steal to live," Kincaid said. "I think a treaty with the Sioux is worth a try."

"I have to agree with you," Dodge said. "Besides, we won't have to placate them long. Once the tracks are laid, there isn't much those heathens can do to stop the natural progress of things."

Kincaid felt a surge of irritation at Dodge's attitude. Then he realized he was seeing the situation with a new awareness, one Reb had given him. He recalled her anger at the Yankees who did what they pleased, and the locals be damned. It made him even more determined to pursue this mission. Perhaps he and Blue together could find a way to make progress a little less painful for everyone involved.

"Son, are you sure you're well enough to make this journey? If not, speak up. This mission is too important to jeopardize because of one man's ill health," his father said.

Kincaid's mother had already told him how his father had aged ten years when the false news of his death had come, so Kincaid wasn't fooled by the seeming callousness of his father's speech.

"I'll be fine, Father," he said reassuringly. "I'd like to leave right away. We'll be expected to provide gifts as a sign of our good faith with the Sioux. Would you make the necessary arrangements, General Dodge, so I can pick up what I need from Miller's Dry Goods here in Denver?"

"I'll be glad to, so long as Lyle will open his purse strings for the supplies," Dodge said with a wry smile.

"I knew I could count on you to come to the meat of the matter," Lyle replied with a chuckle. "What about the ball tonight, son? A lot of pretty young belles will be there."

The last scene in their parlor sitting room before Kincaid had come west flashed across Lyle's mind, and he chastised himself for even mentioning the dance. His son had made it very clear to both his parents that he wanted nothing to do with women after the death of his wife. To his amazement, a sad smile appeared on Kincaid's face.

"As a matter of fact, I think I might indulge in just one waltz."

Reb stood alone next to the wall of the brightly lit ballroom of the hotel while the orchestra played waltz after waltz. Nearby, Dillon entertained an entourage of eligible men who battled to sign her dance card and to bring her a cup of punch between dances.

Kincaid wasn't coming, Reb decided. It was well past nine o'clock, the time that he'd told Dillon he would attend. In fact, it was nearly ten. Reb had watched the doorway eagerly for an hour and had rebuffed all male attention so soundly that the young bucks now warned each other away from the "thorny red rose." She felt more like a florid wallflower.

For the past fifteen minutes she'd observed a nearby group of gentlemen arguing, and she occasionally caught enticing snatches of their discussion. Words like "railroad" and "mountains" spoken in conjunction lured her closer and closer until she stood at the edge of their party.

"There's no mistake, gentlemen," a dignified older man with flinty gray eyes topped by bushy white brows repeated to the assembled group. "The best route for the railroad, the route we will take, is through the Laramie Mountains."

"What if we don't want your railroad in our mountains?" Reb startled him and herself by saying.

The gathering parted to locate the source of the husky voice. There was considerable surprise when it turned out to be a poised, elegantly dressed young woman. Dillon had done her job well. Reb's crimson gown revealed soft shoulders and the tops of softly rounded breasts, then tapered to a point in the front at Reb's narrow waist, before belling in luxurious folds of ruby satin.

Reb's extraordinary intervention in what was so obviously a male conversation impressed the men as much as her loveliness.

"Who's going to prevent us?" Lyle Kincaid challenged, somewhat perturbed that a female, and quite an attractive one at that, would dare to question what he'd just convinced the Denver merchants was an accomplished fact.

"People like me who respect the wilderness the way it is. You have no right to impose your Iron Horse where it isn't wanted!"

"Bravo, miss! You should listen, Father, and believe me when I tell you there are differences of opinion about the advantages of a railroad."

Reb recognized the timbre of the well-known voice behind her. She watched in bewilderment as a pleasant woman with salt and pepper hair and deep smile lines at the corners of her eyes looped her arm in that of the distinguished man Kincaid had addressed as Father.

"Lyle," she chided, "stop talking business and give these ladies and gentlemen an opportunity to dance."

"Wonderful idea, Mother." Kincaid leaned in to speak softly in Reb's ear. "Shall we?"

Kincaid had been delayed by the need to make additional arrangements for his departure for Blue's cabin the following morning. When he'd finally arrived at the ball, he'd found the girl he'd talked with earlier in the day surrounded by her admirers, with no sign of a "friend" anywhere near.

Disgusted with himself for being so gullible, Kincaid was about to leave when he noticed the crowd around his father part for a tall, raven-haired young woman in crimson satin. There was something vaguely familiar about the woman's proud stance.

Kincaid guessed from the increasing aggravation on his father's face that the woman must be disagreeing with him. That he didn't want to miss. Not many people willingly crossed Lyle Kincaid.

Kincaid surprised himself when he asked the woman to dance, but there was something about the single ebony curl that fell down her neck an inch or two on the left side that awakened a memory. The woman smelled of roses, and he closed his eyes to absorb the essence at the same time he placed his hand on her elbow to turn her around. The woman trembled under his fingertips.

Kincaid's eyes widened at the vision standing before him.

Reb's mahogany eyes, rimmed by thickened black

lashes, looked anxious, and her sharp white teeth had
caught her full, rosy bottom lip. Her raven locks had
been curled in soft ringlets that framed her face, one
curl falling tantalizingly over her peach-skinned
shoulder.

Kincaid noted that she'd carefully concealed her
boyish freckles but smiled in pure pleasure at the
enchanting blush that the powder couldn't obscure.

The gown was cut low enough in front for the gentle swells of flesh to titillate his imagination. He put
one hand firmly on the cool satin that hugged her
narrow waist and took her white-gloved palm in his
other hand.

"Dance with me."

The mellow richness of the voice flowed over Reb,
as welcome as honey on a flapjack. She obeyed willingly, stepping into his arms until the satin-covered
tips of her breasts dipped into the silk ruffles of his
white evening shirt. They circled the dance floor
gracefully, both floating in a heaven of their own.

Neither spoke, unwilling to let reality intrude on
the magic of the moment. They didn't hear the music
stop, nor did they hear it start again, so lost were they
in each other.

Kincaid knew Reb must have changed her mind
and sought him out. He felt humbled by the sacrifice
she was willing to make for him and blessed by the
beauty that she offered to him. He danced her

through the open French doors to the shadowed balcony, coming to a stop only when they were far away from the music and the light streaming through the doors.

He brought the gloved hand he held up to his lips, then set it upon his shoulder so that Reb's arms encircled him. Reached with one hand to tip her chin, while the other grasped her waist possessively, he used his thumb to brush away the powder on her cheekbones, until he could see a hint of the freckles he'd missed so much.

"Rebel," he breathed. His lips claimed hers gently, asking forgiveness. When her lips parted in response, he eagerly pulled her close. The kiss deepened, and Kincaid's hands roved along Reb's satin-clad form.

He could hardly believe she was real, and that he was holding her in his arms, so great was his surprise at finding her in Denver. Reb's satin skirt was gathered so full that it provided a substantial barrier to their touch, and Kincaid's frustration mounted when he was unable to bring her as close as his awakening manhood demanded.

Admitting that the dress stood in the way of satisfaction, Kincaid broke the kiss and stepped back to try to draw rein on his rampaging senses.

Reb held on by a thread to the voice of reason. "I have something to say to you," she said breathlessly. "Is there somewhere we can be alone?"

"Come with me." He put an arm around her waist to lead her back to the ballroom.

In her naïveté, Reb had no idea of the devastating effect she'd had on Kincaid. She thought the gleam in his eyes was simply a mirror of the excitement she felt. Glad he was willing to discuss their relationship, she followed him with alacrity.

As the bright lights lit their faces, Kincaid stopped. "Shall we dance our way back through the businessmen?"

Reb laughed. "I should let Dillon know I'm leaving," she said, "or she'll worry."

"Your sister Dillon is here?"

"You spoke to her this afternoon. Don't you remember? The girl with a 'friend.' I'm Rebecca." Reb grinned mischievously as Kincaid's eyes widened in comprehension. "Where were you, anyway? You were supposed to be here at nine."

Kincaid had been watching Reb's mouth as she spoke and was afraid if they didn't get off the balcony soon, he would take her right there. "I'll tell you later. Let's go."

They whirled across the room, Reb safely tucked in close to Kincaid's body as they disappeared out the main ballroom entrance.

"Dillon will worry," Reb protested as Kincaid urged her down the hall toward his room.

"With all the male worship she's enjoying tonight,

she'll never know you're gone. We're here. Come in."

Kincaid opened the door to a room that must have been the finest the hotel had to offer. The crisp white sheets had been turned down on the four-poster so Reb could see only half of the colorful quilt bedspread, with its pattern of blue stars. Dazzling crystal prisms reflected the rosy glow of the cut-glass kerosene lamp that sat on a table next to the bed.

The jeweled reflections enticed Reb closer, and she let her fingers trace the stars and blazes etched into the pink glass at the lamp's base.

Reb turned to begin the task of convincing Kincaid to stay. The ferocity of the avid desire in his eyes left her speechless.

Kincaid enfolded Reb in his embrace. He laid his cheek next to hers and let his fingers toy with the single curl that lay against her slender neck.

"Kincaid, we have to talk," Reb murmured dreamily.

"Yes, we do," he agreed. "I love you, Rebel. I want you to be my wife."

17

The words "I love you" rocketed back and forth inside Reb's head, careening off all her carefully planned arguments and leaving everything a confused jumble. There was no time to sort things out before Kincaid's lips grazed her cheek on their way to her mouth.

"I love you," he repeated huskily.

The phrase settled as softly on Reb's soul as Kincaid's lips on her own, setting in motion a metamorphosis from passivity to aggression that stripped her of her inhibitions as spectacularly as a butterfly shedding its chrysalis.

This time Kincaid didn't hold in check the passion she aroused in him. "Turn around," he commanded.

Reb pivoted so that Kincaid could unfasten the crimson gown. It had served its purpose well, and she felt no regret when it pooled at her feet. She kicked off her shoes, rolled down her stockings, and discarded her bulky underskirt, then spun back to face Kincaid in chemise and pantalets.

"Your turn," she purred with a lusty grin.

She disrobed him, slowly loosening his formal evening coat from his broad shoulders, then freeing the diamond studs from his silk shirt. She let her forefinger drift down his chest until she finally reached the line of black curls on his belly. Sitting him down on the bed, she relieved him of his boots and socks. He obediently stood again while she skinned him out of his trousers.

Reb blushed at the burgeoning manhood that saluted her efforts and, in a rush of shyness, kept her eyes averted, waiting for Kincaid to make the next move.

"I remember seeing you at the pool that day we walked in the forest as vividly as if I were there right now," he said quietly. "You're beautiful, Rebel. Let me see all of you again." He moved forward and slowly slipped the chemise off her shoulders.

Reb's surprise at Kincaid's revelation turned quickly to incensed rage, and she punched Kincaid in the stomach as hard as she could.

He emitted a resounding, "Ooof!"

"You knew! You knew I was a woman, and you didn't tell me," she shouted. She alternately assaulted his chest with both her fists and recited the particular incidents for which she punished him in such righteous indignation.

"*That's* for the phony act you put on when you needed your boots off. And *that's* for the 'Doctor, I

need you,' and *that's* for the description of your perfect wife, you braying mule-headed Romeo. You wolf
in sheep's clothing. You faker! Why didn't you tell me
you knew I was a girl?"

Kincaid grabbed both her hands in one of his.
"Stop it, Reb."

She used her feet to kick out at him. "No!"

"You asked for this," he snapped. He picked her up
and threw her over his shoulder, heading for the bed.

"Don't you dare," she warned.

He threw her on the bed so hard she bounced
twice, ripped the chemise up over her head, and
pulled the pantalets down over her kicking legs
before she had a chance to get away.

When she was naked, Reb scurried to the head of
the bed, pulled her knees to her chest, and grabbed a
pillow to cover as much of her as she could.

"While we're talking about phonies and fakers," he
said heatedly from where he stood at the foot of the
bed, "what about you? I specifically remember asking
you if you were Adam's *brother*."

"I didn't lie."

"No, but you didn't tell the truth, either."

"I couldn't."

"Why the hell not?"

"I was in love with you!"

Kincaid's hands went to his hips in triumph, and a
huge grin stole across his face.

"You don't have to be so smug," Reb said haughtily. "I didn't *want* to be in love with you."

"Rebel, Rebel," Kincaid said lovingly.

When Reb opened her mouth to argue further, Kincaid wagged his finger at her as though she were a naughty child.

"I'm not a kid," she said, throwing the pillow at his head. "I'm a woman!"

"Act like a brat, get treated like a brat," Kincaid responded good-naturedly as he flattened Reb under him on the bed. "Act like a woman, get treated like a woman," he added in a voice that had thickened in passion.

Reb was pinned beneath Kincaid, unable to move, yet it never entered her mind to struggle. She'd been waiting a lifetime for this moment. She could see the unconcealed desire in the eyes of the man she loved, the man who loved her. Her trader's soul was satisfied. She'd given her love and received fair measure in return.

She caressed Kincaid's hips and felt the sinewy muscles tighten under her hands.

Kincaid let his lips wander from Reb's willowy neck across her shoulders and down between her breasts. He kissed each rosy crest once reverently, then lifted himself up to drink the nectar from her lips.

With her hands freed, Reb could satisfy her own need to touch. When their eyes locked, she brought her hands to Kincaid's face and let her thumb brush the scar on his cheek. She splayed her fingers through the errant curls on his forehead, then ran her fingertips across his temple and down behind his ear, finally reaching his corded neck and shoulders, causing him to shiver.

She brought her hands back to his chest to skim his nipples before aiming her fingertips downward and letting her hands follow where her fingertips led. Kincaid quivered when Reb reached her destination. Her lips curved in an impish smile as she watched his features grow rigid with tension.

"Reb," he said throatily. "Do you know what you're doing?"

"No," she replied with a saucy smile. "But that's never stopped me before. And I don't see why it should now."

Kincaid managed a crooked grin. "I can give you one good reason."

"What's that?"

"Because turnabout is fair play."

Reb gasped when Kincaid made good on his word.

They pleasured each other teasingly until their need had heightened beyond what mere teasing could satisfy. Abruptly Kincaid rolled over on his back, bringing Reb with him so that she was now lying on top of him.

Heavy-lidded with desire, she pushed herself up to

a sitting position so her naked thighs straddled his waist.

"You are so beautiful," he said softly.

Reb's brows furrowed and she shook her head.

"Yes, yes, you are," he insisted.

"I wasn't contradicting you," she said with a wry smile. "I just had the feeling for a moment that I'd been here before. Of course that isn't possible, is it?" she said, her fingertips smoothing his rising brow. She leaned down to kiss him, and he rose with her so he was seated on the bed with Reb straddling his lap.

"Come, love," he coaxed gently. He lifted Reb enough for her to impale herself on him.

"All for your delight," he said, winking roguishly at her.

Reb blushed wonderfully, but took advantage of the opportunity he'd given her to guide their love-making. She pushed him down so he was lying flat once more, then rode him as breathtakingly as the wildest bucking stallion.

Kincaid matched her move for move. The rider could not tame the mount, the mount could not shake the rider. The frenzied duel raged, each moment bringing them closer to fulfillment.

Reb cried out in ecstasy, then felt the pulsing release of Kincaid's seed within her as he also exclaimed his exultation.

Reb dropped forward to lay panting on Kincaid's

chest in exquisite exhaustion. "You are so warm," she sighed.

He turned sideways so they lay together, side by side on the bed, her head cradled in his shoulder. He kissed her hair and murmured, "It is always so, no matter how cold the weather."

Reb was reminded of Kincaid's parting words at the base of the mountains. She'd known the warmth of a man's love. But how long would it last? She was too tired to worry about that right now. Maybe later.

The lovers slept, unaware that the witching hour approached.

Kincaid awoke with a start when the first fireworks exploded outside their window, then relaxed when his hand brushed a soft thigh, reminded of his pleasant circumstances. He nuzzled Reb's neck lazily, enjoying the recognizable flame of excitement that ignited when he touched her.

Reb felt the tightening knot of pleasure that radiated across her loins when Kincaid lowered his mouth and gently suckled her breast. She lay still, pretending to sleep, waiting to see what he would do.

Kincaid lifted his head to study Reb's face and knew she was awake when her eyelashes flickered against the bombarding lights and sounds from outside their safe haven. "You're missing the celebration," he reminded her lazily, as his hand possessively caressed her hip.

"Oh, no!"

Reb instantly pulled free of Kincaid's embrace and scrambled from the bed. She grabbed for her underclothes, scrambling to get them on, then reached for her crumpled crimson gown, yanking it up over her shoulders haphazardly.

"What's wrong?" Kincaid jumped up anxiously and pulled on his underwear and trousers to face whatever emergency had propelled Reb out of his arms.

"Dillon and I were supposed to meet my father and Adam for the fireworks at midnight," she wailed. "When I'm not there, he'll come looking for me. I have to go."

"When will I see you again?"

"Tomorrow."

"I'm leaving tomorrow for Blue's cabin. I've got another assignment for the railroad," he said, unsure of Reb's reaction and unwilling to destroy the peace they'd found.

"That's wonderful!" she exclaimed. "I'll meet you here, and we can go together."

Reb wasn't any happier about Kincaid's involvement with the railroad, but at least he wasn't returning to New York right away. She was practical enough to know that they would need some time together to work out their differences.

"You can't come. It's out of the question."

"Why not?" Reb asked.

"I don't want you exposed to the danger. I'll be asking Blue to take me to Chief Spotted Tail to see if he'll agree to come down and sign a treaty in the spring. It's too dangerous."

Kincaid saw the ominous clouds building on Reb's face and took her in his arms before he continued earnestly, "Reb, I'm so pleased you changed your mind and decided to come back east with me. I couldn't bear it if anything happened to you now."

Chills ran up and down Reb's spine. "I haven't changed my mind," she said, tugging herself free from his hold and facing him with hands perched on her hips. "In fact, I came here tonight to convince you to change *your* mind. Even if I had changed my mind about going east, I can't change what I am."

"Exactly my point," Kincaid said. "You're a *woman*, Reb. This is a man's job."

Reb counted to ten, a trick she'd taught herself that usually allowed the reasoned thought to be spoken rather than the reflex one. This time ten wasn't high enough.

"You know damn well I'm just as capable as you are of taking care of myself in any situation. In fact, I'd even go so far as to say I can take *better* care of myself than you can," she spat.

"That's something we'll never find out. Because you're not going," Kincaid said flatly.

"We'll see what Blue has to say about that!"

"Blue will agree with me," Kincaid shot back.

"See you at the cabin," Reb retorted. She jerked open the door and slammed it closed behind her.

He yanked the door open and bellowed at her down the hall. "Reb, come back here! Your dress isn't fastened!"

She pulled the dragging skirt up in her hands and ran faster down the hall.

Kincaid furiously slammed the door. "Damned woman doesn't know when to quit!"

Reb hurried to her room, hoping that she wasn't too late to change her clothes and be downstairs before she was found out. When she opened the door, she knew the worst had happened. Her father towered over Dillon, who was still dressed for the ball and who'd obviously been in tears for some time.

"Where the hell have you been?" her father demanded.

"Damn, Reb, you're only half dressed!" Adam exclaimed as he came up behind her.

Reb stood flushed and breathless at the knowledge-able stares of her family, but exhibited no signs of shame at her shocking behavior.

When Reb and Dillon hadn't met them as

planned, Adam had told Matt about the ball that was in progress upstairs. It was there he'd found his younger daughter, surrounded by rogues and rake-hells. He'd grabbed her wrist and marched her back to her room, demanding to know where Reb was.

Dillon had admitted that her sister was supposed to meet Kincaid at the ball, but she had no idea what had happened to her since. Worry that some calamity had befallen his elder daughter had keyed Matt to a level of anxiety that made him incautious in the handling of his stubborn child.

"Where have you been?" Matt repeated irritably when Reb remained mute.

"I've been with Kincaid," she answered, undaunted. "He's leaving Denver tomorrow on another mission for the Union Pacific. I'm going to Blue's cabin to wait for him."

"You're not going anywhere with that Yankee," Matt gritted out furiously. "*Especially* not to Blue's cabin."

"Yes, I am!" Reb replied.

Matt slammed the fist of one hand into the palm of the other. "That bastard Blue has seen the last of you." Then he ordered, "Adam, take Dillon to our room. I want to talk to Reb alone."

"If you try to stop Reb from seeing either Blue or Kincaid, Dad, you'll find I'm on her side," Adam said.

He stepped up to stand next to Reb. Dillon moved over to join them, presenting a united front.

An expression of frustrated pain flitted across Matt's face before he let his hatred of the mountain man show. "I don't want you near that son of a bitch Blue, because he can't be trusted," he grated menacingly.

His fierce animosity alarmed his children, who protested vigorously.

"Quiet!" he commanded. "I'm not finished."

Matt took a deep breath before continuing. "Blue violated your mother."

"That can't be true," Reb breathed.

Reb's support for the mountain man fueled Matt's anger. *Couldn't they see through the man? Did he have them all fooled?*

"It is," Matt said stonily. In a last desperate attempt to forestall any contact between Reb and Blue, Matt let out the secret that had been tearing at his heart for six years, ever since he'd found out.

"I'm not your father, Rebecca. Blue is."

At that moment, a blazing cascade of fireworks exploded violently outside the window, lighting the room like day and bleaching the color from their faces. They stood frozen in horror, like figures in some ghastly wax museum.

Reb took the moment before the room returned to shadowed darkness to let her father's words sink in.

He wasn't her father, Blue was. How was that possible?
Her mother had been "violated."

"What about the rest of us?" It was a painful question to ask, but Adam had to know.

"You're all my get except Reb."

A poignant sense of loss seized Reb. Precocious Dillon was only her half sister, and Adam, dear protective Adam, only her half brother, as were the quiet Garth and the ebullient Jesse. She felt hurt and shut out.

"You see why I don't want you near Blue," Matt said, pleading for understanding. "You're going home."

Reb didn't see at all, and her confusion frightened her. In desperation she sought escape. "If you're not my father, you have no right to tell me what I can and can't do," she said.

Reb turned to Adam and said, "May I borrow your horse?" She let the wilted gown fall, found her buckskins, and hurriedly put them on.

Adam looked from his father to Reb. His father looked stunned, Reb shocked. Both remained dry-eyed. He knew there must be more to the story than his father had told, but if his father's tight-lipped expression was any guide, the only way Reb was going to find out was to ask Blue.

"Ricochet is in the stable," Adam said. "Good luck, Reb."

Reb hugged her brother and sister, but couldn't bring herself to go near her father. She rubbed the familiar knobby beads on her knife sheath. That simple act had always given her courage because it reminded her of her father's love.

Yet he'd known, even when he gave her the gift, that she wasn't his own daughter. Had he meant what he'd said about loving her? Or was it all part of some hideous lie?

Reb's eyes sought her father's—no, Matthew Hunter's—with the questions she couldn't bear to ask. Then she turned quickly and left before he could answer them.

Matt started to follow her, but Adam blocked his way. "She has to go," he said simply.

Matt debated whether to try to get past his son, but realized that even if he finally won free, Reb would have the head start she needed to reach Blue's cabin ahead of him.

Perhaps it was for the best that Reb have time alone with the man who'd sired her. If only Rachel were here, maybe she could explain to Reb how such a thing had happened.

Matt could not, for he didn't understand himself. He'd been a good husband, kept Rachel's bed warm, been a good provider, done everything he knew to make her happy.

Evidently, it hadn't been enough. He didn't know what he'd done wrong. He didn't know why his wife had created a child with his best friend.

Matt turned his back on Adam and Dillon to watch the magnificent sparklers through the window. He crossed and leaned his forehead against a cool, clear pane, while his palms pressed against the smoothly painted frame on either side. He closed his eyes to shut out the brilliant light. *"Oh, Rachel, why?"* he cried soundlessly into the blackness.

Dillon let the tears that no one else would shed fall freely from her eyes. She was a proper fairy godmother, all right. She glanced at the crimson gown lying in a wrinkled pool on the floor. It was midnight, and everything in Reb's fairy tale had turned into rags and mice and pumpkins.

18

Blue glanced over his shoulder to be certain Reb and Kincaid still followed. He wouldn't have put it past either one to have done away with the other when he wasn't looking. He'd played referee for three days now, and his patience was wearing thin.

They were nearing the Powder River region and had reached the beginning of the thick forest that led into the valleys between the Big Horn Mountains on the west and the Black Hills on the east. He was certain, with all the shouting going on between the two irate lovers, that the Sioux would discover them long before they reached their objective.

He only hoped it was Spotted Tail and not Standing Buffalo who sighted them first.

Blue had heard Reb's side of the story, and then Kincaid's. The Yankee had been very persuasive about the inevitability of the railroad coming through the mountains, and Kincaid's proposal for a treaty with the Sioux had sounded intriguing. Blue wasn't unwilling to try to save Indian lives if he could. He'd informed Kincaid that he'd be willing to act as a guide, but only if Reb came along. He'd also concluded that the couple's spat would be resolved only if they stayed together.

The Yankee had stormed and sworn, but ultimately had had no choice.

Blue began to have doubts about his matchmaking decision the first evening they made camp. Reb had been alternately sullen and sharp with him, and when he'd tried to tease her out of her uncharacteristic temper, she'd burst into tears. Things had gone steadily downhill from there.

Reb hadn't spoken two words to him the rest of the trip, but Kincaid's hide must be bleeding in a dozen places from the constant tongue-lashings she'd given her Yankee. Blue grunted disgustedly when he heard the couple begin their childish bickering again.

"You expect me to give up everything to marry you. What are you giving up?" Reb demanded.

"My peace of mind," Kincaid replied sarcastically.

Kincaid felt tricked. He would never have admitted to Reb that he loved her if he'd had any inkling she was going to pull a stunt like this. Fear squeezed his heart every time the wind rustled the bushes, for his mind's eye saw an arrow headed for Reb.

He was furious with himself for caring. He didn't want to love a woman who took the kind of chances with her life that could get her killed. But how did one stop? He couldn't help loving her, but he didn't have to marry her if she insisted on staying out here.

"I won't live my life worrying constantly whether my wife is on the brink of some disaster," he said crossly.

"How can you say that?" Reb argued. "I'm perfectly capable of taking care of myself."

"God protect me from women who can protect themselves," Kincaid railed derisively. "Laurie said the same thing, and now she's dead! I warned her there might be repercussions if she married a Yankee, even if her Confederate friends didn't know I was a Union Army officer. But she wouldn't listen to me.

She made the mistake of trusting some Johnny-come-lately who professed undying loyalty to the cause and then took money to set her up for the Union Army ambush that killed her.

So don't tell me how safe it is to love you, how we can look forward to a long and happy life together if we marry and stay in this godforsaken wilderness!"

"I'm not Laurie," Reb yelled in frustration.

"No, you're a hundred times worse!" he retorted. "I'd have to be crazy to marry a woman who traipses around the mountains looking for an opportunity to get her scalp lifted by some Sioux."

"You want me to act like something I'm not," Reb charged peevishly.

"I want you to act like a woman," Kincaid corrected.

Reb's face flushed furiously. "Being a woman and being able to handle yourself in any situation are *not* mutually exclusive," she grated out. "I have no plans to change my way of life."

"You will if you're married to me."

"Like hell I will!"

"Those are my terms, take them or leave them," Kincaid said, issuing his ultimatum.

Before Reb could form a sufficiently caustic response, Blue interrupted the wrangling pair.

"Kincaid," Blue called. "I'd like you to ride ahead a couple of miles and see if you can find a good place for us to bed down for the night. We should be getting pretty close to some of the streams that lead into the Powder River. Find a campsite near the water. Take Trapper with you. He'll help you keep a lookout for the Sioux."

Kincaid handed the leads on the seven pack-laden mules to Reb without speaking, then obeyed Blue.

Reb stuck her tongue out at Kincaid's back as he kicked Satan into a lope.

"Reb, I wanted a chance to talk to you alone," Blue said.

"Wanted to give me a little fatherly advice?" Reb snapped back.

"You could use some," Blue replied testily. "You've

been acting like a spoiled brat. Your father should have taken your drawers down and tanned your bottom a long time ago!"

"Why didn't you?" Reb asked.

"Why didn't I what?"

Ever since she'd learned Blue was her father, Reb had been trying to decide whether and how to broach the subject. Afraid of what she would learn but desperate to know the truth, she stood at the edge of a high precipice. She took a deep breath and jumped, praying that something would break the fall.

"Why didn't you tan my hide—Father?" She turned to see Blue's reaction to the title.

His eyes narrowed to slits, and she watched a muscle jerk in his jaw as it tightened. "What is that supposed to mean?"

Reb agonized before she blurted, "Did you rape my mother?"

Blue yanked back so sharply on the reins in his stunned surprise that his horse neighed and reared. He swore vehemently and jerked the bit as he manhandled the horse back under control.

When the gelding had steadied, he kicked his mount viciously over to Reb and snatched the reins of her horse near its mouth. "Get down off that horse!" he said.

"No."

"Rebecca, get down off that horse by yourself, or by God I swear I'll knock you down!"

Reb clambered off the animal and darted as fast as she could through the thick trees away from the furious man.

Blue swung his leg over the saddle and quickly slid off his mount, rapidly overtaking her. She already had her hand on her knife when he yanked her around, grasped her by both arms, and shook her so hard that she was dizzy when he finally threw her away from him. She fought for equilibrium as she reached again for her bowie.

"That knife will only keep you from the truth. Or don't you want to hear the truth?" he said fiercely. Blue marveled at how like Matt she was in some ways. Matt had reached for his knife, too.

Reb bowed her head and let her hands fall to her sides in desolate submission. They stood facing each other without moving for some moments before Blue could control his rage enough to speak.

Blue had always feared that someday Reb would discover he was her father. On the one hand, he'd always been proud of her and would gladly have acknowledged her. On the other hand, it could only be a painful experience for everyone involved. He'd had no idea just how painful it would be. Until now.

"Who told you I raped your mother?" he asked harshly.

"I think 'violated' was the word my fath—Ma—" Reb shuddered and couldn't speak. What should she call Matt Hunter now? She couldn't call him Father, because he wasn't. She wouldn't call him Matt, because she couldn't. The pain in her chest was a tangible thing. She groaned in distress.

"It's all right. I know what you're trying to say." Blue empathized with the agony, as great as his own.

"He said you're my father," she said in a whisper.

"It's true. I am your father."

Reb's whole body sagged defeatedly. Deep down she'd been hoping against hope that there was some mistake, that this was all some cruel hoax.

"But there was never any force involved. I loved your mother, and she loved me."

That possibility was too foreign to everything Reb believed about her mother to go unchallenged.

"You're lying! My mother loved my fath—" Reb pressed the heels of her hands hard against her throbbing temples as her piercing shriek of frustration rent the air. When the eerie echo had died, Reb forced her words out over the huge lump in her throat. "My mother loved the man she was married to."

"At first, yes, she did. And later, afterward, she was a good wife," Blue agreed quietly. "Your father wanted a woman to bear his children, to cook his meals, mend his clothes, and keep his backside warm on a cold winter's night. It would be hard to fault him for that. Your mother provided all that and was beautiful, too.

"After she married Matt, your mother missed the world she'd left behind in Philadelphia more than she'd ever thought she would. Matt could never understand that."

"Rachel never complained, because she had something to prove to your grandmother and to Matt, too. She did a helluva job of adjusting to what they both expected from her."

"Your father demanded that she do all the changing, and she did. But she was never happy because of it."

Reb opened her mouth to speak, but Blue's look defied her to interrupt.

"He saw a future that was the same as the past. She saw a future that included everything she'd left behind. He didn't want to face the fact that his world was changing. She taught you kids everything she knew, in spite of Matt's attitude. He didn't thank her for it," Blue said accusingly. "He thought it was a waste of time. Matt held on tenaciously to the past rather than grow into the future with your mother.

"When he found out about Rachel and me, he could never understand why she'd turned to someone else. Matt never realized how lonely she was, how much she needed someone to share her hopes that you children would embrace the changes that were bound to come and her plans for helping you to accept the new ways.

"Our relationship started innocently enough. I visited Matt's cabin frequently because I had no home of my own, and Rachel and I became friends. You see, I knew all about her world, because I came from there, too."

Reb looked up at Blue. She'd never thought of him anywhere but in the mountains. Now he was admitting he'd lived another life.

"Gather the horses and the mules and tie them up. Then we can sit and talk," he said with a sigh.

The profusion of fir and pine had provided a soft pillow of needles onto which Blue dropped. Reb hobbled the animals, then returned and squatted across from him on her haunches and picked up a pine branchlet, pulling it apart in agitation. When she'd torn each needle away, she picked up another to give her nervous hands something to do.

Blue picked up a perfectly formed pine cone and tossed it up in the air and caught it several times, letting the prickly points lend a stab of reality to the nightmare in which he found himself.

Neither one really wanted to begin the distressing discussion again, but Reb finally broke the silence. "What's your real name?"

"Cabell Ashton. It's a good Virginia name. I was born and raised there and went to the university at

Charlottesville. My father and I had a falling-out over the matter of whether men should own other men, and he disinherited me. It has been a bitter comfort to me that the North has finally settled the question in my favor."

"Your mother and I talked about our pasts a lot, about that other world back east. Our friendship deepened, and we fell in love." There was a long pause before he added, "You were the result of that love."

Reb stood and walked away a few steps to put some distance between herself and Blue. She couldn't bear the tears that had risen in the intense mahogany eyes of the invincible mountain man sitting across from her.

"I begged your mother to come away with me," Blue continued softly. "She wouldn't take Adam and Garth away from their father. Once she'd made up her mind that she wasn't ever going to leave Matt, she wouldn't see me alone anymore. She decided that Matt deserved better, that so long as he was her husband, she owed him her love and respect.

"She kept that promise to be faithful to Matt until the day she died," Blue said bitterly.

Reb whirled and spat out disbelievingly, "Then how did my—how did he find out?"

Blue rose to confront her sadly. "Sometimes the fates aren't kind. I wrote a note to your mother when you were born, telling her how happy I was. Apparently she saved it."

He paused, remembering that joyous time so long ago, then said, "Matt found the note six years ago."

"That's why we left the mountains!" Reb exclaimed. She felt a sharp stab of pain in her chest when she thought what such a discovery must have been like for her father. "You were his partner. He trusted you. How could you and my mother betray him like that?"

"Betrayal is a pretty strong word," Blue said. "When you're in love, you don't always do the 'right' thing. Sometimes the need to be with each other is so strong, it takes over. We made the mistake of letting our love rule our actions," he said hesitantly, his brow furrowed in torment.

"Haven't you ever done anything that seemed so right at the moment, and then regretted it later?" Blue asked, distressed at her intolerance. His voice rose angrily. "Your mother stayed with Matt because he needed her, and she'd vowed 'to love, honor, and obey till death us do part.'

"She knew a few things about what it means to love someone that you could stand to learn," Blue snarled savagely. Without pausing, he challenged, "Do you love Kincaid?"

"Of course!"

"Enough to change for him? Enough to try to be more like what he wants you to be?"

"If he loved me, he'd take me as I am," Reb countered.

"No, Reb." Blue contradicted her with a harsh laugh. "The truth is, both of you have to give a little bit. It's called compromise. One person can't give everything like Rachel did. It cuts the heart away," he said, begging her to understand.

"If you love Kincaid, you'll give a little. And if he loves you, he'll know when you've given all you can, and he'll give the rest of what it takes for you both to be happy."

Kincaid galloped his horse up to the two people faced off against each other in the wilderness and vaulted from the saddle on the run. Trapper almost bowled Blue over in his excitement at the frenzied pace of their return.

"I heard Reb's scream. What happened?"

Reb flew into Kincaid's arms and grabbed him desperately around the waist, burying her face in his shirt, hiding from the suffering Blue had let her see.

"What happened?" Kincaid repeated anxiously. He was pleased that Reb, who'd been fighting with him constantly for four days, suddenly clung to him for dear life. But he wanted to know who, or what, had threatened the woman he loved.

"You'll have to ask Reb," Blue said curtly. "Take her as far as the river and set up camp. As much noise as you two have been making, it's a wonder we aren't already surrounded by Indians. I'm going to see if I can locate Spotted Tail before Standing Buffalo finds us."

"If I'm not back by morning, stay headed northeast, and keep your eyes peeled for trouble. Come on, Trapper," he called to the large dog.

After Blue had galloped off, Kincaid pried Reb's hold loose and stepped back.

"What happened, Rebel?" he questioned tenderly.

"It's about Blue and me. Blue is my . . . He's my . . . My father isn't . . . My mother . . ." Reb said incoherently.

"It's all right, Rebel," Kincaid said, kissing her softly on the mouth. "I can wait."

He walked over to the mules and unhobbled them, then took the lead to the animals and mounted Satan, waiting patiently for Reb to mount.

Reb felt dead inside. She grabbed the reins of her horse and mounted stiffly. Then she and Kincaid followed Blue's faint path through the thick forest.

Blue had barely ridden out of Reb and Kincaid's sight when he backtracked around the couple and picked up the trail they'd previously traveled. He found a comfortable spot where he could remain concealed and waited.

Now that Matt had told Reb that Blue was her father, it was a safe guess he was somewhere behind them, waiting to see the results of his stick in the anthill. Blue had given Reb the best advice he knew, and now he intended to see that she had the time to think over that advice, and to act on it without Matt's interference.

Sure enough, in less than two hours, Blue heard the telltale sounds of shod hooves on rock and the crunchy jangle of horses trying to chew grass around a bit. Blue moved his horse into the path of the oncoming riders and waited.

Matt and Adam both saw Blue at the same time. Matt reached to pull his rifle from its leather case on the saddle, and Adam caught his hand.

"He's Reb's father," Adam said.

Matt let the rifle slide back down in its boot and kicked his mount to urge it closer to Blue. The air bristled and popped with the tension that streaked between the two men.

"Where's Reb?" Matt asked.

"With Kincaid."

"Where are they?" Matt persisted.

"Ahead. It was a cruel thing you did, telling her." The only sign Blue had that Matt acknowledged the criticism was the slight narrowing of his eyes. "Only you left out some of the facts," Blue added coldly.

"I told her what she needed to know," Matt countered angrily. "I've come to take her home."

"I can't let you do that," Blue said. "Reb has finally found a man she can love. He's a good man, a strong man, as strong as she is. They need time alone to work out their differences. And I intend to see they get it."

"How the hell do you propose to stop me?" Matt reached for his rifle again, but Blue kneed his horse to reveal his own loaded, aimed Spencer.

"Reb and Kincaid are headed for Spotted Tail's camp. We're going to take a short cut and meet them there. I have some talking to do with Spotted Tail before Kincaid arrives, anyway. You can come along peaceably, or I can make the trip very unpleasant. It's your choice."

Matt scowled, but Adam wasn't at all displeased.

"Dad," Adam said quietly, laying his hand on his father's shoulder, "I don't pretend to know how you feel right now. I only know that if there's any chance at all for Reb and Kincaid to come to an understanding, they deserve to have it. There'll be plenty of time for you and Blue to kill each other later," he finished sardonically.

Matt glanced over at the son who could find humor even in this tense situation, then back to Blue. "We'll go with you. But she damn well better arrive at Spotted Tail's camp in one piece."

Secretly, Blue acknowledged that Matt's concern bore merit. There were risks that Reb and Kincaid would run into trouble if left to themselves. But when he weighed those risks, even the risk of death, against a lifetime of happiness together, Blue had no difficulty making his choice.

"Don't worry," he said. "Reb can take care of herself. And I expect Kincaid will have a care for her as well."

Reb and Kincaid had lost Blue's trail but were continuing northeast through the sun-speckled forest when, without warning, they were startled by the screeching, war-painted Indians that dropped onto them from an outcropping of rock.

The weight of one attacking brave knocked Reb from her horse. Once on the ground, she was quickly overwhelmed when two Sioux appeared from the underbrush and joined the first.

Kincaid was the victim of the same kind of surprise attack. The two Sioux who'd leaped from the cliff above him, together with two others who'd joined them from their hiding place in the heavy thicket along the trail, sat on his extremities while he swore vigorously but fruitlessly at his captors. Concern for Reb was foremost in his mind, since he couldn't see past the four Sioux who surrounded him.

"Rebel, are you all right?" he shouted.

"Kincaid!"

The fear in Reb's voice galvanized Kincaid, and with superhuman effort he managed to free one arm. He swung his huge fist savagely at the nearest Sioux and broke the warrior's cheekbone. Kincaid heard a guttural command from somewhere behind him, and the wounded Sioux was replaced by two more. He struggled vainly against the increased restraint.

"Reb? Reb?" he called anxiously. He got no answer.

Reb had been gagged with rawhide after she'd severely bitten one of her attackers. Her hands had been pulled back viciously and tied behind her. A brave, naked except for breechclout, moccasins, and a war vest of bone and feathers, rode up before the pair. He gestured, and Reb was jerked up on her feet and a rawhide rope placed around her neck. The lead was handed to the arrogant Indian.

Kincaid had been so concerned about Reb that he hadn't paid attention to his own plight. Each wrist had been secured with a long rawhide thong, and the thongs handed to mounted Indians on opposite sides of him. Another noose of rawhide had been tightened around his neck and handed to the same vividly war-painted buck who held Reb's line. He appeared to be the leader of the war party.

The two Indians holding the rawhide that bound each of Kincaid's arms simultaneously applied pressure. The pull in opposite directions yanked him to his feet, stretching his arms out and wrenching the sockets. A younger brave made the mistake of coming too close, and Kincaid lashed out with a booted foot, catching the foolish man in the groin.

The line around Kincaid's neck snapped taut, and the band started homeward with their prizes, not the least of which was Kincaid's magnificent black stallion.

The lead around Reb's neck was longer, so she ran ten paces behind Kincaid. When she stumbled over a rotting log, she was dragged by the neck for a few paces before a passing Indian snagged her excruciatingly by the crook of her elbow and dropped her back on her feet.

Kincaid looked over his shoulder and met her eyes, willing her to stand. He saw her stagger for a few steps, but she managed to keep up with the spotted pony trotting ahead of them.

The Indians laughed among themselves, speculating how much they could get in barter for the goods on the confiscated mules, and wagering their share of the loot on whether the smaller captive, whose face already showed the first bloody scrapes from the trail, would survive the forced march back to camp.

Reb watched Kincaid jogging ahead of her, his arms stretched out painfully on either side, one occasionally jerked backward or forward when the available space between the trees narrowed so the Indian riding on one side couldn't keep pace with the one on the other. She could tell by Kincaid's darkened features when he turned to check on her that he wasn't happy about the situation. Reb knew the extent of her love's ire when he started ranting furiously at their predicament.

"Dammit, Reb! I warned you something like this might happen. You better, by God, do your damnedest to stay alive until I can get us out of this mess."

Kincaid clung to his anger desperately; it left no room for the fear and despair that clutched at him with fierce talons. He forced his mind away from the pictures that rose before him when he imagined what would happen when the Sioux discovered Reb was female. Where the hell was Blue when he needed him?

Reb formed an appropriate retort, but couldn't speak because of the gag. None of this was her fault. He was supposed to be watching out for Indians. She had no intention of rolling over and playing dead, either. She would prove to him that wilderness women were raised to survive anything that man or nature threw at them.

Standing Buffalo turned back proudly to gaze on

his two captives. The Great Spirit had given back not only Too-Big-For-Horses but also one of the two trappers who had set him free. He would not be cheated again of the vengeance owed for the death of his brother. All in the village of Spotted Tail would be witness to how well Too-Big-For-Horses met his death.

19

Reb lay facedown on the rocky ground, her hands still tied behind her back. The gag had been removed the previous night, so that the Indians could tease her with the promise of water that wasn't delivered. Her tongue lay swollen in her mouth as though it didn't belong there.

The red rims of her eyes burned, and her eyeballs screamed their disapproval when she raised her shielding eyelids. She could hear the guttural bark of shouted commands but couldn't seem to make her body obey her will.

It was the morning of the third day of their captivity, and she had had no food or water and very little rest for two days. A vicious kick in the ribs rolled her over on her back, and she squinted her eyes at the very ugly Indian blocking her view of a partially overcast gray sky. She grunted as the brave leveled another kick that brought tears to the corners of her eyes.

"Get up, Reb," she heard Kincaid plead.

She turned her head and saw that two Indians were working on the knots that had tied him stretched out between two pines during the night. How her life had been changed since that first felicitous meeting, when she and Adam had found Kincaid tied spread-eagled in the forest, as he was now. Would some passing stranger rescue them? she wondered. She snorted to herself at the poor odds she would give to the sucker who bet on that.

She realized then just how fortuitous it had been that she and Adam had found Kincaid. She smiled beatifically at the thought that, thanks to Kincaid, at least she wasn't going to die a virgin. The smile split the skin on her lower lip, and a trickle of blood spilled down her chin.

Kincaid was sure Reb's mind had gone when he saw her grinning like a Cheshire cat, but he said nothing, because whatever she was thinking about had started her moving.

Reb called on her cramped stomach muscles to pull her into a sitting position and, though they protested, she rose. She felt sure she must have at least one broken rib. She pulled her bruised knees up and laid her forehead on them, trying to gather the courage to face another day. There was no part of her aching body that wasn't sore. Her shoulders and wrists throbbed. The smell of urine on her clothes bespoke the most wounded part of all—her pride.

For she'd been forced to wet herself like a child and then endure the Indians' mocking laughter at her shame.

Reb lifted her head and rolled onto her knees, trying to rise. The same ugly Indian put a foot on her buttocks and pushed her back down on her face with a croaking laugh. Reb wanted to cry when he replaced the awful gag. She lay unmoving after he was done.

"You red-devil son of a bitch! Do you want her up or not?" Kincaid shouted hoarsely. "Dammit, Reb, get up or I'll kick you up myself!"

Reb's resentment at Kincaid's threat provoked her to rise unsteadily on her feet to confront him. She wanted to shout that it wasn't fair. Kincaid hadn't had so much as a finger laid on him since he'd been captured. The Sioux all seemed to keep their distance from him, as though he were some special kind of demon. Their respect had increased after one of the braves had tried to ride Satan and been thrown and trampled to death.

Reb, on the other hand, had been the brunt of every cruel trick or unsporting joke the fiendish Sioux bullies could think up. It was easy for Kincaid to stand there and shout "Get up!" when he didn't have a mark on his body! She'd like to put him in her moccasins and see how well he'd fare.

Reb's eyes shot sparks at Kincaid from a face that

was a patchwork of bloody scrapes and scratches, before her tether jerked her away.

In the blindness of her own pain, Reb couldn't see the agony Kincaid stoically endured. The scarred muscle in his thigh had tightened over the past three days, and the excruciating ache in the old wound caused him to limp badly. It had become a hellish struggle to pick the leg up and put it down again.

Kincaid also suspected that sometime during the journey he'd torn the muscles in the recently knitted flesh of his left shoulder, for the jerking pull of the rawhide thongs had become a throbbing torture. He had no other explanation for the kaleidoscope of black-and-blue discoloration. Worst of all, he'd been reduced to shallow panting, for he couldn't take a deep breath without encountering the damnable constriction in his chest that visited him each time he thought of losing Reb.

Kincaid struggled painfully with all the ferocious strength of his sinewy back and shoulders against the rawhide thongs that bound him. He wasn't unaware that Reb bore the brunt of the Indians' vindictiveness. If he could have brought their fury down on himself and spared Reb, he would have done so. But nothing he did seemed to provoke the Indians to grapple with him. He vented his frustration by raining imprecations down on the heads of the Sioux.

Throughout the early morning, Reb dragged at the

end of her tether in exhaustion. The terrain had become rockier. The majesty of the tall peaks all around them would have been breathtaking if she'd only had the strength to lift her head to view them.

Those among the band who'd bet that Reb would not complete the journey contributed to her labor, for they frequently tripped her, then struck her meanly when she was down or cuffed her roughly when prodding her to rise.

Each time Reb fell, Kincaid alternately murmured cajoling words of encouragement and threatened dire punishment if she didn't succeed in getting up. Kincaid was heartened that, after all they had been through, Reb was somehow still doggedly on her feet. Still alive.

That meant there was still hope.

Some of that hope vanished when he detected the distant cacophony of barking dogs and playing children that meant they'd reached the Indian village. He realized then that he'd been counting on Blue to rescue them before they were ensconced among the Sioux. There was still the remote chance Kincaid would be able to find someone to get a message to Spotted Tail. There were numerous tribes camped in the Powder River region, though, and Kincaid had no way of knowing which one had captured them.

The Indian camp was nestled in a grassy valley in the shelter of two enormous rocky bluffs. A rushing stream wound in and out among the tepees. Wooded thickets rimmed the edges of the bluffs, hemming in the camp.

The Indian women stopped cooking, tanning hides, and crushing dried buffalo meat for pemmican to stare. The children dropped their hoop and pole game, and all came from the tepees, dotted here and there as far as the eye could see down the valley, to congregate around the renegade leader and his two captives.

"Stand back," Standing Buffalo warned. "Lest Too-Big-For-Horses send you to the Happy Hunting Ground before your time."

The awed faces of the children bore mute testimony to the stories that had already been told about the fierce white warrior.

The Indians bound Kincaid as securely as beef on a roasting spit to a stake at one side of the main circle of tepees, and he was left strictly alone. Reb, on the other hand, was a hub of unwelcome attention. She bunched her face to her chest and curled herself into a ball on the ground to avoid the blows aimed at her by the women and children.

Standing Buffalo planned to wait for the return of Spotted Tail, who'd gone to powwow with the Oglala Sioux in another village, before he began his test of Kincaid's merit. There was no reason, though, to delay their torture of the other captive.

"Let us make an example of this trapper," Standing Buffalo ordered curtly. "Strip him."

Someone produced a knife, and Reb's bonds were cut. Then the women and children tore at her, ripping her buckskin shirt away. Gales of crowing laughter and pointing fingers revealed the fact that Reb's sex had been discovered.

Kincaid's eyes closed, and he swallowed convulsively.

Reb blessed the Indian who'd cut the gag from her mouth, even while using her now freed tongue to revile the rest. She hugged her arms to her breasts to hide herself from view, welcoming the million pinpricks in her arms and shoulders that signaled the returning flow of blood to her numbed limbs. She felt herself being yanked to her feet. She couldn't help shivering at the threatening voices of the Indian braves, who pulled her hands away to reveal her femininity to all.

Standing Buffalo observed Reb with more than a little admiration. Of course, the woman had been gagged so she could not cry out, but he had been witness to her travail on the journey, and the bruises on her chest and ribs evidenced the hardship she had endured. When he remembered that this female had also been responsible for the initial escape of Too-Big-For-Horses, he acknowledged that her medicine must be very powerful. Such a woman would breed very strong, brave sons. He reached out to run a forefinger appraisingly down her cheek.

Even though Reb knew she was making a mistake, it was too good an opportunity to pass up. When Standing Buffalo's hand neared her mouth, she snapped her teeth down hard on the fleshy part of his palm, near his thumb. The renegade chief howled in surprise and tried to shake her off. She held on like a bulldog and had drawn blood before he freed his hand by cuffing her in the head with his other fist, knocking her unconscious.

"She be a wild she-cat all right!"

The Indians parted like the red sea for the burly mountain legend.

"Ah, girl, I hadn't expected to see so much of ye again so soon," Breck O'Hanlan chuckled to the unconscious form. "Too bad yer pa is me friend," the redheaded giant added, *tsk*ing his regret as he looked her up and down appreciatively. "But I guess since he is, I'd better see what I can do to get ye out of this."

"I have captured a very bold woman," Standing Buffalo boasted to the mountain man in the Sioux tongue. "She will make an excellent second wife when she is tamed." He gestured to several of the women and gave instructions that Reb be carried to his tepee.

Kincaid had watched Reb attack the Sioux and watched her be knocked out with equal parts of pride and terror. When he saw the redheaded behemoth appear, a portion of hope was added to the other two emotions. His eyes narrowed as he watched Reb be carried to an Indian tepee and Standing Buffalo follow her inside.

Breck calmly made his way to the trussed-up man, the cogs turning furiously in his mind for some way to save Reb from the fate Standing Buffalo had planned. So far no bright idea had emerged. Judging from the man's size, for there could not be many in the territory to match it, this must be the Yankee that Matt had told Breck he'd found with his daughter. How had the two gotten back together again? He was sure Matt had told him the lad had left for parts unknown. "Why be ye travelin' with the colleen?" he demanded sternly.

"She wouldn't stay home where she belonged!" Kincaid snapped.

Breck let go with a great belly laugh. "That fits me first impression of the girl," he agreed. "That there brawny buck be wantin' her to wife," Breck drawled teasingly.

"Standing Buffalo? Never!" Kincaid raged.

"Calm down, lad. Ye'll get yer chance to fight soon enough. What be the young miss to ye?"

"I love her."

Breck pondered this admission with great interest. Perhaps there was a way to rescue the she-cat and save the Yankee, too. "Be ye willin' to marry the colleen?"

"Marry her?" Kincaid said incredulously. "Here? Now?"

"Aye, unless ye be wantin' to give her to Standin' Buffalo for his second bride. He figures he'll breed hisself brave sons with a she-cat like her."

"You're not making it sound as though I have much choice," Kincaid said, giving the redheaded man a withering look.

"No, lad. No, I'm not. So then, you agree?"

"I agree."

"Good. Now, here's me plan."

After discussing with Kincaid what he would have to do, Breck made his way to Standing Buffalo's tepee. He entered and waited at the opening to the buffalo hide dwelling for an invitation to join Standing Buffalo, who was sitting cross-legged facing the doorway.

When Standing Buffalo welcomed him in, Breck was careful not to cross between his host and the fire burning in the center of the circular space. He seated himself on Standing Buffalo's left as an honored male guest. Breck asked in the Sioux tongue to be allowed to speak to Reb and received Standing Buffalo's permission.

Reb had been completely stripped and was lying naked on a huge buffalo robe. Her head was cushioned on a fox skin stuffed with grass. She'd been carefully washed, her ribs strapped with lengths of deerskin, and her cuts and scrapes bathed with a soothing salve. Her need for water had been met with the supply kept in the rawhide water pail in the tepee, but her stomach rumbled in hunger.

A kettle of buffalo meat stew sat warming on the fire, so any who were hungry should be able to fill their bellies at will, and the smell had set Reb's saliva to flowing. She stared up at the small opening that vented the smoke from the fire, feeling as impotent as an animal caught in a steel trap.

Reb didn't attempt to hide her nakedness when Breck squatted next to her to speak, and the mountain man couldn't restrain his wandering gaze. He brought his mind back to the business at hand when Standing Buffalo grunted in displeasure.

"How feel ye 'bout an Indian husband, girl? Standin' Buffalo has a mind to claim the spoils of war as his second wife."

"I'll choose my own husband," Reb spat, rising painfully to a sitting position and knocking away the woman's hand that tended her.

"That's the fightin' spirit!" Breck said. "I spoke to the man ye came here with, and he says he be willin' to take ye for wife hisself."

"That's very generous of Kincaid," Reb said wryly.

"Kincaid, is it then? Of the railroad Kincaids?" Breck asked in surprise.

"Yes, blast his hide," Reb snapped.

"What be ye doin' up here?"

"Kincaid plans to talk to Spotted Tail on behalf of the Union Pacific about a treaty with the Sioux."

"Mary, Joseph, and Moses," Breck said, crossing himself. "Did Spotted Tail know ye were comin' fer that purpose? From the looks of this reception, I'd guess not," Breck said, answering his own question. "All them rifles I brung from Denver," he muttered to himself, then said, "Well, let's get one problem settled before we look fer more."

"Ye must tell Standin' Buffalo that Kincaid has also asked ye to be his wife. Do it where his braves will hear yer words. I'll be there to translate. Say that ye'll take whichever man proves stronger in combat."

"That means Kincaid will have to fight!"

"Of course, girl. What did ye expect?"

Standing Buffalo had not been able to resist showing off his prize, and later the same afternoon had paraded Reb around the village dressed in a light, fawn-colored buckskin dress decorated with an intricate blue-and-white beaded design. Breck was on hand to translate when she made her announcement.

"I am already promised in marriage to this man,

Kincaid," Reb said, when they were within a few feet of the white captive.

"Too-Big-For-Horses is my prisoner," Standing Buffalo replied.

"You have stolen my woman, as you stole the gifts I brought to Spotted Tail," Kincaid accused.

A murmur of alarm ran through the assembled Indians when Breck translated this message, and the group of onlookers began to grow.

Standing Buffalo had frequently challenged Spotted Tail's authority, but had always submitted to the chief's supremacy rather than leave the tribe. He was unpleasantly surprised to discover he had apparently committed a blunder by claiming the pack-laden mules of this tall man.

If the gifts really were intended for Spotted Tail, he would have to give them up. He might be allowed to keep the black stallion, but that was little comfort, because it was death to ride the animal.

Now the woman contended she belonged to Too-Big-For-Horses as well. Standing Buffalo's temper flared. It looked as though he would come away empty-handed.

He was also confused. Hadn't the Great Spirit placed Too-Big-For-Horses in his power so that he could wreak vengeance for Smaller Bear's death? Could he have so totally misjudged the Great Spirit's intent?

Breck saw the furious indecision that plagued Standing Buffalo and used his knowledge of this particular Sioux, who shared his love of wagering, to take advantage of the situation.

"If the gifts belong to Too-Big-For-Horses until he presents them to Spotted Tail, then he can wager them if you have a contest."

"That is true," Standing Buffalo mused.

"Ye could insist the she-cat be part of the bargain," Breck continued.

"I could only honor as my husband a man who has proved himself strongest in combat," Reb said on cue.

Standing Buffalo crossed his arms. He could see all sorts of advantages to a competition with his captive. He believed the white man had been worn down sufficiently by the journey to be easily defeated, especially if the contest took place soon, before his powerful adversary had a chance to regain his strength. It would only enhance his image among his people to have conquered this mythical enemy in battle.

If the white warrior wagered the pack-laden mules, and Standing Buffalo won them from him, no demands for the gifts could be made by Spotted Tail. Perhaps, in defeating his enemy, he would also learn the secret to mastery of the great black devil stallion.

Most importantly, when he had vanquished Too-Big-For-Horses, he would be able to claim the white woman, who would bear him strong sons. Perhaps that was what the Great Spirit had intended all along, he told himself.

"I will fight Too-Big-For-Horses," Standing Buffalo said. "If he wins, he may have his freedom, the mules and packs, his black devil horse and the white woman, and there will be a tepee for his lodging until Spotted Tail returns.

"If I win, the woman and all else shall be mine, and Too-Big-For-Horses forfeits everything, including his life, in payment for the life of Smaller Bear."

The crowd shifted uncomfortably. The stakes were very high.

"I accept the challenge of Standing Buffalo," Kincaid said gravely.

"We will fight before the sun leaves the sky," Standing Buffalo said exultantly.

Reb waited alone in a tepee that was stuck away in a thicket, so hidden that one might pass within a few yards without seeing it. She'd been moved there while Standing Buffalo danced himself into a fighting frenzy. The thudding drums and the wailing howls of the Indians thrummed on her nerves. Her senses had been heightened to such a fever pitch that she nearly jumped out of her skin when she heard a noise at the opening to the tepee.

"Shhh. Do not be afraid," a soft, delicately accented voice called to her.

Reb watched a lovely Indian girl come forward into the flickering firelight. The tiny child couldn't have been more than ten or eleven, Reb guessed. She had long black hair held in place by a rawhide band at her brow that was plaited in two long braids.

"You speak English?" Reb asked surprised.

"Shh," the girl warned again. She came around the fire and sat next to Reb. "I am Morning Dove. The guard's back was turned, so I sneaked in. I was curious to see the white woman captive. You are not so beautiful," she said matter-of-factly.

"I've never thought so," Reb answered honestly.

"But two brave warriors will fight each other to see which will claim you as wife."

"That's true," Reb replied, her heart lurching with fear for Kincaid. "I wish it weren't."

"I do not like Standing Buffalo. He would not be a kind husband."

"Then perhaps you would do a favor for me," Reb asked. "Do you know whether they've given the white man any food or water?"

"I do not know. I do not think so, though. Everyone is afraid to go near him."

"Are you afraid?"

"Me?" The child's eyes were as big as saucers, and it dawned on Reb suddenly that they were as blue as

Dresden china. "I'm not afraid of anything," the girl said with false bravado.

Reb located a buffalo-calf's-head skin filled with water and handed it to the maiden. "Then I ask you, as a friend, to be sure the white man gets some water before he fights. Will you do that for me?"

The child looked troubled, then seemed to make up her mind. "I will have to find a way to be tall enough to reach his mouth, but I am smart. I will think of something," she said confidently.

The sprite left as quickly as she'd come.

Moments later, moving cautiously from between two closely pitched tepees, Morning Dove urged Satan closer to the post where the white warrior stood tied. The pounding of the drums and the frenzied dancing of Standing Buffalo kept the Indians entranced. They had given Kincaid a wide berth, and by stealth the Indian maiden maneuvered the horse so she was hidden in the heavy thicket behind the tall man.

Kincaid felt cool hands tip his stubbled chin up and then force his mouth open to dribble in some warm water. His mouth opened wider, and he craned his neck toward the refreshing liquid like a baby bird seeking worms from its mother.

"Not too fast," a girl's voice whispered.

Kincaid stopped drinking and turned his head in astonishment to peruse the tiny child sitting bareback astride his huge black stallion.

"Satan has never let anyone on his back except me," he said in amazement.

"Do not worry. All animals are my friends," the girl told him. "The white captive woman sent you this water."

"And you weren't afraid to bring it?"

"Only a little," she replied in a small voice. "Now I can see, though, that you are not a devil, only a man. For would a devil from the fires of hell really crave water?"

"Your logic is impeccable," Kincaid said, smiling through cracked lips at the precocious child.

"What is 'impeccable'?" she asked.

"It means 'without fault.'"

"That is not a good word to describe anything I do."

"Why not?"

"Because I am always causing trouble," she answered frankly.

"I can believe that," Kincaid said with a grin.

Morning Dove frowned at the white captive. Why did he smile at one who admitted to being a worrisome burden to her master?

"May I have some more water?" he asked.

The girl complied with his request, but broke off hastily when the drums stopped beating. "They will come now." The child ran a small, inquisitive hand timorously over Kincaid's muscular biceps, then up the taut, steely sinews that ran across his shoulders. "I do not think you will need it," she said at last, "but I wish you good luck."

In the awesome silence that descended on the Indian camp, Reb rose and paced the hazy, smoke-filled tepee. *Damn Breck O'Hanlan and his bright ideas,* she thought. Imagine two men butting heads over her like rutting stags! Reb shivered in fear and excitement.

Soon Kincaid and Standing Buffalo would fight for the right to claim her. No matter which man won, tonight she would be a wife.

20

With the two rivals standing before her in the center of the camp, Standing Buffalo dressed in breech-clout and Kincaid stripped down to his buckskin pants, Reb was almost willing to admit that she'd been wrong to come along on this journey. It was the first time since their capture that she'd taken stock of Kincaid's condition, and she was horrified by what she discovered.

His naked chest revealed the rainbow of bruises on his shoulder. She saw tight lines of pain around his mouth each time he took a hitching step. She had no way of knowing whether he'd received the water, but his lips looked parched, and his face showed the gaunt signs of hunger.

"You don't have to do this for my sake," Reb said.

"What would you suggest I do Rebel?" Kincaid replied grimly. "Walk away? Let him make you his wife?"

Reb remained mute, but her mind was working furiously. She just might prefer life as an Indian bride to marriage with Kincaid under these forced circumstances. Assuming he won.

The whole tribe, women and children included, surrounded the pair that was poised to fight. Some held torches in the event the twilight contest extended into darkness.

"The object of the competition is merely to prove yer superior prowess," Breck explained, working with both hands to try to loosen the muscles on Kincaid's scarred thigh. "In order to win, ye must force Standin' Buffalo to yield. There'll be a single knife and if ye can get possession of it, ye can use it to defend yerself, but not to kill. Understand?"

Reb tied one end of a six-foot rawhide thong to Standing Buffalo's left wrist as Breck instructed her to, and then knotted the other end of the thong around Kincaid's wrist. A single knife had been stuck in the ground about ten feet behind the two combatants.

When Reb stepped back, the contest would begin. The Sioux yelped their encouragement to Standing Buffalo, who'd been a participant in many such contests in the past, and had always come away the winner.

As he watched his opponent warily, Kincaid massaged the muscle of his leg. It was still stiff enough to hamper his mobility. His enforced three-day fast had left him lightheaded, and he knew his reactions

would be slow. He played for time, giving his shriek-
ing joints and sinews a chance to loosen and his
adrenaline a chance to flow.

When Standing Buffalo leaned all of his weight
against the thong and then let go, Kincaid seemed to
lose his balance, and he stumbled backward to the
ground.

Reb kept her features absolutely blank, even
though her heart had leaped to her throat.

Standing Buffalo grabbed the knife from the
ground and grinned lecherously as he strode toward
Kincaid's inert form. The fight was going to be over
almost before it had begun. He stepped up confidently to claim his victory and paid for his careless-
ness when Kincaid jerked his feet out from under
him.

"Let's see how you fare when your enemy's hands
aren't tied," Kincaid muttered. He barreled his right
fist into the stocky Indian's gut.

Standing Buffalo stabbed reflexively with the knife
when Kincaid hit him and was pleased to see the gash
left by the blade.

Reb watched the line of red grow and begin to drip
freely down Kincaid's iron-thewed arm. She tried to
convince herself that Kincaid would have had to fight
even if she hadn't come along, but she knew she was
only making excuses to assuage her conscience.

After measuring the mettle of the man, Breck had

wagered heavily on the Yankee to win this battle against the many braves who believed the extensive scar on Kincaid's thigh would hold him back. The legendary Irishman had been mildly irritated when Kincaid seemed to fall like a green farm boy for Standing Buffalo's first trick, then gloated when he saw the tables turned.

Breck vigilantly watched the two strong men exchange blows for a few minutes. For a thickset man, Standing Buffalo was amazingly agile. But Breck decided that Kincaid's devastating right fist was doing at least as much damage as the Indian's slashing knife.

Kincaid could tell Standing Bill was tiring, and took a chance he wouldn't otherwise have taken. He kicked out suddenly with his unreliable scarred leg, disarming the Sioux renegade. Kincaid had no time to enjoy the astonishment on Standing Buffalo's face. He merely took advantage of his longer reach to catch the Sioux in a stranglehold around the neck. His bulging muscles strained with the effort of holding the squat, struggling Indian, whose short arms couldn't reach Kincaid.

"Yield," Kincaid commanded.

With a chortling laugh at all the furs he was going to win, Breck translated Kincaid's demand.

"I—will—not—yield," Standing Buffalo rasped. He could see all the prizes and glory he had possessed when he had so proudly ridden into camp earlier in the day flowing through his fingers like so much sand. Desperate, he kicked backward with his right heel, catching Kincaid square in the middle of his old wound.

Kincaid yelled out loud and saw stars. Before the renegade could repeat the very effective attack, Kincaid tightened his grasp, cutting off the Indian's supply of air until the limp body of the Sioux marked his capitulation.

Kincaid stepped over Standing Buffalo's still body. Taking Reb's hand possessively in his own, he turned to face the deathly quiet crowd of awed Indians, who observed in fear and dread the invincible white warrior who had defeated their champion.

"I have defeated Standing Buffalo and have won my right to this woman. I claim her as my wife." Kincaid turned a stony visage to Reb and waited.

She looked to Breck, and he nodded insistently.

"I accept this man as my husband," she said.

"I will stay in the village of Spotted Tail and await his return. I offer my hand in friendship to any who will take it," Kincaid said.

Such an unprecedented turn of events took the Sioux aback, and Breck's translation was greeted with utter silence. "I think they be afeard of ye, lad," Breck said.

"I am not afraid."

The crowd parted, and Morning Dove walked

slowly and surely forward. When the tiny girl stood before the tall man, she held out her hand to him. He clasped it firmly. "Thank you," he whispered gratefully.

"See. He will not eat you," Morning Dove called with a burbling laugh to the dumbstruck Brulés who surrounded them. She shot Kincaid an impish grin.

Several of the older braves slowly approached, offering their friendship to Kincaid. Among those who sought him out was the ugly brave who had so viciously mistreated Reb. Apparently the brave was willing to let bygones be bygones.

Kincaid hadn't considered that possibility, and he hesitated before offering his hand to the Sioux.

Breck translated as the Indian spoke.

"A woman so brave must bring honor to your lodge. May she give you many fine sons."

When Kincaid embraced the grotesque, softspoken man warmly in friendship, so many others rushed to follow suit that Breck finally had to shout at them to stand back.

When she was certain that Kincaid's welcome was secure, Morning Dove joined Standing Buffalo's wife in reviving the fallen braggart. Standing Buffalo awoke to find Kincaid being touted as friend by all. He took his ill temper out on the nearest object, slapping Morning Dove vindictively.

Kincaid heard the distinctive sound and turned to

locate the source. He discovered Morning Dove on the ground next to the sullen Indian.

"Why do you mistreat this child?" Kincaid asked menacingly.

"I need no excuse to punish this girl," Standing Buffalo said. "She belongs to me."

Kincaid waited for Breck to translate, then said, "Come here, girl."

Morning Dove looked fearfully from Kincaid to Standing Buffalo and back again, but didn't move.

"Ye can't just take the girl," Breck protested.

"Then I'll make a wager for her," Kincaid said, smiling cold-bloodedly. "Tell Standing Buffalo that I dare him to ride Satan. If he can stay atop the horse, he wins all the mules and the packs. If he can't, I get the girl."

Breck translated the challenge.

A cold sweat broke out on Standing Buffalo's forehead. He had seen the bloody pulp the devil horse had made of the foolish brave who had attempted to ride him. He was not stupid. He was certain the white warrior had the same fate in mind for him. If he refused the challenge, it would mean a loss of face. Yet what choice did he have? The white man had tricked him, and he saw only one way out.

"It is not necessary for us to make such a wager. If you want her so badly, I will make a gift of the girl to you."

Kincaid didn't let his triumph show, but the sprite was not so discreet.

"You are a coward, Standing Buffalo," she taunted as she skipped over to Kincaid.

Standing Buffalo's fist caught the girl behind the ear, and she went flying.

Kincaid engulfed Standing Buffalo's fist in his own and stepped close to the squat Sioux.

"Breck, come here. I want you to translate this so there's no mistake," Kincaid said with a feral growl. "Tell him that if he ever so much as lays a finger on Rebel or that girl, either one, ever again, I'll kill him."

Kincaid waited until Standing Buffalo's slitted eyes revealed he'd gotten the message, then turned his back contemptuously on the defeated bully. He gathered Reb and the girl and allowed the excitedly chattering tribe to escort them through the stand of timber along the creek to the secluded tepee where Reb had waited before the fight.

Kincaid held the flapped doorway decorated with porcupine-quill designs open for Reb and the girl to enter, then followed them in himself, shutting the village out behind them.

He walked past Reb and the tiny girl, then turned around to the two expectant faces. Kincaid let the fury he'd been hiding show in his flashing eyes, his rigid jaw, and his aggressive spread-legged stance. He wanted to grab Reb and shake her and tell her what a fool she'd been to come along, so he'd been forced to marry her.

He was married to Reb!

The realization hit him in the stomach like a vicious punch, and he wavered slightly on his feet. All of his swearing and promises had come to nothing in the end. He determined to get her the hell out of this place as quickly as possible.

Yet hadn't Reb done everything she'd said she could do in the wilderness? Hadn't she stayed alive in the most brutal circumstances imaginable? He studied the patchwork of scratches on the beloved face and felt a surge of pride in what she'd accomplished.

She'd done even more. Though a captive herself, had she not thought of his agony of thirst and sent the girl to bring him lifesaving water?

Kincaid couldn't deny he wanted Reb physically. Just thinking about caressing her rounded breasts, skimming his hands down her slim hips and thighs, touching her in places where he knew no man had been before him, awakened his body so that a hardened ridge was visible along the buckskin leggings.

Having let his thoughts get so far out of hand, his eyes slipped to the small child who stood between his desires and his action. His sense of humor rescued him from irritability. It was going to be a very crowded honeymoon, he thought wryly.

The fierceness of Kincaid's glower when he'd

entered the tepee had rocked Reb's confidence. What if, in retaliation for the forced marriage, he wouldn't touch her? Watching him waver, she wanted to reach out to him, to hold him and love him. But she stood her ground warily, waiting.

She would not beg him to love her. She had her pride. Then she detected the avid gaze that raked her body and the rising need that followed it, and she knew a fear greater than the first. What if he did take her, and there was no love in his touch? She couldn't help shuddering.

Kincaid perceived Reb's shudder and believed she'd caught a chill from the night air. His sexual desire vanished with the advent of his concern. "Are you all right?" he asked.

When Reb nodded slowly, he crossed to put his arm around her shoulders. But her trembling increased.

"Hand me that pail of water near your feet," he said to Morning Dove.

The girl fetched the rawhide pail, and Kincaid held it while Reb drank, then drank the rest himself. Then he said to the girl, "We'll need more water to drink and some food, a broth, nothing solid. Can you take care of that?"

Anxious to be of help to her savior, Morning Dove grabbed another pail and raced from the tepee to get more water and to procure the herbs she would need for the broth.

When she'd gone, Kincaid turned again to Reb.

He suddenly felt a desperate need to claim her body, to make her totally his, but was horrified that he could even consider such a thing when she wasn't well. Self-consciously, he dropped his arm and stepped back, breathing deeply to stem his rising desire.

"I'm glad you're safe," he said.

I love you, Rebel, he thought, searching her eyes to see if she felt the same way.

"You're hurt. Let me see to your cuts," Reb replied.

I love you, Kincaid, she thought, avoiding his glance, afraid that the love she felt wouldn't be mirrored there. She concentrated instead on the blood, mixed with dirt and sweat, that streamed from a dozen places on Kincaid's body.

"There's a slash on my side that may need stitches," he said. "But the rest don't seem to be serious."

Reb's heart was in her eyes when she finally looked up sideways under her long, inky lashes and said, "Go lie down over there on the buffalo robe, and I'll take a look."

Relieved at having found in her adoring gaze the love for which he'd searched, Kincaid obeyed, suddenly enervated in the aftermath of the forced march without food or water and the fight with Standing Buffalo. After he lay down, he closed his eyes.

"Kincaid," Reb cried anxiously, kneeling down beside him.

His eyelashes fluttered open.

"Oh," she said sheepishly. "I was afraid you were hurt worse than you said and were hiding it from me."

"I'm only very tired, love," he said tenderly.

Reb's heart skipped a beat at the endearment, but her voice was steady when she urged, "Then rest. I'll take care of you."

Kincaid closed his eyes again, thinking, as he allowed sleep to give surcease to his pain, how pleasant it was to be married to a woman so capable and caring.

By the time Reb sat down next to Kincaid with the rest of the pail of water and a cloth to wash him, his regular breathing signaled that he was asleep. The blood had dried on the cut he'd asked her to check, and she decided, after looking closely at it, that it didn't require stitching.

When she'd removed as many of the signs of the previous days' hardship from his body as would come off with a cloth and water, Reb laid her head down next to Kincaid's on the buffalo skin for just a moment to wait for the return of Morning Dove.

When the Indian girl entered the tepee, she found the couple sleeping contentedly. Knowing that they would both be hungry and thirsty when they awoke, she continued her preparations for the meal.

Several hours later Kincaid tried to turn on his side and rolled onto Reb.

"No more! No more!" Reb cried, waking Kincaid.

"Wake up, love. You're dreaming. It's all over."

Reb awoke to find Kincaid's concerned gray eyes watching her anxiously.

"I thought I was tied up again, and that someone was kicking me," she said, letting the tears fall freely.

"It's over now, Rebel. You're safe. We're together, and I'll keep you safe from now on," he vowed, damning again the cruelty of Standing Buffalo's band of renegades.

"I'll try to stay out of trouble, Kincaid," Reb promised, hiccupping as she tried to halt the tears.

"I don't know if that's humanly possible for you," he said with a sigh. "But yes, by all means, Reb, do try."

He kissed the tears from her eyelids, then followed the wet paths down her cheeks to her mouth. He let his hands roam down her silhouette, curving in at the waist and out again at the hips. Then he pulled the fringed buckskin skirt up to expose Reb's long legs to his exploring touch.

She cried out once, when even the weight of his hand was too much for a bruised area on her hip, and he rose to gently soothe the tender spot with a kiss.

A giggle from the other side of the room made them both sit up in alarm.

"I have water and food for you," Morning Dove said. "Unless you have other needs to attend to first," the girl added, too knowingly for a child her age.

Reb was surprised and then amused to see Kincaid blush.

He frowned at Reb's smirk and cleared his throat, as though to erase the uncomfortable knowledge that their prior amorous activity had been observed by the child.

"We'll eat now," he said gruffly.

It was amazing how refreshed they both felt after the rest. They consumed as much water as they could drink and as much broth as they could swallow.

"I feel as stuffed as a chick with caterpillars," Kincaid said when he set his empty bowl down. "Thank you for the delicious meal," he said, praising Morning Dove.

"You never complimented by broth," Reb said archly.

"I think I'll give my leg some exercise. Would you like to come with me?" he asked, ignoring the jibe.

"I'd love to," Reb and Morning Dove both answered together.

For a child who'd seemed all-knowing half an hour ago, Morning Dove now appeared totally unaware of any desire on the part of the newlywed couple to be alone. It was insane for Reb to be jealous of a ten-year-old girl, but she wasn't sure what other term accurately described her feelings.

Kincaid gave Reb a helpless shrug when Morning Dove's back was turned and mouthed the word, "Later."

Reb had to be satisfied with that promise, as the three stepped from the tepee for a stroll by moonlight through the quiet Indian village. Morning Dove turned out to be pleasant company, acting as a guide and explaining the unusual sights, such as the strips of buffalo meat hung up to dry high out of the village dogs' reach on long poles held up by wooden scaffolds.

They reached the stream that ran through the village and sat down on the bank to skip stones into the moonlit water.

"How did you learn to speak English?" Reb asked the girl.

"My mother taught me." At Reb's inquiring gaze, Morning Dove explained. "I have not always belonged to Standing Buffalo. My mother is the wife of an Oglala Sioux. My father's name is Silent Water," she said proudly.

"Does your mother also have blue eyes?" Reb asked.

"Oh, yes," Morning Dove agreed. "And yellow hair."

Reb and Kincaid each acknowledged to the other the significance of that statement. Morning Dove was at least half white.

"My father treats my mother well," the girl continued. "Nor did he beat me. Unless I was bad and deserved it," she added as an afterthought.

"Last summer Standing Buffalo visited our village. He saw me playing and asked my father if he could have me as his wife when I came of age. My mother begged Silent Water not to consent to such a thing when I was so young, to wait at least until I was grown. My father agreed."

"But Standing Buffalo was cunning. He played a gambling game with Silent Water until my father had nothing left to wager. Standing Buffalo urged him to wager more, and when my father did, he lost. Then he had nothing left to pay with except me. Silent Water was ashamed of what he had done, but there was nothing he could do.

"To save my father's honor, I was forced to come to the lodge of Standing Buffalo. Now I belong to you," she said to Kincaid. "Does that mean when it is time you will take me as wife?"

Kincaid turned to Reb in consternation before he spun the small girl to face him, took her shoulders in his hands, and spoke in as paternal a voice as he could muster.

"It is the custom of my people to take only one

wife. I have chosen my woman." Kincaid saw the crestfallen posture of the child and looked to Reb for some suggestion as to what he should say next.

Reb put her hand on the girl's shoulder comfortingly. "I have several brothers," she offered, "who will also be your brothers and who will protect you until the time comes for you to choose your mate."

"I too will always be your protector should you ever need my help," Kincaid assured her.

With the fickleness of youth, Morning Dove accepted the lost opportunity to have Kincaid as her spouse, but asked, "Will you still let me ride your horse if I am not your wife?"

Kincaid laughed out loud in relief. "Of course. If you will ask permission first. And if you promise to be careful!"

"I will go and see him now and tell him what good friends we will be," the girl said as she skipped away.

"She's a delightful child," Reb said when Morning Dove had gone.

"But too much for me to handle," Kincaid said. "Especially since I already have my hands full." He let his actions suit his words, unlacing the buckskin dress and cupping Reb's breasts gently in his palms. He let his hands drift lower and encountered the strapping that bound Reb's ribs.

"Are any broken?"

"Just cracked, I think."

"You were very brave," he said solemnly. It was as close as he could come to admitting that maybe Reb could take care of herself in the wilderness.

"I didn't want to die," she answered simply. She ran her fingers through his wavy locks and caressed his cheek with the back of her hand. "I love you, Kincaid," she said.

Blue's words went caroming through her mind. *Enough to change? Enough to be more like what he wants you to be?*

"I'll try to be the kind of wife you want," she whispered. She saw the acceptance of her offer in Kincaid's eyes as he moved his lips to capture hers. Reb gasped when Kincaid ran his thumbs across her nipples, and shivered when he put his lips to the pulse point behind her ear.

They both groaned when they heard Morning Dove's approaching footsteps.

"Come quickly," she called. "Spotted Tail has returned!"

21

❦

Breck had made a good deal when he purchased the new-model Sharp rifles and ammunition that he'd been paid by the Denver merchants to bring to the Sioux. Those "peace-loving" businessmen hoped to help the Indians to undermine the Union Pacific's attempts at a northern route.

Breck had just traded his own Henry rifle to Standing Buffalo and kept the last of the batch of new Sharps for himself. He and Standing Buffalo could hear the commotion start at the edge of camp and work its way toward the center. They stepped outside at the same moment Spotted Tail rode past.

When Breck saw who rode beside the Indian chief, he crossed himself and said, "Mary, Joseph, and Moses. It's time fer me to take a little trip." He turned to make a hasty exit, but was stopped by a harsh voice.

"Breck O'Hanlan, you conniving Irishman! Where are they?"

"Now Matt, don't be blamin' me fer any of this. I only did what I could to help."

"Where are they?" he roared.

"Honeymoonin'!" Breck answered, with a roguish grin.

Matt turned to Blue, who rode beside him. "See the result of your meddling?"

"It sounds to me as though everything turned out all right," Blue said.

"I think it's great," Adam said, beaming his approval.

Blue, Matt, and Adam had reached the Indian village, discovered that both Spotted Tail and Standing Buffalo were gone, and located the Brulé chief with the Oglala, all in the time it had taken Reb and Kincaid to make their forced march back to the village. Matt had spent the past few days with his heart in his throat. No one knew exactly where Standing Buffalo was, and O'Hanlan's flip answer hadn't done much to assuage his fear.

At that moment, the couple in question appeared. Reb looked from one to the other of the two men who had both been her father. It was an awkward moment. She nodded in greeting to Matt, then to Blue.

At last she flashed them both a grin and quipped, "It's about time you showed up. Two fathers, and neither one here to give away the bride!"

Both men were still too furious with each other to realize that Reb had made her own peace with the fact they both claimed fatherhood.

Matt eyed the patchwork of scabs on Reb's face and the red welt that the thong had left on her neck. Blue made the same survey, and the two eyeballed each other with enmity.

It didn't take much imagination to surmise why Reb and Kincaid hadn't reached the camp before Blue and Matt. The marks on Reb's face and neck spoke for themselves. Breck's presence helped explain why the couple were no longer held captive. Each man blamed the other for the harm that had come to Reb.

Matt thought that Blue had no business taking Reb along on such a dangerous journey in the first place.

Blue thought that if Matt hadn't come along, he would have been with the couple, and they would have avoided capture.

Both men glared at each other until Spotted Tail interrupted the unspoken hostilities.

"I am Spotted Tail," the Indian announced to Kincaid in English. "You wish to speak with the Council?"

"Yes. I've brought gifts on behalf of a group of men who want to build an iron road for a great Iron Horse on a ribbon of land south of here. We want to do this peacefully, with Spotted Tail's help."

"My friend Blue has spoken to me of your desire. It is late. Let us rest. Tomorrow we will speak more."

Blue accepted an invitation to enjoy Spotted Tail's hospitality, and Matt and Adam accepted a similar invitation from Breck, leaving Reb and Kincaid alone—except for Morning Dove, who volunteered to make one last trip to the stream for water.

Standing Buffalo watched the departing white men with gritted teeth. He should have killed Too-Big-For-Horses when he had the chance. Spotted Tail was always too ready to believe the white man when he offered gifts and promised peace.

If the white warrior convinced the Brulé chief to sign a treaty, in the end they would only be cheated again, just as he had been denied his vengeance against Too-Big-For-Horses. He would not be robbed by the white man any longer.

Standing Buffalo formulated a very simple plan. He would take the white woman and deal with the tall warrior when he came to get her back. But how could he get the woman away from Too-Big-For-Horses?

Just then, Morning Dove passed him on her way to the stream.

Standing Buffalo stepped boldly into the path of the Indian girl.

"What do you want of me?" she asked, confident that the Indian would not touch her while she was under the protection of Too-Big-For-Horses, but nonetheless leaning away from him cautiously.

"Tell Too-Big-For-Horses that, since he has betrayed the Sioux with his talk of a treaty with the white man, I take back my gift and will touch you as I please."

With that, Standing Buffalo slapped Morning Dove, knocking her down so that one of the sharp stones along the bank cut her cheek. He turned and left, smiling triumphantly as he assessed the certain success of his plan.

Morning Dove picked herself up and filled the water pail before she returned to the tepee. She'd tried to staunch the flow of blood on her face, but, when she entered the tepee, Kincaid noticed immediately that she'd been hurt.

"What happened?" He took her face in his hand, turning it into the firelight to see the cut.

"Standing Buffalo . . ."

"Did he do this to you?" Kincaid raged.

"Wait!" Morning Dove said. "I do not want to make trouble. He said he is taking back his gift. I must go back to him."

"You stay right here. I'll settle this with Standing Buffalo once and for all," Kincaid said coldly. "Reb, you take care of Morning Dove. And stay out of trouble!"

Reb caught her lower lip in her teeth to avoid hurling a childish retort. She'd made up her mind to try to be more like Kincaid wanted her to be. If he said stay, she would stay. At least, for a little while.

Kincaid had been gone only a moment when Standing Buffalo stepped inside the tepee. He reached for the girl close to the door and put a knife to her throat.

"Tell the white woman that I will kill you if she makes a sound."

As soon as Reb heard the first guttural word, she reached for the knife she'd been using by the fire and turned with it in her hand, ready to attack. The sight of Standing Buffalo with his blade pricking the skin on Morning Dove's neck brought her up short.

"He says he will kill me if you make a noise," the terrified child said.

There was more guttural barking from the squat Sioux, and the tiny girl translated. "He says to drop your knife and come with him quietly. He says there will not be a second chance to obey."

The Indian's eyes gleamed wickedly as he pressed the point a little deeper into Morning Dove's flesh. Reb dropped her knife as though it had caught fire.

"Tell him I will do as he asks."

Standing Buffalo gestured for Reb to go ahead of him and followed with Morning Dove. His plan was working perfectly. He would have the white woman as bait and the girl to serve his needs while he waited for Too-Big-For-Horses to come meet his fate.

Standing Buffalo escorted the two women out of the village on foot to a spot where he'd hidden two horses. He pulled Morning Dove up in front of him while indicating that Reb should mount the other horse.

Reb had felt helpless tied and gagged, but it was nothing to her feeling of powerlessness now. Nothing kept her from speaking, nothing kept her from saving herself, except the certainty that if she made one wrong move, Standing Buffalo would kill the small girl.

Standing Buffalo took the lead on Reb's horse and headed for the craggy mountain bluff closest to the village. He did nothing to soften the imprint left by the horses' hooves on the mossy rocks. He didn't need to hide his trail, for he wanted the white warrior to be able to find him.

Meanwhile, Kincaid had searched the entire Indian village for Standing Buffalo. When he couldn't locate him, he decided that the cowardly Sioux must have realized he would come after him, and had left the village.

As Kincaid walked back to the tepee, he was wondering how he could get enough privacy with Reb to have a proper honeymoon without hurting Morning Dove's feelings. By the time he arrived back at the tepee, he'd made up his mind that he didn't care about the child's feelings.

He lifted the decorated tent flap and entered. His mouth was open to speak, but no words came out.

Nothing inside was disturbed. All was as he had left it. Reb's knife lay on the cutting stone beside the kettle slung over the fire. But the tent was empty. After he'd told them both to stay put! Kincaid rued the day he'd fallen in love with his hellcat in buckskins.

"All right, Rebel," he gritted out through clenched teeth. "Where are you?"

Standing Buffalo stopped the horses when they reached a small stone cave set into the side of the mountain.

"Get off your horse," he ordered Reb. Morning Dove translated.

"You, girl, take this rope and tie her hands," Standing Buffalo said to Morning Dove. He replaced his knife in its sheath, picked up the Henry rifle he'd just bought from Breck, hefted it, and then cocked it.

Morning Dove worked quickly. When she'd finished, Standing Buffalo checked the knots. "Go inside," he ordered. He turned to watch Reb, and at that moment Morning Dove shoved him as hard as she could and ran.

The stocky Indian recovered his balance quickly and swung the rifle up to sight on the fleeing girl.

Just as he pulled the trigger, Reb flung herself into him, knocking him to the ground, where their momentum rolled them over together several times.

Reb gasped at the pain that assaulted her already bruised and battered body but strained her shoulders up off the ground to see if Morning Dove had escaped safely.

Nothing moved in the darkness.

"She is dead!" Standing Buffalo said maliciously. "I saw her fall. You will pay for your stupid action," he threatened, "after I kill Too-Big-For-Horses."

He pulled Reb up and dragged her into the cave after him.

⸎

Kincaid had waited a half hour for Reb and Morning Dove to return and then decided that he would have no peace of mind until he knew what they were doing.

The etiquette that forced him to wait for permission to enter Spotted Tail's tepee tried Kincaid's patience. He could see Spotted Tail, with Blue on his left, seated before the fire, talking. Exiled from the tepee, but guarding the doorway, Trapper thumped his tail on the ground in welcome to Kincaid.

When Kincaid finally entered, Spotted Tail was coldly polite.

"I have said I will discuss the treaty tomorrow. What brings you here?"

Kincaid was furious with Reb for the embarrassing position in which he found himself. "I'm looking for my wife," he said in chagrin. "I thought she might have come here to see Blue."

"I haven't seen her," Blue answered with an amused smile. "Perhaps she went to visit Matt and Adam."

Kincaid remembered what Reb had said about her brothers being Morning Dove's brothers, too, and thought that she'd probably had some brilliant idea of getting Morning Dove and Adam together tonight. He would kill her when he found her.

"You're probably right," he answered ruefully. "I'll check there. I'm sorry to have broken your peace," he said to Spotted Tail.

"She is a new wife," Spotted Tail said sympathetically. "Be patient and make your wishes known to her, and she will learn to please you."

Kincaid only wished it were that easy. Feeling more foolish with every step he took, the angry newlywed made his way to Breck's lodging. The mountain man had set up a tent, which was really no more than a piece of hide to keep the sun off during the day. There were no sides to the shelter, and Kincaid could see as he neared that Reb and Morning Dove weren't there. Where the hell were they? he thought in exasperation.

When Kincaid approached the three men, it was

anxiety, not embarrassment, that beset him. "Have you seen Reb?"

"Lost her already, have ye, lad?" Breck said with a chuckle.

"Standing Buffalo attacked Morning Dove, so I went looking for him to make good my promise. I never found him, but when I got back to the tepee, Reb and Morning Dove were gone. I thought they might have come here."

"We haven't seen them," Adam said.

All four men heard the distant echo of a single shot, and each one knew with a chill of certainty that Standing Buffalo had Reb and Morning Dove. Each man searched the others' faces for the answer to the same question. Which one had been shot?

"Rebel," Kincaid whispered. The name floated on the night air, drifting toward the craggy bluffs from which the bullet's echo had come.

"Ye won't be able to see yer way to follow him tonight. Even if ye do find the trail, he'll be waitin' fer ye somewhere in the dark," Breck warned.

"We have to try," Adam said.

Kincaid put his hand on Adam's shoulder. "I agree. I'll get Satan."

"It's yer funeral," Breck said with a shrug. "Ye'll be needin' a weapon. Here's me good new Sharps rifle." He offered Kincaid the spanking new gun. "It's loaded and ready to go. I'll join ye at daybreak."

"I'll get Blue. We'll need all the help we can get," Matt said.

Matt and Blue joined Kincaid and Adam, and the four men headed toward the closest mountain, each using all his skill to search the ground for signs that would tell them which way Standing Buffalo had gone.

It was Blue who first saw the hoofprints that let them know they were on the right track. They followed the trail for another half hour before Matt raised his hand for all to be still. Then they all heard the noise. Something was coming through the undergrowth.

The men dismounted and spread out behind whatever cover they could find to await whoever was proceeding so hurriedly and noisily toward them. The tension mounted as the crash of broken branches drew closer.

Adam saw the black braided hair and buckskin shirt and attacked, bowling over and subduing his struggling victim with a minimum of effort. That achievement had put his hands in contact with two mounds on his opponent's chest.

"It's a girl!" he said in amazement. "And she's hurt," he added when his hand came away from the girl's arm sticky with blood.

"Morning Dove?" Kincaid knelt beside the girl, who still lay between Adam's knees.

"Yes," the girl cried in relief.

"How badly are you hurt?"

"Only shot a little," she answered Kincaid. "Standing Buffalo has taken your woman prisoner. They are at the cave a little way up the mountain. He means to kill you. And her, too, I think. I will take you there," she said, trying to get up. She didn't have much success because Adam hadn't moved from his position straddling her.

Kincaid put his hand on her shoulder and said, "You've done enough. We'll do the rest. Adam, will you take Morning Dove back to the village? Adam?"

Adam was entranced by the large, luminous eyes revealed by the moonlight. He hitched his knee over the girl so he knelt to one side, then lifted her easily into his arms. She was so tiny!

"I can walk," Morning Dove murmured. Caught by Adam's intense gaze, she held her breath, waiting for him to speak.

Adam stood up, then shook his head as though to clear it. He handed Morning Dove to Kincaid. "Hold her until I mount up, then hand her up to me."

When Adam had settled in the saddle, Kincaid passed the girl up into the bewildered man's arms. Adam cradled the girl as though she were a small child—and indeed, he thought, she wasn't much larger.

"Good luck," he said to the other three men as

they all mounted up. "I'll see you back in the village."

Kincaid heaved a sigh of relief that Reb hadn't been shot. As he thought back on Morning Dove's words, though, a shiver ran down his spine. The one thing that had kept him sane was the belief that Standing Buffalo didn't want to kill Reb, that he wanted her for himself.

Morning Dove had suggested that the Indian wanted to kill them both. He considered calling Adam back to question the girl further, but realized he would have his answers soon enough. Arguing voices brought his attention back to the immediate situation.

"You had no business letting Reb come on this trip," Matt railed at Blue. "She would have been safe at home now, if it hadn't been for you."

"You never learn, do you?" Blue countered. "You don't understand Reb any better than you did Rachel."

"Don't you dare bring Rachel's name into this!" Matt said savagely. "I should have killed you six years ago, and I would have, too, if you weren't Reb's father."

Kincaid digested that juicy tidbit of information and felt his stomach roll with the punch of it. So that's what Blue had told Reb that she hadn't been able to talk about. No wonder the concerned faces of Reb and Blue that had greeted him when he'd opened his eyes in Blue's cabin had borne such identical features. Blue was Reb's natural father!

"If Spotted Tail hadn't come along and found me where you left me, I would have been dead," Blue retorted. "Matt, you were my friend. I didn't mean to fall in love with Rachel, it just happened. I'm sorry you were hurt. I've been sorry for a long time. But I have no regrets about Reb. I love her like a daughter.

"She's as wild and as free as the mountains she was raised in. Believe me when I say you can't tie her down. You have to learn to swallow your fear and love her as she is."

The speech could have been aimed at the tall Yankee, and perhaps it was. But neither Matt nor Kincaid had a chance to reply; at that moment the silence was shattered by an otherworldly scream.

22

For some reason, Standing Buffalo hadn't tied Reb's feet or gagged her. He'd merely gestured to Reb to sit in a back corner of the dark cave. She would have obeyed the rifle in his hands no matter the condition of the cave floor, but she was glad to discover, that the ground was dry, and it didn't crunch with little bugs or scurry with little animals.

Standing Buffalo lit a fire with flint and tinder he'd brought in his rawhide bag-for-all-possible-things, and the cave began to reflect the cheery light. The Indian continued talking to himself in his guttural tongue, eyeing Reb every once in a while. He seemed to be working himself up to something, and judging by the lascivious leers that were frequently visited upon her, Reb could make a pretty good guess of the particular activity he had in mind.

Reb had thought for a while now that, if there were just some distraction, she might be able to get past Standing Buffalo and run for safety. She'd decided to create her own diversion when she heard the voices arguing in English and knew that help was on its way. Unfortunately, Standing Buffalo heard them, too, and walked to the front of the cave to look out.

Reb cursed the stupidity of the lumpkins who would take the time and trouble to rescue her and then botch it by letting their presence be known in such a clumsy way. Well, as long as they were close enough for her to hear them, the reverse was also true.

Reb let go with an earsplitting shriek and charged Standing Buffalo like a billy goat. Caught unawares, the Indian was sent twirling by Reb's butting shove. She was in the open air in moments and running.

"I'm here!" Reb yelled at the top of her lungs. "Help me!"

The three men urged their horses dangerously fast in the darkness toward Reb's voice.

"I see her!" Matt yelled. Just then, he saw Standing Buffalo's silhouette in the firelight, taking aim on Reb.

At the instant Standing Buffalo fired, Reb tripped and fell.

"She's down!" Matt threw himself off his horse and ran to Reb, who rose unsteadily.

"I just fell," she mumbled breathlessly. "I'm not hurt."

Matt pulled her into his arms and rocked her back and forth as tears of relief streamed down his face.

Seeing that Reb was with Matt, Kincaid let Satan thunder on toward the Sioux renegade. He shouldered the Sharps rifle Breck had given him, but when he tried to fire the gun, it jammed.

Standing Buffalo saw Too-Big-For-Horses on his devil steed barreling toward him and leveled his gun at the big man's heart. Then he thought how much better his revenge if the white man should be robbed first of that which was dear to him.

Kincaid watched in horror as the Indian turned the gun on Reb.

"No! Rebel," he screamed. He yanked hard to turn the black stallion into the path of the Sioux's fire, knowing as he did that there was no way he could get there in time. His eyes were riveted on Reb, expecting to see a repetition of the tragedy he'd experienced once before.

Both Matt and Blue heard Kincaid's warning yell, but it was Blue who acted first. He grasped Reb so she was sandwiched between the two men who'd raised her and loved her and both been her father.

Kincaid jerked when he saw Blue take the bullet that was intended for Reb, then cling to his daughter, guarding her from further harm.

Standing Buffalo screeched his rage at Blue's interference and pumped two more shots into the white man. Out of the corner of his eye, the enraged Indian perceived a streak of gray fur. He wheeled and barely had time to fire his gun before Trapper crashed into him with a yelp of pain.

The weight of the dying animal bowled the Sioux over, and the Henry clattered away across the stony ground out of his reach. Standing Buffalo threw off the carcass just as Kincaid launched himself from Satan's back.

The two enemies rolled from the force of Kincaid's thrust, but it was Standing Buffalo who came out on top, his knife poised to kill the white devil who had so plagued him. A ghoulish leer was frozen on the Sioux's face as he anticipated his moment of glory.

Standing Buffalo had underestimated the fury of his adversary. It was the last mistake he ever made.

Kincaid grabbed Standing Buffalo's wrists, and the muscles of the two men bulged with the strain as Kincaid slowly but surely turned the blade up to the savage's heart and then inexorably pressed it home.

Kincaid pushed the hated body away and rose to stand over the fallen Sioux. Standing Buffalo's eyes glazed, and a trickle of blood ran from his mouth.

"I always keep my promises," Kincaid growled ferally to the dying Indian. He turned and staggered back to the huddle around Blue. The mountain man was stretched out on the ground, his head cradled in Reb's lap.

"How is he?" Kincaid rasped.

"Don't talk as though I'm not here," Blue said irritably. Blue grabbed his chest with his hand as though to stop his life's blood from pouring out, but it seeped through his fingers. "Rachel and I will finally be together for the first time without causing pain to anyone else," he whispered.

Reb watched Matt reach for Blue's other hand and take it in his own, then saw the forgiveness in her father's eyes as he held on tight to his dying friend.

Blue coughed, and his lips tightened from the pain. "Damn, that hurts," he rasped. "Remember what I said," he admonished Reb. "I meant it."

"I will," Reb answered, smoothing the silver-streaked black hair back from his cool forehead.

"I will," Kincaid answered.

Blue looked at Kincaid and smiled. His voice had weakened, so Kincaid had to lean in to hear him. "I thought you might get the message. I'm glad you did."

Kincaid heard Blue's expiring breath and reached over to close the lifeless mahogany eyes.

"I'm sorry, Reb," Matt said in a voice thick with grief. "I never had the courage to tell you when I first found out he was your father. I was so jealous of the love Rachel gave to him. And I was afraid of losing yours, too."

"I'll never stop loving you, Daddy," Reb whispered. She leaned across Blue to hug her father tight.

Matt cleared his throat, then pulled Reb's hands

free and stood. "I'll take Blue back to his cabin to bury him."

"Take Trapper, too, Daddy, and bury him next to Blue," Reb said quietly.

Matt nodded his agreement, then asked Kincaid, "Will I see you when your business here is finished?"

"Of course. Reb and I will come to visit you before we go—" Kincaid stopped in mid-sentence and glanced down at Blue, whose head still lay cradled in Reb's lap. Kincaid saw that, for the second time, Reb bore her loss dry-eyed. "—before we make our final plans," he finished.

Reb helped Kincaid and Matt place her father across his horse and tie him down, with Trapper alongside him, then mounted her own animal and waited while Kincaid strapped the Indian down in similar fashion.

It was a sadly pensive party that made its way back toward the Indian village. When they arrived, Reb went directly to their tepee, where she found Morning Dove and Adam.

"Blue is dead," she said. "So is Standing Buffalo."

Adam took his sister in his arms to comfort her. Kincaid entered the dwelling and walked over to tap Adam on the shoulder. Adam nodded and stepped aside to let Kincaid take his place.

"We'd like to be alone," Kincaid said. "Adam, do

you think you could find a place for Morning Dove to spend the night?"

"The girl can stay with me." Adam took Morning Dove by the hand and led her from the tepee.

When they were alone, Kincaid walked Reb over to the buffalo robe and made her lie down. He lay down beside her and took her in his embrace, laying his cheek against hers.

"I'm sorry, Rebel. Blue was a good man."

The words were the catalyst that released Reb's tears. She buried her face in Kincaid's chest and cried until sleep overtook her.

Kincaid was careful not to hold her too tight for fear of hurting her bruises. But soon he, too, lost the battle with fatigue and slept.

They woke to the cheerful voice of Morning Dove, who was trying to convince Adam that the couple would be grateful to have a hot breakfast and not mind the intrusion.

"She's right, Adam," Kincaid called from his pallet.

"Oooh," Reb groaned as she sat up. "I'm so sore."

"Me, too," Kincaid agreed, giving Reb a light kiss on the nose. "The sooner my business is done, the sooner we can be out of here and on our way home."

Reb chewed on her lower lip to keep from asking where Kincaid thought home was. She reminded herself of Blue's sacrifice, and her mother's, and determined that her love was at least as strong as theirs. She decided to say nothing.

"You're looking well this morning," Kincaid said to Morning Dove as the girl entered the tepee.

"The bullet only scratched my arm. This man" — she gestured to Adam — "took good care of me."

"This is Adam, one of my woman's brothers, who will be your brother also until you choose a mate," Kincaid explained.

Adam looked confused. "What's this about me being her brother until she chooses a mate? The girl's just a child!"

"That shows what you know," Morning Dove sniffed. "I have passed fourteen summers."

"Fourteen!" Adam, Reb, and Kincaid all exclaimed together.

Kincaid turned to Adam ominously. "Where did you two spend the night?"

"By the stream. But you can just forget whatever you're thinking. She's a kid!"

"A kid who knocked you off your skids the first time you saw her."

"I was just surprised because she was so tiny and because . . . because . . ."

"Yes?" Kincaid asked aggressively.

"Because she had breasts," Adam blurted. A blush spread up his cheeks at the admission.

"Damn!" Kincaid muttered. "Where Reb and I are

going, we can't take any extra responsibilities. So you'll take this . . . tiny child with breasts home with you and take care of her like the good *brother* Reb promised you'd be. Understand?"

"I already have two sisters," Adam said sullenly.

"Well, now you have three," Kincaid said.

They'd completely forgotten that Morning Dove was listening to every word they said.

"I will not go where I am not wanted," she spat at Adam. "Besides, I would not like to have a brother with green eyes like a cat and a broken nose!"

"Last night you told me that my eyes reminded you of the prairie grass in summer, and that my broken nose made my face look strong," Adam contradicted.

Kincaid and Reb exchanged amused glances.

"Well, maybe I was wrong," Morning Dove shouted. She scooted out the door before Adam could answer, and he raced after her.

Reb resisted the urge to ask again where it was they were going that they couldn't take extra responsibilities. They sat down to the breakfast Morning Dove had brought, and shortly thereafter, Kincaid was called to meet with the Council.

Kincaid entered the Council lodge with trepidation, since he wasn't sure what Spotted Tail's reaction would be to the death of Standing Buffalo. He knew the answer to his question when he was seated at Spotted Tail's immediate left as an honored guest. No word was spoken of the Indian's death as they smoked the ceremonial pipe that was passed to the left from man to man.

"Tell us of your iron road," Spotted Tail finally invited.

"It'll change the face of the mountains near the Platte," Kincaid explained. "We can't know what the future will be, but it's possible for both our peoples to share in the good things the Iron Horse can bring along the iron road. It'll join this nation together from east to west. That is a good thing, after the strife of the years past.

"In peace, your people and mine can learn much from one another. Will you join me at Fort Laramie in the spring to decide the terms of a treaty?"

There was some discussion of whether Too-Big-For-Horses could be trusted. But Spotted Tail was supportive of the idea and reminded the Council that his friend Blue had also been in favor of sitting down to talk with the white man. Spotted Tail turned to the circled Council, and they took a vote.

"We will come," he said.

Kincaid left the Council feeling satisfied with the results of his mission and very thankful to Blue for the ease with which the Indians had agreed to his suggestion.

Anxious to spend some time alone with Reb, he was unpleasantly surprised when he arrived back at the tepee to discover they had company. Kincaid sat down next to Reb and made it clear from the glare he gave Breck O'Hanlan that the Irishman wasn't welcome.

"I came to give me condolences to Reb and to bring ye a little weddin' present," Breck said. The burly mountain man fished around in his pocket and came up with Kincaid's gold pocket watch.

Reb watched anxiously to see how Kincaid would react to the vivid reminder of Laurie.

"Where did you get this?" Kincaid asked, smoothing the engraving on the back with his thumb.

"I gave Standin' Buffalo me Henry rifle, and he gave me that. I saw yer name etched in the gold and thought ye might like to have it back."

"Thank you. It meant a lot to me," Kincaid said. He looked up at Reb with all the love he felt for her in his heart and said, "I thought I would never be as happy again as I was when I received this gift the first time. I'll always carry it now, remembering that the gift has been given again."

Reb nodded imperceptibly, yet Kincaid saw her gesture and acknowledged it by bringing the golden symbol to his lips.

"I was sorry to hear 'bout Blue," the mountain man said. "I heard ye done in Standin' Buffalo with his own knife."

It took Kincaid a moment to focus on what the redheaded man had said. Then he let out some of his anger over the tragedy of the previous night. "If your damned Sharps had fired, I could have saved Blue. When I checked it this morning, I discovered it has a defective firing mechanism."

"Mary, Joseph, and Moses," Breck muttered, crossing himself. "Be ye sure?"

Kincaid nodded solemnly.

No wonder the Sharps had been so cheap! Breck wondered just how many of the rifles he'd been trading were faulty. He sure didn't want to give up any of those prime pelts he'd acquired.

"I think I'll check the lay of the land out west over Fort Bridger way," the burly man said.

"Good luck, girl," he said after he had risen. "Take care of yerself," he cautioned Kincaid. "If ye ever get out to Fort Bridger, come see me."

"We just might do that," Kincaid said.

Reb glanced at Kincaid. When were they ever going to be as far west as Fort Bridger? That was on the other side of the Rocky Mountains. Weren't they going back east to New York?

When Breck left, Kincaid turned back to Reb with a grin. "Now that we're alone, how about a walk?"

"A walk?"

"I have in mind a place with a little more privacy." Kincaid led Reb to the stream, and they strolled north along the bank. As they meandered past the rushing water, Kincaid said, "When I was in Denver, my father offered me a job."

Reb's first thought was that they were going to be leaving the wilderness, and fear rose up to choke her. She managed to ask, "Did you accept?"

"Not at the time, but I'm going to."

In panic, she wondered how long she had before he wanted to leave. "When will you start?"

"Right away," he answered. "He needs someone to survey the rest of the Union Pacific route west, and then to act as an advance man for the track gangs."

Reb caught Kincaid's gaze, and her eyes widened in disbelief. "You're not going back to New York!" Then she bubbled with laughter, and began to leap and dance in a circle around him. "You're going *west!*"

"*We're* going west." Kincaid opened his arms to her, and she threw herself into them. He swung her in a circle until they were both dizzy and giddy with joy. Blue had been right. She was special and wild and free. He swallowed the lump of fear in his throat and hugged her tighter.

"It sounds like a wonderful job," Reb whispered in Kincaid's ear.

They'd reached a point where the creek widened and deepened into a pond that was surrounded by stone cliffs on three sides and rimmed in cat-o'-nine-tails. A stream of water glistened along one wall, and green moss had grown along either side of the slick wetness.

Kincaid released Reb, and she immediately began unlacing her dress. She let it fall, then strode boldly into the cool water. She whirled to confront Kincaid, who still stood on the bank watching her.

"Come in. The water is refreshing," she called.

Kincaid unlaced his buckskin shirt and carefully pulled it off over his sore muscles, then slipped out of the buckskin pants as well.

Reb waited patiently for him to walk the few paces into the water to her. "Hold me," she said quietly.

Kincaid gently embraced Reb, and she encircled his waist with her arms.

The feel of flesh against flesh in the soothing water left them strangely contented.

Reb turned her face up to Kincaid and bathed in the love that radiated from his eyes. He brought his mouth down gently to cover hers and sipped delicately of the nectar that was Reb.

Reb leaned forward to touch her lips to Kincaid's chest, which tasted distinctly salty. Then she twirled her tongue around each of his nipples, noticing with delight that they hardened into buds, as hers also had in mere anticipation of Kincaid's touch.

"You're asking for trouble, Reb," Kincaid growled low, when Reb kept up the teasing titillation.

"When have I ever run from trouble?" Reb

taunted. "Besides, you'll drown if you try to kiss me like I'm kissing you!" She laughed, knowing her breasts were under water.

"We'll see about that," he said.

When Kincaid took a deep breath as though he were going to dive under water, Reb lunged back and splashed furiously away from him.

"Catch me if you can," she shouted merrily.

Kincaid swam powerfully toward her, then disappeared underwater. Reb turned in circles, searching for the telltale ripples that would reveal his presence. But the pool remained so calm that a green dragonfly lit on the surface nearby.

Just as Reb was beginning to worry, Kincaid burst upward with Reb cradled in his arms so her rosy crests were accessible to his mouth. He smacked kisses noisily across her face and neck.

"Now, what was that about drowning?" he asked smugly, threatening to drop Reb.

She screamed and grabbed his bruised shoulder for support. Kincaid yelped at the sharp pain and flinched away, losing his balance so that they both went under.

Reb shot up, breaking the surface with a surge of excitement, then hunted for Kincaid. She felt his kiss on her navel moments before he appeared before her.

Kincaid lifted Reb up out of the water by her waist, flicking the crystal drops from her breasts with the tip of his tongue, then working his way up her neck to her mouth, as he slowly lowered her into the water. The touch of lip to lip caused them both to shiver in pleasure.

They let the world pass unnoticed as they loved playfully, tugging on just an upper lip or lower lip, or running tantalizing tongues along the edges of lips, each learning what most pleased the other.

Reb ran her hands through the wet curls at Kincaid's nape, then traced the line of his strong jaw and the familiar angled planes of his face. "I love the feel of your skin," she murmured.

"I feel your touch in my heart, Rebel. It warms me, it soothes me, and I'm content." He hugged her to him, reveling in the way their bodies molded together.

Reb stood in the sparkling water with her arms around Kincaid and her head leaned quietly against his chest so his voice rumbled in her ear when he said, "You're getting all wrinkled."

"I just wanted proof that you'll still love me when I'm old," she whispered against his flesh.

"I'll love you forever, Rebel," he said. He lifted her chin with a forefinger and sealed the promise by touching his lips to hers.

"Are you two going to stay in there all day?" an irritated voice called from the bank. Adam paced back and forth anxiously. "It's Morning Dove. She's run away. I need your help to find her."

Reb looked up mischievously at Kincaid. "He should have known better than to try to boss her around," she said. "We'll be right there," she called to Adam.

"I'll be right there," Kincaid corrected. "Humor me," he said when Reb opened her mouth to retort.

She smiled sweetly at him, then dashed a huge scoop of water into his face. "Hurry back!" she said, grinning broadly, "and maybe I'll give you a chance to get even."

Kincaid snatched a quick wet kiss before he splashed from the water. He pulled on his buckskins while Adam ranted and explained to a very understanding Kincaid how Morning Dove had been impossible to talk to.

"I'll be back soon," Kincaid shouted to Reb. "Go back to the tepee and wait for me. And stay out of trouble!"

When the two men had left, Reb stepped slowly from the pool, letting the rivulets of water cascade down her sleek form. She felt so loved she could have purred in contented she-cat satisfaction.

She would go back to the tepee and wait for Kincaid's return. And she would do her best to be good and to stay out of trouble, as he'd asked. At least for a little while.

Enjoy the following excerpt from

Joan Johnston's next Bitter Creek novel

THE NEXT
MRS. BLACKTHORNE

coming soon from Pocket Books

"I can't believe Dad's marrying that uppity French-speaking redheaded bit—" Kate Grayhawk cut herself off before she called her father's prospective wife the B-word. She glanced at her uncle North, who was brushing down his horse in an adjacent stall. "You've met Jocelyn Montrose, haven't you, Uncle North. What do you think of her?"

"Are you done grooming that animal?" he asked.

Kate turned back to the bay gelding she'd ridden across her uncle's Texas Hill Country ranch that morning, sending the brush down the animal's back in long, soothing strokes. "Jocelyn is only twenty-five—just six years older than me," Kate continued. "Dad was married to her sister, for heaven's sake."

"If I'm not mistaken," he said, "Jocelyn's sister died two years ago, leaving your dad a widower."

Kate flushed. "He should be marrying Mom."

That was the crux of Kate's problem. She couldn't believe her forty-six-year-old father and thirty-five-year-old mother were going to throw away this last chance at finding happiness together. "If Grandpa King hadn't kept them apart, Mom and Dad would have gotten married before I was born, instead of never getting married at all."

Her uncle gave a noncommittal grunt and continued grooming his horse.

Kate lifted the bay's black mane and brushed the animal's sweaty neck. "I wish I knew how to make Dad change his mind about that French ambassador's daughter he seems to think is so perfect for him."

"I believe her father was ambassador *to* France," her uncle corrected. "She was born in Connecticut."

Kate shot her uncle North a narrow-eyed look. "Whatever. Dad shouldn't be marrying some blue-blooded eastern tenderfoot. If that wedding happens next month, Mom's heart is going to be broken into so many pieces, it'll never mend."

Kate watched for another look of censure, but her uncle seemed totally absorbed in the glossy black stallion he was brushing. She'd learned over the years that Uncle North never sympathized, never offered advice, never offered to solve her problems. In fact, sometimes his ice-blue eyes were so cold, they made her shiver. When she was a kid, she'd dubbed him North *Pole*, he'd seemed so remote and unfeeling.

She'd also noticed that whenever she poured out her troubles to her uncle, they somehow miraculously got resolved. She was sure Uncle North was paying attention, listening to every word she said. She knew he cared about her and wanted her to be happy. He just had a little trouble showing his feelings.

Which wasn't surprising, considering that King Grayhawk was his father, and he'd had two really bad stepmothers after Grandpa King had divorced North's mother. Kate knew for a fact that Grandpa King didn't listen. And he didn't care about anyone but himself.

The situation between her parents would have been resolved long ago if her two grandfathers, King Grayhawk and Jackson Blackthorne, hadn't been mortal enemies. But Blackjack had stolen away Eve DeWitt—the woman King loved—and married her, and the two men had been on opposite sides of the fence ever since.

It was no wonder that when her father got her mother pregnant all those years ago, Grandpa King had taken advantage of the situation to exact revenge by forbidding them to marry.

But her parents were meant to be together like oatmeal and raisins. Like eggs and bacon. Like pancakes and syrup.

Kate realized she was hungry. Her horseback ride with Uncle North had started at daybreak, and the sun was well up. She had an hour's drive ahead of her, to get back to her dorm room at UT. She was finishing her freshman year at the University of Texas at Austin, and she'd left her homework sitting when she'd come to spend the weekend on Uncle North's ranch. Her brushstrokes came faster until her uncle lifted his head and pierced her with a look from his ice-blue eyes.

"You giving that horse a good brushing?" he asked.

"Yes, sir." Kate slowed her hand, but her mind was still working a mile a minute. "What if I pretended to break a leg?" she said. "That would get Mom and Dad here in a hurry."

"It also might make your mom take chances getting here," North said.

Kate bit her lower lip. When she'd called and left a message that she was in trouble a year ago, her mom had caused an accident because she was driving too fast, trying to get home to help Kate. "I see what you mean," she said. "Maybe you could tell Mom you need her help with something, and I could ask Dad to come help me with something."

"I manage fine by myself," North said. "And your mom knows it."

Kate's face twisted in disgust. "You could pretend—"

"No."

The curt word sounded final. Absolutely, positively firm. Kate would get no help plotting from Uncle North, that was for sure.

"You finished?" he asked.

Kate ran her hand along the bay's glossy back and said, "Yep."

North slapped his horse on the rump, left the stall and headed out of the barn without another word.

Kate chewed on her lower lip, staring at her uncle's broad, powerful back and long legs as he strode into the sunshine. In the past, she'd been happy to rely on one of Uncle North's miracles to accomplish the impossible. But he hadn't seemed the least bit interested in helping her get her mother and father back together. And she knew for a fact Uncle North didn't like the Blackthornes—which included her father—one little bit.

Kate squinted as she stepped out of the barn into the blistering Texas sun. She waited for her eyes to adjust as she stared out over the grassy hills dotted with the purple remnants of April bluebonnets. There wasn't much time before her father's wedding—to the wrong woman. Just one month. Her mother's—and father's—happiness was just too important to leave to chance.

She was just going to have to come up with a miracle of her own.